THE END OF THE AGE

WRAK-WAVARA THE AGE OF DARKNESS
BOOK FOUR

LEIGH ROBERTS

CONTENTS

Editing by Joy Sephton http://www.justemagine.biz
Cover design by Cherie Fox http://www.cheriefox.com

Sexual activities or events in this book are intended for adults.

ISBN: 978-1-951528-30-0 (ebook)
ISBN: 978-1-951528-31-7 (paperback)

Dedication

For those who know the joy of exploring undiscovered worlds and wondering—

What If?

CHAPTER 1

The community at Lulnomia was settling into a routine. And as the Mothoc became more comfortable in their new home, more interaction took place. But not everyone welcomed fixing up broken relations. Tyria, least of all.

Tyria had left her family to follow Straf'Tor's teachings. It broke both her mother's and father's hearts, and her siblings resented her leaving because of how much it upset their parents. She had not sought them out, leaving it up to them to make contact since they were the ones who were angry with her. But it seemed that none of them wanted to reunite, which left her very uncomfortable knowing a chance reunion was inevitable—and apparently unwelcome.

It was Tyria's brother who first came across her. She was down by the stream, fishing rocks out of the cold water for Fahr to play with. It was a common pastime of the younger offling, who enjoyed arranging them in patterns or stacking the stones as high as they would go without toppling over.

"Tyria."

Her stomach twisted as, even after all this time, she recognized her brother's voice. She turned from where she was squatting down to look up at him.

"You have not sought us out; why not?"

"Probably for the same reason none of you has sought me out?" Tyria answered. "I fear hurt feelings remain, maybe even anger still?" She stood up and brushed the snow from her legs, flicking the water off her hands.

Nodnak scuffed his feet. "It is true. Mother and Father never got over your leaving. They want to see you, but at the same time, they do not."

"And Aerbo and Costan?" They were Tyria's sister and her other brother.

Nodnak did not answer.

"I see," she said.

"I will tell them I ran into you."

"Tell them—tell them I am sorry I hurt them. I never got to tell them that."

"I will." Nodnak turned away.

Tyria found herself relieved that she did not have her son with her. She wondered if word had gotten to her family about her having an offling. Had Fahr been present, her brother would have asked who her mate was. It was a topic Tyria had avoided talking about at Kthama and did not want to talk about at Lulnomia either. But she knew it would come up out of natural curiosity. The last thing she wanted was for some type of stigma to fall on Fahr's shoulders because his father had poisoned Ushca.

It was not Fahr's fault who his father was. Still, there would always be those who judged. And there was nowhere else to go; they had to make their life at Lulnomia, one way or another.

The Healers were on their way to locate a new sacred spot where they could connect with the Great Mother in protected isolation. Several locations were suggested by individual members, and they had set out as a group to tour each of them.

The first they came to was a small cave down close to the river. It was large enough for them to hold meetings in, though its true purpose would be to serve as a place of worship and renewal. Though nondescript, the fresh humid air from the river created a soothing energy within its walls, even in these winter months. Next, they traveled far up one of the paths to a small clearing that overlooked much of the surrounding area. It was pleasantly private with lots of soft grasses and songbirds, but there were concerns over the climb during winter months for the older Healers as it was up a fairly steep incline.

The third place they went to was an alcove rimmed with high rocks. It was not on one of the regularly traveled paths, so far enough away to avoid foot traffic. Because of the large boulders that created a bit of a feeling of enclosure, it reminded Pan a little bit of the Healer's Cove at the High Rocks. The group milled about the area longer than they had any of the others.

Pan was taking in the energy with her eyes closed when someone addressed her.

It was Irisa, and she opened her eyes to look down at the small elderly female.

"The answer you seek is closer than you realize."

At a loss, the Guardian just blinked at her.

Before Irisa walked away, she reached out and patted Pan on the arm.

It was a breach of protocol for anyone out of the family circle to touch a Guardian without permission. Yet Pan was not offended. If anything, she felt comforted. She watched Irisa leaving, wondering who the female was and why she, a Guardian, was so drawn to her. Pan decided to wait no longer; she had to find out all she could about this enigmatic older female.

❀

"Irisa?" asked Hatos'Mok. "The older female who seems to come and go at will. She never stays anywhere for a long time. She visits one community, stays a while, then disappears. Then we eventually hear she has turned up at another of our communities. Often a great deal of time passes in between. Of course, now there is only this one Mothoc community."

"What else do you know about her?"

"She is older than the dust of Etera."

Pan could not help but laugh.

"Seriously," Hatos'Mok continued. "It seems she has always been old. No one knows anything about her. She keeps to herself. There are rumors that she speaks to Shi—" He stopped.

"She speaks to *Shissu*? Those who have returned to the Great Spirit?"

Hatos'Mok nodded. "As far as I know, it is not a claim anyone but Irisa has ever made."

"So people think she is out of her mind?"

"If they do, it is not something they fear. She is always welcomed and in the past has been a great help wherever she turns up."

"Someone has to know something. She cannot have been old forever."

"That is all I know," said Hatos'Mok. "Perhaps the Healers will have more answers for you."

Pan did not want to ask the Healers; she had concerns that it would get back to Irisa. Still, since Irisa seemed to be part of the Healer community, it was the logical place to start.

"I do not remember her coming to Kthama other than when Lor Onida gave birth to Liru—"

"Guardian, she is harmless, and if anything, she is revered among those she has visited—others will tell you the same. I do not know why she only ever came to Kthama that one time when Lor Onida returned to the Great Spirit."

A great help.

"Before you go," he stopped her, "I would like your ideas on how to unite the community further. I am pleased that, for the most part, our People are mingling and renewing old ties. And I do not seek to diminish each community's separate identity. That is the last thing I want to do. I do not want to undermine the Leaders' authority over their own people, but I would like to create a more cohesive vision of us all as Mothoc, as you once spoke of, instead of being only the previous populations of the High Rocks, the Far High Hills, the Little River, and so on. And it might help to heal some of the rifts that are still alive between estranged family members."

"You are speaking of the people from Kayerm? That there are still some hurt feelings over the division? I will give it some thought."

Pan collected Tala from Jhotin and sought out her mate. But Rohm'Mok was out with a crew in some of the branches of Lulnomia that they had not yet investigated, so she returned to her quarters to play with her little daughter.

Tala had an inquisitive nature. She was into everything and no matter what Pan brought in for her to play with, the offling had an inexhaustible interest in every aspect of it. She felt whatever it was all over with her hands, sniffed it to see if it had a smell, and licked it. Sometimes she would hold it to her heart as if to see if she could get a feel of its essence. Pan wondered if perhaps their daughter would become a Healer at some point as she seemed very in tune with everything on Etera. It was inevitable that at some point, Tala would become interested in the 'Tor Leader's Staff.

"No, Tala. You must never touch it. Remember?"

Tala frowned at her.

"I mean it. This is something you have to accept and not test me on." Pan got up and went over to the Leader's Staff. "This is for Mama only to touch. No one else. Ever. Not Papa, not *anyone.*"

I had better find another arrangement. Then Pan remembered where her father had kept the Leader's staff while she was growing up. She decided to have an insert carved high up in the corner into which she could place the staff, far out of her daughter's reach for many years to come. Or until Tala decided she understood the importance of the directive. In the meantime, she would be sure not to let Tala out of her sight when they were in the same room as it was.

Pan stood in front of the staff, thinking of who to ask to carve the insert, and then heard Irisa's words in her head. "The answer you seek is closer than you realize."

Of course. The scroll. The unifying factor that Hatos'Mok was looking for. The scroll had been created at a time when all the Mothoc were united. It symbolized the Sacred Laws that bound them together. That united them.

She sat back down with Tala, whose attention had turned to the collection of gourds Pan had given her to arrange and to hide other toys inside.

⚘

When Lor Onida found him, Moc'Tor was in one of the private meeting rooms.

"May I interrupt?" She stepped inside.

"What do you need, Healer?" He asked, noticing she held something in her hand.

Lor Onida reached out and offered the item to Moc'Tor.

"Why are you giving this to me?"

"Because the time of division is upon our people, and this cannot be the cause of further widening the rift."

Moc'Tor unrolled the piece of hide she had given him, the symbols that recorded the laws the community had agreed upon. Yes; that which was meant to unite them could only be a source of more division.

He nodded. "There is only one scroll. And now two groups of Mothoc, those who follow me and those who follow my brother, so to whom does the scroll belong? You are right. It is perhaps one of the most sacred items we now have. To give it to either group would create animosity, more strife. But it is too precious to be destroyed."

"Then hide it well, Adik'Tar. Hide it where it will only be discovered by one who has the wisdom to know what to do with it when that time is at hand," Lor Onida said.

Moc'Tor instantly knew where it could go. "I have a place where it will be safe and discoverable only by the one with the wisdom to know when to reveal its existence," he said. "Does Oragur know?"

"Only you and I know that it is now in your keeping. We need only be silent about it until the community is split up. Then its existence will dissolve into confusion, and eventually, it will be decided it was lost in the commotion."

"At some point, someone will ask you directly," the Guardian pointed out.

"It is simple; I will tell them I gave it to you."

Moc'Tor was not sure how he would handle that when the time came, but he trusted that some answer would occur to him.

As it turned out, Lor Onida was right, and in the turmoil that was to come, the scroll became a topic of lesser importance, easily skirted. When she died years later, it had not yet been disclosed that the guardian had the scroll. In the end, with both Moc'Tor and Lor Onida gone, no

one knew what had become of it. Well, almost
no one.

⚜

Pan thought long and hard about telling Hatos'Mok
of the whereabouts of the scroll. She knew it would
unify the community, but was this the time to reveal
it? Would animosity develop against her father, and
perhaps her, for hiding it from them for so long? It
could be perceived as a betrayal, and Pan knew she
must wait until she was sure the time was right. For
now, they would have to find another way to unite
the Mothoc.

⚜

Tyria, upset by her brother's approach, was suddenly
overcome with homesickness for Kayerm. Needing
some answers, she sought out Kayerm's Leader,
Norland. He sat next to her and listened patiently.

"Do you wish to reunite with your family?" he
asked after she was finished.

"I do not know. Part of me, yes. I am lonely; I
admit it. I did not want to leave Kayerm, but I feared
persecution for carrying Ridg'Sor's seed. Now, I am
living here at Lulnomia not only with Kayerm's
community members but also with my parents and
siblings. I am the Healer of the High Rocks, but in

my heart, Kayerm is still my home. Now there is nowhere to go to escape my fears."

"Then perhaps you should face them. You feared condemnation from us at Kayerm because of what Ridg'Sor did, but I think you sold us short. There was a lot of concern when you disappeared. Many thought at first that perhaps you had tried to follow the rebel group and had either caught up with them or gotten lost. Luckily, we quickly learned from Wosot that you had left for the High Rocks with Straf'Tor. Your people were sad you had gone, but they understood why. The only reason they do not approach you is out of respect for your decision to leave. I think if you came to one of our meetings, you would experience only welcome, not judgment."

Norland's words were like a balm to Tyria's soul. It had not occurred to her that there would be forgiveness and understanding. She had assumed they would turn against her and her offling in retribution for her mate's crime of murdering Ushca.

"Healer, no one believes you had anything to do with what Ridg'Sor did. No one. I understand your panic and why you left—I think we all do. Please, meet with us and find out for yourself."

Tyria suspected that Norland was right, though if he was not and they did reject her, it would be no worse than what she had imagined a thousand times. And if he was right, and they accepted her back into the group? She had been welcomed at Kthama, but she would not have gone there had it not been for her mate's actions.

"Oh, why did I pair with Ridg'Sor. I ask myself that over and over again." Tyria hung her head in shame.

"I supposed that, as a Healer, perhaps you saw his inner pain and anguish, and your heart went out to him. Perhaps you thought you could help heal him of his suffering."

Tyria lifted her head. "I am surprised you can feel any compassion for him. After what he did."

"I am not old enough to consider myself wise by any means, but the years I have lived have been hard. I suppose it gives one a sense of humility, seeing how difficult our paths can be. Perhaps, in our own ineffective and distorted ways, we are each doing the best we can, no matter how misdirected. Ridg'Sor paid for his crime; it is not yours to pay for as well."

The Healer rose and asked Norland to let her know when their next assembly would be.

Norland sought out Wosot and Kyana and told them of Tyria's visit. "Do you think she is right? Would the community have rejected her?"

Kyana shook her head. "I want to believe you are right, Adik'Tar. That everyone would have been able to separate Tyria from Ridg'Sor's crime. But in retrospect, I am not so sure. Everyone was devastated when Ushca died and when Straf'Tor abandoned us right after. I think that at the time, she made the correct decision.

"But now, I would say that the acceptance you speak of will be there now. Everyone suffered at Kayerm. It was not just the harsher conditions, which Ridg'Sor made sure to rub into everyone's wounds as often as he could. It was the pain of leaving our families and friends over the division in philosophy. I am not saying it should not have happened. Had we not left Kthama, it is possible that harm might have come to the Akassa as emotions were stirred up to an almost unbearable level. Could it be possible that Moc'Tor and his brother saw that the division had to happen and orchestrated it themselves for the protection of the Akassa? Sometimes I wonder."

The two males looked at each other. "I am always amazed at your wisdom," Wosot said to his mate. Kyana smiled and reached over to take his hand.

"I have invited Tyria to the next assembly," said Norland.

Like every other Mothoc community in the past, Lulnomia only had one entrance and there was no way completely to avoid members from the other communities. So it was inevitable that one day Pan would run into Liru.

Krin was returning from her daily tasks and had Liru with her. Pan stopped cold when she spotted them making their way up the main path to Lulnomia. She waited for their approach.

"Good morning, Guardian," Krin called out and waved. Liru, at her side, looked up and stared at the white figure towering above her.

Krin looked down at her little sister. "Liru, this is the Guardian. She protects Etera and all of us."

Liru gave a little bow, to which Pan smiled. "I am pleased to meet you, Liru."

"How do you know my name?" Liru asked.

"I have known you since you were born, but you do not remember."

"Oh," Liru said.

"Pan took care of you for a while when you were first born," Krin explained. " She loved you very much." Krin looked at Pan and said softly, "She still does."

"That is true, little Liru. If you ever need help, I want you to know you can ask me. Understand?"

Liru nodded. Her eyes were wide with wonder at the distinctive silver-white coat of the Guardian of Etera. "You look like my toy."

Pan thought of the little hide toy she had made for Liru and sent with her to the Deep Valley. One she had fashioned out of white fur, intentionally making it look like herself. "Yes, I made that for you," she said softly.

"Thank you," Liru said. "It is my favorite."

"I am glad. I will let you be on your way, then." Pan stepped aside so they could pass, then she turned and watched them walk on up the path to Lulnomia. She dropped her eyes as sadness filled her heart. She wondered why that offling got to her so. She had her own daughter now, but still, the heartache lingered over having had to give Liru back to Oragur. *Mother said help would come to me.* It could not possibly be Liru—could it?

Months passed, and it was time for the next assembly. Though Tyria trusted Norland, she left Fahr in Jhotin's care. Jhotin had become the community carer, often looking after many of the offling when needed. He had a way with the young ones who found him delightfully funny and very entertaining.

Norland had earlier described to Tyria where the meeting would be held. As she made her way through the hall of what was Kayerm's piece of Lulnomia, her heart was beating hard. As much as she longed to see familiar faces, she feared seeing their rejection.

Norland had started the meeting by the time Tyria arrived. Everyone was seated on the rock floor in a semi-circle radiating out from the front where Norland stood. He saw Tyria and nodded to her. Others, seeing his gesture, turned to see who had come in.

"Tyria!" Pagara rushed to her feet and ran back to embrace the Healer. "I am so glad to see you. I knew you were here, but I did not know—"

"I understand; you do not need to explain."

The two females embraced warmly. By then, others were on their feet and had come to join them.

Beala was the second to reach Tyria. Tyria looked over Pagara's shoulder, still in her embrace, to see the older female. Beala had been Ushca's best friend. If there was any animosity, Beala would be one of those she would expect it from.

"Tyria," Beala said softly and reached out to pat her arm. Pagara released her, and Beala put her arms around Tyria. "I am so glad you have returned. You have returned, have you not? Have you come to live among us?"

"I— I do not know," she stammered. "I do not know yet."

"You would be welcome. Here, look around you." Beala turned Tyria so she could see the smiling, welcoming faces.

Tyria scanned the group and saw welcome on all the females' faces. She was reluctant to look at the males, though she did not know why.

In the next moment, Kyana and Wosot approached her.

"Welcome," said Wosot.

"Yes, welcome!" Kyana added.

By now, everyone was engrossed on the scene at the back of the room, which Norland had just reached. Teirac, taking Norland's cue, now stood next to Wosot and Kyana.

"We all welcome you, Tyria," said the Leader. "We are glad you are here."

Toniss stepped forward to speak. As one of the oldest females and the mother of Straf'Tor's son, as well as grandparent of the current Leader, she held special status among them all.

"We heard you had an offling," she said.

Tyria cringed. She had not wanted Fahr to be mentioned yet. Finally, she stammered, "Yes, I do. A son."

"Please bring him to meet us," said Beala.

"Whether a son or a daughter, offling are always a blessing," said Toniss.

Noticing that most of the males had not welcomed Tyria back, Trak spoke. "On behalf of the males, I welcome you, Healer. We were grieved when you left us and were relieved to hear that you were well and living at Kthama."

"How did you know?" Tyria asked, looking up at Norland.

"The Guardian, Pan, told us when she came to explain her plans to reunite the Mothoc," Norland said. "You have a lot to catch up on. The evening is young so why not stay a while after we are done and visit with your friends. They will be glad to tell you all that happened after you left. There is a great deal to tell."

Norland returned to the front of the room while

the others remained at the back and sat with Tyria.

After the meeting was over, the friends told Tyria everything that had happened after she and Straf'Tor left, and Tyria was saddened to hear of so much pain and suffering. Before leaving, she promised to come back again.

Wosot and Kyana walked Tyria back to the Great Chamber of Lulnomia, from which tunnels branched off to the separate communities.

"Thank you for your kindness," Tyria said.

"I do not want to wait until the next meeting to see you again. Could we not see each other in between?" asked Kyana. "I am sure others feel the same."

Tyria agreed with the suggestion, and after Kyana and Wosot had disappeared back down the tunnel, she practically ran to find Jhotin and retrieve Fahr.

Tyria rushed over, snatched up Fahr, and hugged him tightly. "I will never let anything happen to you. Ever."

"What has upset you?" Jhotin asked.

"I went to visit my friends at Kayerm," she answered, her voice muffled in Fahr's neck.

"Were they unkind?" he asked.

"No. No. They welcomed me. I am just so turned around in my thoughts and my feelings. I have feared their anger ever since I learned we were all to be reunited here. And none of it happened. It was all my imagination—or so it seems."

"But you are not sure. And you fear for your son if you are wrong? Why would they reject you, Tyria, just for leaving?"

Tyria was so grateful for a listening ear that she told the Helper everything and how she feared retribution against their offling for Ridg'Sar's crime.

"I understand. I believe I would feel the same as you. You are wise to take your time to decide because you have a home here with us. Everyone at Kthama welcomed you, and perhaps you can be part of both communities. I see no reason why not."

CHAPTER 2

Laborn waited anxiously for enough time to have passed before claiming that Dak'Tor had not tried to seed Dara. He was almost licking his lips at the idea of forcing Dak'Tor to mount Dara in front of him as proof that he was trying to seed her. Whether it was a perverse interest in watching others mate, or his pleasure at publicly humiliating Dak'Tor, or both, was not certain. Laborn suspected Dak'Tor's problem, and if he was right, the pressure of the public display would make it irrefutable. Laborn would do anything he could do to discredit Dak'Tor because, in the back of his mind, he feared the Guardian's brother.

There was a rumor that Gard had challenged Laborn early on when the leadership of the rebels was not assured, and this was how Gard had gotten the deep scar on his face. Laborn let him live because Gard was strong and he needed him, and Gard never crossed the new Leader. But this male, Dak'Tor, who had no history with the group and who was a mystery, did present a possible challenge. Laborn knew that the Guardian was revered among all Mothoc, and despite his efforts to discredit her, he suspected he had failed. And by association, and due to his silver-white coloring, Dak'Tor gained power and status.

Luckily for Dak'Tor, the roots Useaves had given him did work. He had successfully mounted Dara, and now it was a matter of time. But would she become seeded before Laborn decided their time was up?

✿

Laborn spoke to Useaves one morning, "It has been long enough. The cold weather is breaking. If the female is not seeded by now, I doubt she will ever be."

"It took a while for Iria to be seeded. Why are you so impatient for this one?"

"I am not impatient. I just do not like being fooled. And he thinks he is fooling me. I know the problem, even if you do not," he snapped at the older female.

Useaves just smiled wryly. "Take care with your words, Laborn."

It was as close to an admonishment as she could give, and Laborn backed down. He did not understand why Useaves was so confident and would stand up to him, but he did not want to find out. He knew Healers had knowledge that others did not. She could easily slip something into his food or drink that would do away with him quietly and efficiently, and no one would know the difference.

He sighed. "If we did not need his seed, I would have put an end to him when he first came."

"I told you when he arrived, he is a gift from the Great Spirit. But not all gifts are easy. Sometimes we must earn the gift through overcoming our own challenges." Then she declared it, "You fear the Guardian."

Laborn clamped his mouth shut. When he had calmed down, he said, "I do not fear the Guardian. I was with Moc'Tor. As were you. I watched him fight Norcab, and he bleeds just as any of us do. Yes, he eventually killed Norcab, but I witnessed no special powers. The Guardian has others fooled, but not me."

"Then you have nothing to fear from her brother." Useaves was baiting Laborn. Waiting for him to reveal his weak spot, and he did.

"I do not fear her brother!" he practically shouted. "I have waited long enough!" He got to his feet and went to find Gard.

Word quickly traveled that something was afoot, and by the time Gard had returned with Dak'Tor and Dara, a crowd was tailing them.

Laborn was pleased to see the group gathering to watch the spectacle he was about to make of the Guardian's brother. The more who witnessed Dak'-Tor's public humiliation, the better. Dak'Tor's friends were also there, along with Iria. Kaisak, never too far away, watched from where he was standing next to Laborn.

"I have waited long enough," shouted the Leader. "You think you can outsmart me. I challenge you to prove yourself with her now in front of all these witnesses." He dragged Dara out by her arm and pushed her to the ground on all fours.

"Now. Mount her now and prove yourself a male!" he shouted.

"This is barbaric!" Dak'Tor looked to Useaves for help.

"It is reasonable. Laborn must be sure you are able to seed the female," she answered.

"Are you saying I would allow another male to mount me in his stead?" Dara glared up at Laborn and started to rise, but the Leader shoved her back down.

Dak'Tor stepped between Laborn and Dara. "Leave her alone! I have nothing to prove to you. The female is seeded. Ask her!" He reached down to help Dara to her feet.

Laborn grabbed Dak'Tor's arm and jerked it away.

By instinct, Dak'Tor pushed Laborn back.

"You will pay for that," the Leader shouted.

Dazal came forward to help his sister up.

Once on her feet, she announced, "I am seeded. It is true."

"You are lying," Laborn accused her. Dazal pulled his sister partially behind him for protection. Dak'Tor stepped next to Dazal.

"Why would I lie? That would be stupid as time will prove if I am or not," she answered.

"Come here. I will find out if you are still a maiden or not," Laborn threatened, reaching out his hand toward her.

"No! You are insane. Do not dare even to think you have the right to touch me so!" Dara yelled at him.

At Laborn's lewd suggestion, even Useaves had taken a step forward as if to move between him and the female. He saw Useaves' intention and growled and bared his canines. She and everyone else could see he barely had himself under control.

Laborn pointed at Dak'Tor. "You have no control over your females. They are insolent. Rude. I am the Adik'Tar here. I make the rules. I decide who lives—and who dies." His gaze locked on Dak'Tor at the last part. His eyes were wild, and a drop of saliva ran from the corner of his open mouth.

The crowd shifted nervously, and some took a

few steps backward. Suddenly, Laborn seemed to realize how out of control he was. He shook his head quickly as if to snap himself out of his sudden derangement and wiped his mouth on his forearm.

He stared at Dak'Tor as he said, "*Va!* You are right. Time will tell. And when it proves that you are lying, you will all pay." He then turned to the group of Dak'Tor's friends. "All of you. And if you wish to be spared, you had best re-think your association with this *PetaQ*."

"This serves none of us," Useaves announced. "Go on your way now," and she dispersed the onlookers by stepping forward and waving them all away.

Seething inside, Laborn turned his glare in her direction. How dare she determine when they should be dismissed? Perhaps this old female had served her purpose. Perhaps it was she he should make an example of.

Kaisak walked after the group, hurrying them up.

After they were all gone, Laborn turned on Useaves. "You overstep your place, female. You had no right to declare the assembly over. I was not done making an example of that troublemaker."

"You were going too far. You have no right to suggest touching a female as you threatened to."

"I am the Adik'Tar. I can do as I wish!" his anger was rising again.

"Not without consequences. If you continue to harass the Guardian's brother and mistreat the females, threatening to use them Without Their Consent, you will lose the respect of everyone."

"Females are here for our bidding. I give them the level of respect they have earned by their service to us males. That includes you," he snarled.

"Every male here has a mother, if not also a sister. Some have a daughter. Your disregard for us is not as deeply shared by the other males as you think," she snarled back.

Just then, Laborn noticed movement in the background and realized Gard had seen the whole exchange. "Go away now, Useaves. I have no time to waste arguing with a *female*."

Useaves followed Laborn's glance and also saw Gard. "As you wish, *Adik'Tar*," she said bitterly and walked away as briskly as she was able.

Once Useaves was out of earshot, Laborn called Gard over.

"My apologies for intruding," Gard said. "I heard raised voices and came back to investigate."

"No matter. I have something to discuss with you. Sit down."

Dak'Tor's group went back to their usual meeting place. "Are you alright, Dara?" Dak'Tor asked her on the way. Dazal was walking next to his sister with an arm around her shoulder.

"Just angry, that is all."

"So you are seeded?" her brother asked.

"No, no, I am not. I am sorry, I know I said I was. But I wanted to buy some time and I needed Dak'Tor to be convincing. And I certainly was not going to let that monster touch me."

"What do you think Laborn will do to us?" asked Zisa. She was still defiantly refusing to let Dazal mount her and now Dara had said she was seeded when she was not. "For one thing, it is going to become obvious in time that you are not seeded."

"I will say I lost it."

The usually shy Vaha spoke up. "We all need to calm down. Laborn is full of empty threats."

"What do you mean?" Dazal was surprised.

"What can he do to us? We are the future of the community. If he harms us or impedes us in any way, his goal of removing the Akassa and Sassen from Etera is dispersed on the wind like the kahari seeds in spring. And since his mate was killed, that is all he cares about in life."

"He can make our lives miserable," said Iria. "He can make us stop challenging him by punishing us."

"That is true," said Dazal, "but if we can gain the support of the others in the community, it will be unpopular. I think he made a big mistake today by threatening what he did. I think he fears an uprising. That is why he is so obsessed with you, Dak'Tor; you are the only one who could challenge him, but as I said earlier, he needs you. Not only for your seed, because despite what he says about not fearing the

Guardian, he could use you as leverage if the Guardian came here to unseat him. However, only if you are still alive."

At the mention of Pan, Dak'Tor thought for a moment. He had grievously wronged his sister. But she was the better person, and he had to believe that in time she would forgive him, so he could not completely rule out her support if it came to that. Their father had made a terrible mistake by choosing him to lead. *That is the only good that came out of what I did.* Pan was the rightful Leader of the High Rocks.

"So it sounds as if we are saying we need to mingle more with the community," said Iria. "See if we can win over at least enough of Laborn's followers to keep him from making our lives harder than they already are. But how do we do that?"

"However we do it, we must do it slowly, so it is not obvious," said Vaha. She turned and caught Dazal staring at her.

"What do you think about Useaves?" asked Dak'-Tor. "I know we have talked about her before, but I cannot figure it out. She seems able to challenge him openly."

"Yes, but I have never seen her go as far as she did just now," said Zisa. "And did you see the look he gave her? It was as fierce as the one he gave you, Dak'Tor. A look of pure hatred."

The others nodded.

"If I were her, I would watch my back," Zisa

added, "and if she is not worried for her life, then she has some powerful hold over him—that is all I can think."

✿

"Forgive me, Adik'Tar, but you need to think twice about this," said Gard. "Useaves is difficult, but she is the closest we have to a Healer. She is not expendable."

Laborn knew Gard was right. "Then we have to find some way to manage her. To intimidate her. I do not care how you do it; just get her back under control. She cannot openly challenge me in front of others like that."

"Tell her she went too far. Or chastise her publicly to put her back in her place. You are still the Leader."

"No. It cannot be that direct. It must be a threat to her but not traceable to me—just enough to put doubt in her mind about her position here. Come up with something that will mean she needs my favor; she must be reminded of that."

At that moment, Gard realized there was another reason the Leader did not want to confront the old female himself.

Laborn was afraid of Useaves.

✿

Finally alone with Dak'Tor, Dazal spoke. "If we seriously think you have a chance of unseating Laborn, then you will need my help."

"In what way?"

"You must learn to fight. Fight for your life."

"How do you know I cannot fight?"

Dazal barely stopped himself in time from laughing. "Please. How long have we been friends? I remember the time that cougar started stalking us when we were out hunting. You were terrified. You stood there as if you were helpless, a victim. Her next meal. There was no way she could have harmed us, but it showed me clearly that you have no skill to protect yourself and that your ability to command respect is questionable at best."

More and more, Dak'Tor regretted taking the easy way out all his life. There had been many teachers there for him at the High Rocks, and he could have learned many skills. Instead, he had allowed others to do things for him. Now he was paying for his life of privilege. The only skill he really was good at was tracking. He could hunt enough just to survive. He had hunted deer, but nothing as powerful as a cougar, which Dazal had just called him on.

"We need to train you to be a fighter. A warrior, even. And once we start, you are going to be too sore, too exhausted to do anything else at the end of the day."

"Where can we practice that we will not be seen?

It will not do my reputation any good if they learn you have to teach me what I should by right already know."

"I know a place. It is a way from here, not a place we can travel back and forth to every day. So we will have to make some excuse for being away for a while. Most likely a hunting trip, but that means we will also have to make time to hunt. For as long as we need to be gone, we cannot come back empty-handed. I hope your hunting skills have improved from the first time we met; I had to cover for you then for sure."

"Who will look after the females? And why would Laborn not think we were just running off?"

Dazal thought for a moment. "Laborn knows you care for Iria. He did care for Shikrin, so he will not think you would abandon her or your son. We can ask the females' parents to look after them."

Everything fell into place, and before long, the two males were on their way to transforming Dak'Tor into a fighter.

As they walked, Dazal said to Dak'Tor, "The first thing about being a warrior is that you have to have a fire in you. I do not know if you ever did, but from what I can see, whatever was there has gone out."

Dak'Tor was insulted but tried to turn it into a joke. "Really? Not even a tiny spark?"

"Sorry if that hurts your feelings. What are you? Were you raised as a female? You are more like a sensitive maiden."

"I lived a privileged life, and I am not proud of it. In fact, I regret it now more than you know."

"For one thing," said Dazal, "you have to learn to stop letting your feelings rule you. There is a time and place for those, but you seem to wallow in them. If they always rule, they make you weak when you need to be strong.

"You are good with tracking, but otherwise, you have the most rudimentary hunting skills when it comes down to it. We need to work on your weak areas," he added.

"My father used to tell me that a warrior who nurses his weaknesses will never grow his strengths," Dak'Tor confessed.

"Good advice. You must learn to push yourself past your limits. That is the only way to stretch them."

"So you are telling me never to care about anything?"

"Not what I am saying. Care, yes. Love Iria. Be devoted to her and to Isan'Tor. You need to care about something because you need the power of love to fuel you in a fight."

"You tell me to have control of my feelings, but now you say I have to use them to fuel myself in a fight? Double-talk."

Dazal stopped in his tracks and turned to Dak'-

Tor. "If you do not love, do not value something, then you have nothing worth fighting for. Battle is hard. It is frightening. No one will tell you this, but the fear stirs something in us that gives us extraordinary focus. We can become single-minded. Our love for others or what we believe in gives us the strength to turn that focus into defeating the enemy instead of running away and saving ourselves instead."

Dak'Tor realized he'd had nothing to lose before. He knew his parents loved him. He knew he had a place at Kthama and would only rise in stature and privilege. He never had anything driving him internally as his father had. But what had driven Moc'-Tor? Dak'Tor was suddenly ashamed that he had not really gotten to know his father. He had been too busy trying to get out of responsibility. The wealth of knowledge he could have learned from Moc'Tor—that opportunity was lost for all time.

"As much as I hate hearing this, it is helping me," Dak'Tor admitted.

"Laborn is smart. He will use your love for Iria and Isan'Tor against you. So that is why we must use it to make you strong, instead."

"I know nothing about life," Dak'Tor acknowledged in a low voice. "Next to you, I am an idiot."

"No, you are not. The fact that you can even say that, admit that to me, tells me you are ready to step up and start owning your life. Take the power that is yours. Fight for what you want. Learn what you do not know. Your humility is your greatest asset. Not your pride."

Dak'Tor was thinking. He had prayed for help from the Great Spirit, and Tweak had shown up and led him to the abandoned rebel cave system where Laborn's males found him. Perhaps Dazal's friendship had been sent as part of the answer to his prayers.

CHAPTER 3

As Takthan'Tor had feared, the assembly of Leaders at the Deep Valley was as sparse as at the first meeting he had called at the High Rocks, with only the Leaders from the nearest communities in attendance. If he could not inspire the other Leaders with his vision of using a continuation of the Mothoc High Council meetings to unite the Akassa community, he was at a loss as to how to keep the Akassa from splintering into separate and entirely independent populations.

He also knew the Akassa were charged with re-engaging with the Brothers. To make amends and repair the rift that had occurred from the thousands of years of no contact between them and the Mothoc. The question was, did the Brothers have any knowledge of how their seed had been taken Without Their Consent? Takthan'Tor did not know if it would be easier if they knew or did not. If they did, the resentment might be entrenched. If they did not, then he and the other Leaders would have to break it to them. Both of which would mean a long period of healing. Either way, there was a difficult path ahead of them all. And the Akassa were still struggling over the leaving of their Protectors. They were nowhere near being ready to engage the Brothers.

"For the few of you who have come, I am glad to see you here."

The meeting was being held at the Deep Valley, and he nodded at their Leader, Lair'Mok.

Blank stares met his welcome. There was no energy there. No enthusiasm. How could he inspire these Leaders who seemed to be struggling so themselves?

"Let me get to the point. It falls to us to lead our people into the future." He threw out a challenge. "How are we going to do that?"

No one answered.

"You are here," Takthan'Tor continued. "You at least came to meet with me, so you must care to some extent. I am looking for any ideas."

"We do not know. We have not led before. We were not raised by our fathers to lead as the Mothoc Leaders were," said Gontis'Rar of the Little River.

"Then that is the first lesson," Takthan'Tor replied. "We must raise our sons differently. We must raise them with the realization that they will be expected to take over leadership. Prepare them from when they are young. Make sure they can hunt, forage, track, prepare, follow the magnetic currents, read the night sky. Fight. Have confidence in themselves."

"What need do we have to teach our sons to fight? We have no natural predators," Gontis'Rar said.

"That is not entirely true. We occasionally lose someone to a Sarius snake. But we cannot assume that the past will predict the future. We may not have any need to be warriors now, but if we wait for what we cannot see to prepare for it, it will be too late. We must become Leaders of vision."

There was a slight stirring among the few there and some nodding and affirmations.

"And how are we to learn all this if we do not know how to do it? Our teachers are gone." And Gontis'Rar shrugged.

Pitiful. A pitiful group of people already beaten by their own thoughts of helplessness.

"The same way the females learn how to improve their skills. Experiment. We can learn to fight. We can learn to make better, stronger spears. It is trial and error, and the time is now, while we are not faced with an enemy."

Gontis'Rar spoke once more, his voice raised as if in anger. "You sound as if you know something we do not. Did the Protectors tell you something they did not share with us?"

"I know nothing that you do not know. I was not

given any privileged information. But you all heard the language of the Rah-hora. In time, the Age of Shadows will fall, and that is when the trust test will begin. It does not sound pleasant; it sounds like something we must prepare for. And if I know anything you do not, it only comes from my own experience. We must anticipate what we will need to know that we do not. What if we learn to protect ourselves, and nothing comes of it? So what? Better to be prepared for something that does not happen than to be unprepared for something that does."

"We have enough on our hands as it is. Our people have no faith in us as Leaders. They still talk, incessantly, about the Protectors. Some say that they will return one day, and our lives as we knew them will be returned to us."

"And why should they not speak that way? We all felt safe with them here. As for you, you must give your people a reason to believe in you," said Takthan'-Tor, now walking over closer to Gontis'Rar. "You must prove to them that you are worthy for them to follow. To feel that now you look after and protect them. Give them a vision just as I am trying to do with you. If we isolate, if we do not come together as a unit, as Leaders, our communities will drift apart. And then each of us will be alone in trying to guide our people. As a group of peers, we can learn together and lead together. We must learn to trust and count on each other and carry our people forward together."

He walked a few steps back and turned to address all of them. "No, we are not as strong as the Protectors. We are not as tuned into the Great Spirit as they are. Were. But what does that matter? There is only us now. Stop looking at what we no longer have and look at what we do. Etera provides all we need, and the Mothoc taught us what we need to survive. Now we must teach ourselves to lead. If we fail, we fail from our own weaknesses and lack of vision.

"Who among you is your greatest toolmaker?" he then asked.

Several names were called out. "Why not start an exchange of knowledge? Every community has at least one toolmaker. We send one toolmaker at a time to visit the rest of our communities. We can learn from each other. Or bring them together somewhere for a few days and let them all teach each other at once. We could do the same with our Healers."

"But they only know what they already know," said Gontis'Rar.

Takthan'Tor was losing patience. How did he lead the unleadable? They were so defeated. How could he inspire them to believe in themselves?

"You are right. Forget trying to lead our own people. Forget trying to learn more, grow, become stronger. Let us just sit back on our haunches and wait for the Protectors to return and rescue us."

"That is not what I am saying!" Gontis'Rar shouted.

"Is it not? Because that is what I hear. They are going to come back and save us, so why bother exerting ourselves?" Takthan'Tor now raised his voice.

"Takthan'Tor is right," said Lair'Mok of the Deep Valley. "We cannot wait for the Protectors to return—if they are even going to. I do not know who started that rumor, but it is also circulating here. The rumor grows in strength because that is what people want to believe. They do not know how to move forward. We lived in their shadow all our lives, and we do not know how to step out of it."

"Well spoken, Lair'Mok," said Takthan'Tor.

Culrat'Sar spoke up. "I support Takthan'Tor's idea. An exchange of knowledge is good. They may come up with a new idea just by talking about what they do know. The females do it all the time, and there is no reason to think it cannot happen with the toolmakers or Healers. Let us agree to meet again next full moon. Bring your tool makers; let us start with them. Have them bring their supplies. We have to start somewhere. Takthan'Tor, who is your finest toolmaker?"

It took no time for Takthan'Tor to answer. "Her name is Wry'Wry. She is the daughter of my High Protector."

"So be it. I suggest we meet at my community, the Far High Hills, next time. Bring her with you."

Culrat'Sar went on to ask each of the other Leaders for a commitment to bring their best tool-maker next time. By the time the meeting was over, Takthan'Tor was feeling more positive about the outcome. The only part he was dreading was bringing Wry'Wry to the next meeting. And based on how she felt about him now, he suspected she would not want to spend time with him either.

When he returned to Kthama and told his High Protector, Healer, and First Guard about the meeting, they had a more positive reaction than he had. Vor'Ran, the High Protector, was proud of his daughter's tool-making skills and felt it was an honor to be chosen by Takthan'Tor to represent the High Rocks.

"It is not until the next full moon. But you will tell her—or should I?" Takthan'Tor asked.

"I will let her know so she can be thinking of what supplies she wants to take with her," replied Vor'Ran. "I am sure she has a favorite striking stone. But you should invite her yourself personally at some point. I am sure she will be pleased."

Her father was wrong; Wry'Wry was not pleased to hear this. At all.

"I have to travel to the Far High Hills? With the Adik'Tar?"

"Well, who else would you think? It is a Leaders' meeting. The other Leaders are bringing their best toolmakers. This will be good for you and good for the communities. You may well even learn something new."

"Father, I am not so arrogant as to think I have nothing to learn. I welcome the exchange. I think it is a great idea."

"Then why are you raising your voice?"

"Was I? I did not realize. I am sorry. It is just—"

"It is just what?" her father asked.

"Never mind. It will be fine."

"There is another reason I believe it is time for you to go, my daughter," Vor'Ran said. "You are of pairing age. It will be good for you to mingle with the other communities."

"Pairing age? I am not ready to be paired. I do not wish to be paired."

"Nevertheless, you are of age. Your mother and I have discussed it. It should be brought up at the next High Council meeting, which happens to be the same one to which you will be traveling before long."

"But some male named Kant, who took up after Varos left, now keeps the records. It will come down to bloodlines, so what difference does it make if they see me?"

"I believe it does. It cannot hurt. You are highly skilled and respected by all at the High Rocks. You have a pleasing personality—usually," he added, "and you are beautiful. Your mother and I tell you this all the time."

"Your minds are made up?" she said, crestfallen.

"Yes. It is time for you to take a mate and have offling of your own."

"Very well. May I leave now?" she asked.

"Yes."

Wry'Wry went to their living quarters and tossed herself down on her sleeping mat. She was not ready to be paired, and she did not want to leave Kthama. Her home was there. He was there. Oh, why had his feelings for her changed?

There was a time she had thought Takthan'Tor liked her in a romantic way. Now he always appeared to avoid her, to have no time for her. They had seemed to be getting closer before he was picked to be the Leader, and he became distant shortly after. She had not changed, so what had? Had the burden of leadership altered him so much?

Vor'Ran told Takthan'Tor that Wry'Wry was excited about going to the Far High Hills. Takthan'Tor raised his eyebrows in disbelief.

"Really?"

"Well, alright. No. But she will be when the time comes. Perhaps she is not comfortable leaving Kthama. Her mother and I have decided it is time for her to be paired, and what better time to tell the High Council than at the next meeting. That way, she will not be just a name; the High Council members will have a chance to get to know her a little better."

Paired. Wry'Wry? She would leave Kthama. Be paired to who knows who.

"Did she agree to this?" he asked, trying to sound nonchalant.

"She has no choice. If she waits too long, other younger maidens will come forward, and her chance may be lost. I do not want to see my daughter grow older with no offling and no male to protect and provide for her."

Takthan'Tor looked stricken.

"Is something wrong?"

"No. I am just remembering a conversation we had about bringing together all those who wish to be paired. I am sure there are other maidens and males who would want to be. I think we should call an assembly and find out before the next meeting." Takthan'Tor turned away. "Take care of that, please. I am going to take my daily walk through the High Rocks."

Vor'Ran arranged an assembly for that evening. Takthan'Tor tried to look pleased with his High Protector's efficiency, but as he stood in front of the crowd, he had to fight for control over his inner turmoil.

"You know why we are here," he said. "At the next High Council meeting, our High Protector's daughter is going to be put forward to be considered for pairing. If there are any others, males or females, who are also ready, I want to present all your names and family history for consideration."

As he was speaking, he could see Wry'Wry in the front row, standing next to her parents. He refused to let his gaze drop to hers, knowing it would be his undoing. Publicly.

"Adik'Tar," said Tensil, his Healer. "Forgive my imprudence, but have you yourself thought of taking a mate?"

He could not stop himself; his gaze flickered to Wry'Wry. His heart stopped, and it took him a moment to recover. "Well, of course. It is my obligation to produce offling, someone to pass the leadership of the High Rocks to. But with so much going on, I do not think it prudent to do so at the moment."

"You get to choose for yourself. Perhaps the meetings at the other communities will prove beneficial in that regard."

Wry'Wry said something to her parents and squeezed past her father. She walked briskly out of the room.

Takthan'Tor watched her leave. *I did it again.* Somehow, he had offended her again. Clearly, she hated him now, and he must kill his longing for her. It was impossible anyway, ever since he had made

Vor'Ran the High Protector—the hardest decision he had so far made as Leader.

He thought back to his conversation with Rohm'Mok when he was deciding whether to choose Vor'Ran or Anthram to be his High Protector—

"I need your guidance. I have been unable to decide between two for the choice of High Protector. What qualities should I look for?"

"What does your own counsel tell you?" Rohm'Mok asked.

"That he must be someone the other males look up to. Accomplished in many areas. Fair-minded. Quick to decide, but at the same time not impulsive. Able to weigh all factors and come to a plan of action."

"All solid answers. I am not sure why you are confused?"

"I do not know if I should choose someone who is desirous of the position. Someone who pursues it over someone who is less—driven, so to say."

"That is a common quandary. Who is best suited to lead? The one who seeks it and makes it his goal in life? Or the one who carries the mantle more lightly, who is satisfied without control and influence over others."

"Exactly my problem."

"There is no simple answer," said Rohm'Mok. "And one is not necessarily always the right choice over the other. Perhaps the choice lies not between the two different temperaments but is more wisely based on the integrity of each of the candidates. Above all, the welfare of the people must always be the guiding factor behind

any decisions made by those in leadership. Not the acqui-
sition of more authority, fame, or admiration. Those who
are able to set aside their own self-interests, even with an
internal struggle, will always be the better choice in a
position of authority."

It was not until Rohm'Mok had suggested the
welfare of the Akassa had to be the guiding element
in the decision that Takthan'Tor realized why he had
not been able to decide. He knew Vor'Ran was the
better choice. But he also knew that as the daughter
of his first in command, Wry'Wry would then be out
of his reach. Takthan'Tor felt it would create an
unnatural imbalance as the Leader's mate would be
Third Rank, higher than that of the High Protector
except in times of crisis. In the end, he had chosen
the welfare of his people over his own personal
desires. Now every time he saw her, all he felt was
loss and despair. He had loved her for some time.
Envisioned her in his arms, in his life day after day.
And now, she could never be his. And even worse,
before long, it would fall to him to announce Ashwea
Awhidi over her and another male.

The time passed too quickly. Before long, Takthan'-
Tor, Vor'Ran, and Wry'Wry were on their way to the
Far High Hills. In the end, the Leader had asked
Vor'Ran to go with them. He made some excuse that
he did not want to put Wry'Wry's reputation at risk

by traveling alone with a male, even if he was the Adik'Tar. Vor'Ran could not see any validity in Takthan'Tor's concern as no one would ever think the Leader capable of taking advantage of his position like that, but in the end, he acquiesced and agreed to go with them, much to Takthan'Tor's relief.

As they made their way up the tunnel that snaked along the Great River, Takthan'Tor reached out in an offer to carry Wry'Wry's travel satchel. She looked at him, frowning. "What are you doing?"

"I was offering to carry your bag for you."

"I am not some weak female who needs to be coddled. I can carry my own supplies," she snapped.

"Daughter," Vor'Ran said. "What has gotten into you? Your Leader was only offering out of consideration. How can you turn that into an insult? I swear, this only confirms that your mother and I are right in having you paired. You need something, or someone, to calm you down."

Wry'Wry blushed at her father's indelicate remark. She turned her face away, not wanting either of them to see her reaction.

In spite of himself, Takthan'Tor could not help but chuckle, to which Wry'Wry snapped, "Do you think that is humorous? Perhaps you are in need of a good mating yourself!" she snapped.

"That is enough!" Vor'Ran practically shouted. "You apologize now. Yes, my remark was out of hand, but it was I who said it, not Takthan'Tor. You will treat the Adik'Tar with respect. When you calm down later, you will realize it *was* rather funny, and then you will have the good sense to be ashamed of yourself for speaking to him so."

Takthan'Tor had to say something. "It is I who should apologize. I should not have laughed."

"Whatever is going on with you, Wry'Wry, please get it under control," Vor'Ran continued. "No one wants an insolent female, except one who wants to break her. Trust me, you do not want that kind of male for a mate."

Takthan'Tor had never seen that side of Wry'Wry before. He had known her to be almost always amiable, smiling, a friend to all she met. He wanted to disagree with Vor'Ran. He wanted to tell her how the fire in her did not make him want to break her. It only made him want her more. But he knew he never could say the words he wanted to.

Wry'Wry was silent the rest of the day's walk. When they settled down in one of the nesting nooks along the Mother Stream, she made a place for herself away from both Takthan'Tor and her father and turned her back to them.

They continued the rest of the walk without another word from Wry'Wry. So the males passed the time discussing possibilities for a pairing celebration such as Tensil had suggested some time ago.

Wry'Wry listened but said nothing. The thought of Takthan'Tor announcing Ashwea Awhidi over her and an unknown male just made her angrier. She decided then and there that she would do everything she could to thwart the choosing of a mate for her.

The entrance was busy when they arrived at the Far High Hills as all the Leaders and their toolmakers were supposed to arrive by twilight. Takthan'Tor, Vor'Ran, and Wry'Wry were immediately welcomed and shown into the middle of the group, where introductions were made.

Takthan'Tor was pleased to see there were a few more Leaders present than last time. He did not recognize them all, but he was immediately grateful for whoever had sent messengers out to the other communities about the gathering of toolmakers. That gave him some hope for their future gatherings.

Vor'Ran introduced Wry'Wry, who was not her usual bright self and barely said hello. They were shown to their quarters and told they would be summoned for last meal. Once settled in, Vor'Ran turned to his daughter.

"Why the sullen attitude? You barely said hello to the other Leaders and toolmakers. Tell me you are not still angry at the joke I made on the way?"

"I do not care about the joke. But I do not want to be paired. Why should I have to be? Does every female have to be paired the moment she is of age? For one thing, I do not want to leave Kthama."

"What is the other thing?"

"What other thing?" she frowned.

"You said *for one thing*. That means there is another reason. What are you not telling me?"

"You would not understand. Besides, it does not matter. It cannot be helped, so there is no sense talking about it."

Vor'Ran let out a long breath. "I should have sent your mother with you instead. Perhaps she would be able to understand you. I certainly cannot."

Wry'Wry then moved closer to her father, and as she wrapped her arms around his neck, placed her head on his chest. "Father, please do not make me pair. I do not want to."

Vor'Ran's heart softened toward her, and he laid his head on hers. "I am sorry. I hate to see you unhappy like this. But none of us likes changes. It seems to come hard to our people. But once you have someone in your life and a little offling on your hip, you will realize I was right. We have to keep moving forward."

Wry'Wry had vowed she was not going to cry but could not help herself. As she let out a little sob, Vor'Ran, for the first time, doubted his and her mother's decision. If it was making her this unhappy, how could it be the right thing? Was it not the parents' role to encourage their offling to do what they believed was right, even if they were unwilling at the time?

"Just try to stop fighting the idea. At least try to have a good time while you are here; it is possible they will not make a match for you. Maybe you just need more time to get used to the idea. Perhaps we did not give you time to adjust to it," Vor'Ran said.

"I will never adjust to it!" She tore herself from her father's embrace and flung herself down on the sleeping mat, immediately wishing she had tried it out first before she landed on the hard surface.

Vor'Ran threw his arms up in the air. "I will give you some privacy."

Before long, it was meal time. The guests filed in, selected their food from the customary food counter serviced by older females behind it, and were shown to their tables.

When it was their turn, Takthan'Tor, Vor'Ran, and Wry'Wry were seated near the front. Just as they sat down, Culrat'Sar came over with a becoming female in tow.

"I hope you have found everything acceptable. This is my daughter, Persica. I am introducing her to all the guests since she will be helping me with these gatherings from now on.

Wry'Wry looked her up and down. She was indeed very attractive with generous hips that would bear offling well. Her wavy hair was an unusual mix of black and brown tones. Worse than that, there was a kindness in her eyes that probably made her immediately likable—except to Wry'Wry.

Culrat'Sar introduced his daughter to each of them, ending with Takthan'Tor. Persica seemed to brighten even more when they reached the Adik'Tar.

"The High Rocks has the largest of our populations. You must be wise to lead so many so successfully."

Takthan'Tor answered, "I do not know if I am being successful. Perhaps no Leader does until years have passed. But I thank you for your kind words."

Wry'Wry's eyes narrowed. If she had not liked Culrat'Sar's daughter a moment before, she liked her even less now. And she disliked herself even more for how she was feeling. Why should the female not flirt with Takthan'Tor? He was magnificent. But he did not have to flirt back.

"Well, we will leave you to your meal," said Culrat'Sar. "My daughter and I must go and get some food."

"You are welcome to join us if you wish," Takthan'Tor said. "Though you must have your customary table, and you have many guests."

"We would be pleased to," Culrat'Sar answered. "We will be right back."

Wry'Wry observed that the table they were seated at was fairly large. She wondered if perhaps the Leader had intentionally had them seated there, planning all along for them to be joined by his daughter. Was Culrat'Sar trying to get Takthan'Tor interested in Persica?

"What will you be doing to help your father?"

Vor'Ran asked Persica as the two returned and sat down.

"Just making sure our guests have what they need. Arranging for personal needs, making sure the water gourds are refreshed every day, and the like," she said.

"Ah, so in a way, you are the lead female here?"

"To a point, perhaps. I am also a toolmaker, so there is lots to keep me busy."

Wry'Wry could not stop herself before she rolled her eyes. *So all of a sudden, everyone is a toolmaker.*

"Is something wrong?" Persica asked her.

"Me?" she stammered. "Oh, no. Oh, no, I am sorry. I am just preoccupied."

"I hear you are asking to be paired."

"My parents' idea," Wry'Wry answered, then quickly glanced at her father.

"My daughter has not completely warmed up to the idea. I fear it is our fault; we should have given her more time to adjust, perhaps waiting for the following High Council meeting," Vor'Ran answered.

"What is there to adjust to?" Persica responded. "I cannot wait to be paired. I thought every female looked forward to the day when she would have a strong male to care for her and protect her and give her offling." Then she glanced at Takthan'Tor.

To Wry'Wry's horror, he smiled.

"You are right," Wry'Wry blurted out a little too strongly. "I do not know why I have resisted it. Now that you have said that, I can see that being paired is exactly what I need. Father, though you have no control over it, do what you can to ensure I am made a good match. The sooner I am paired, the sooner I will enjoy all the benefits that the Adik'Tar's daughter has just explained. Now, if you will excuse me, I am exhausted from the trip and am going to get some sleep."

Wry'Wry rose, said good night to each of them, and left with most of her meal untouched.

"I apologize for my daughter," Vor'Ran said. "She usually has a very agreeable personality. Everyone says so."

"It is most likely unsettling being away from home and her mother and familiar environment," suggested Culrat'Sar. "Do not be concerned about it. We hear she is an exceptionally fine toolmaker."

"Perhaps I should go and speak to her. I think it is my words that upset her," said Persica. Before Vor'Ran or her father could stop her, she had left.

Takthan'Tor turned to Vor'Ran and Culrat'Sar. "I am not sure that was a good idea."

"Do not worry about Wry'Wry. My daughter is very kind."

Takthan'Tor nodded and did not say what he was thinking. He was not worried about Wry'Wry. But with the state Wry'Wry had been in lately, he was worried for Persica.

At the sound of the clack on the stone door, Wry'Wry called out, "Go away, Father!"

"It is not your father; it is me," Persica said through the open door. "May I come in?"

This was the last person Wry'Wry wanted to see. "I am fine. I do not know why you are here."

Persica appeared in the doorway. "You are not fine. If my father and your Leader cannot see it, that does not mean I cannot. What is bothering you? Are you truly that much against being paired?"

Wry'Wry sat up and ran her hand over her face. "No. Yes. No. Oh, I do not know."

Persica took a few more steps into the room. "May I stay a while? It seems you could use a friend right now."

Her kindness was unwarranted after how Wry'Wry had behaved, so in her shame, she waved Persica over to sit down.

"It is not that I did not expect to be paired. There was a time when I even wanted it. But—"

"But not to just anyone. Is there someone you care for? Is that it?" Persica asked with a soft voice, leaning in toward Wry'Wry.

Wry'Wry hesitated a moment then admitted, "Yes. That is it. Someone I was close to for some time. I thought we would be together one day. And then, suddenly, he started acting differently toward me.

Cool. Aloof. Even curt. And I still cannot think of a thing I did to cause the change I saw in him."

"Did you think he cared for you at one time?"

"I was sure of it. As sure as I was of anything. That is why it is so painful."

Persica waited for Wry'Wry to continue but when she did not, said, "Are you hoping his feelings will someday return?"

"I do not know. Maybe. Or maybe I just cannot get over him. The idea of being with another male is —oh, I cannot even conceive of it. I guess I had too many daydreams about our life together, he and I. Maybe Father is right; maybe I only need more time. In a way, it feels as if I am grieving."

"I think you should tell your father what you just told me and ask for more time. I think he needs to understand why you are fighting him. Ask him to wait until the next High Council meeting to announce that you wish to be paired. Maybe in that time—"

"His feelings will return? No. I do not think so. I guess it is best if I start accepting it and try to move forward.' Wry'Wry sighed. "But there is no joy in my heart over a future with any other male."

She looked at Persica. "Thank you for coming to talk to me. I miss my mother, and it is good to have another female to talk to."

"You can come and talk to me any time. I have no sisters, and I would enjoy having someone to talk to other than my mother. Besides, we are both toolmakers! Perhaps we can help each other advance our trade. I will see you tomorrow, then," and Persica rose to her feet. She turned to give Wry'Wry a warm smile before she exited the room.

She is so kind. And I was horrible back there. Wry'Wry knew she had disrespected both her father and her Adik'Tar with her behavior. Perhaps that is how she had to start looking at Takthan'Tor, as her Leader and not as the male with whom she used to spend time laughing and taking long walks looking for wildlife.

Wry'Wry turned over and prepared to quiet her mind with sleep. Her last wish before she drifted off was that she knew what she had done to change his feelings for her. Maybe if she knew that, she could move on.

Persica returned to the eating commons to find her father and the other two males engaged in deep conversation. She walked over but then caught herself and turned away.

Vor'Ran noticed her and said, "Please, Persica. Did you speak with my daughter?"

She turned back. "Yes, I did. And perhaps you could speak with her yourself soon. Find out what is really troubling her. I think when you do, you will not think so harshly of her for how she feels. That is all I can say." Then she excused herself and went to join some females at another table.

"Your daughter must have a way with words," said Takthan'Tor. "Forgive me for saying this, Vor'Ran, but I did not think she would be able to get Wry'Wry to talk to her at all."

"My daughter is a very kind person," Culrat'Sar said. "She is humble and caring. She would make a fine mate to any male." Then he added, "You should spend some time with her while you are here, Adik'Tar."

"Perhaps I will, thank you," Takthan'Tor answered. He was torn. Wry'Wry was soon to be paired, lost to him forever. Even though it was inevitable, the thought of her in the arms of another male tore through him like a knife to his heart. But somehow, he had to move on; he knew it. Somehow, he had to put out of his mind all thoughts of her and what might have been between them.

The time at the Far High Hills passed quickly enough. Wry'Wry did her best to avoid Takthan'Tor and turned her back if he entered the toolmakers' forum. Though she enjoyed the time with the other toolmakers, she was anxious to return to Kthama. Several of the High Council Leaders mingled among them, making conversation. She could not forget her father's hope that in getting to know her better, they would choose her the perfect mate. Part of her wanted to be churlish to turn them against her, but she realized that would only backfire. If it was inevitable that she be paired, she did not want an overbearing mate who would take joy in breaking an insolent spirit. In the end, she tried to be as much herself as she could while managing her churning feelings for Takthan'Tor.

Despite the rocky start, Persica and Wry'Wry found they not only had a lot in common but that they enjoyed each other's company. Against Wry'Wry's will, she and Persica became friends. The only problem in their friendship was that Persica seemed interested in Takthan'Tor. So far, Wry'Wry had not told her new friend who the male was who had broken her heart. She wondered what would happen if Persica ever found out it was the very male she kept being extra nice to.

Vor'Ran was pleased to see his daughter making a friend outside of Kthama.

By the end of the gathering, Wry'Wry had shared quite a few techniques with the other toolmakers and learned some new ones.

The coming together to share knowledge had been a success. But the rest of the High Council meeting did not go as well as some had hoped.

Takthan'Tor stood next to Vor'Ran, looking over

the gathering of Akassa. Where the Leader had hoped to find enthusiasm and forward-thinking, he was instead met with pessimism and a sense of defeat. "We are not moving forward," he said to the High Protector.

"Do you mean at the High Rocks? Or here, the High Council?"

"Any of us. All of us. As a people. We are not moving forward. Look at their faces. Where is the enthusiasm? I see only despair. What is it going to take to turn it around?"

"Perhaps time," Vor'Ran remarked.

"Our young males and females, even they seem lackluster. I am not sure time will solve this problem."

As they continued watching, Persica and Culrat'Sar came over to join them. Culrat'Sar strategically positioned his daughter next to Takthan'Tor, close enough that Takthan'Tor would be well aware of her female essence.

Takthan'Tor addressed his fellow Leader. "We will be leaving soon, Culrat'Sar."

"The toolmakers have learned a lot from each other. This was a good idea," replied the other Leader.

"Perhaps there should be another meeting soon?" Persica suggested. "This time with the Healers?"

As she was speaking, Takthan'Tor glanced at Culrat'Sar's daughter and noticed again how attractive she was. She had a mixture of darker and lighter strands in her hair, unusual for their kind. If only he could put Wry'Wry out of his heart and his mind.

He turned back to Persica's father. "Hopefully, those who came will go back and share their experiences with others. Perhaps that will generate interest. Before we disband, I would like to address the High Council one last time."

That afternoon, with the High Council gathered, Takthan'Tor took the floor. "I trust you share my opinion that this was beneficial to the toolmakers and that we should consider bringing together another group to share their knowledge." Many nodded, and some murmured their agreement.

"But before we disband, I want to address the issue of the Others. The Brothers as they are now to be called. It is our charge now to find a way to engage them. To win their trust and make amends for the wrongs of the past. Does anyone have anything to say about this?"

Takthan'Tor waited, and no one said a word.

"What do you say?" asked Culrat'Sar. "Surely you have all thought about this; you all received the Rahhora, just as we did. This is the will of the Great Spirit. We must make amends."

Finally, one of the other Leaders spoke up. Lair'Mok of the Deep Valley. "It is too soon. We are not ready yet. We must wait until we have adjusted to the loss of the Protectors."

Takthan'Tor felt himself losing patience. "And when will that be? And how will that come about?

Do we have a plan to put this great change to rest so we can move on? I hear lamentations but no solutions. It is what it is. It is done. They have left, and they are not coming back."

"With all due respect, you do not have offling, Adik'Tar," someone said. "We struggle not with just our own reactions, but those of our sons and daughters."

"This has shaken them as it has shaken us," added another.

"That may be true, but what is shaking them further is watching you, their parents, their Leaders, struggling with this. You must set a good example. It falls to you to find a way not to just survive this but to thrive in spite of it. You must inspire them. They are the future. How are they to have the confidence they can succeed if you as their Leaders do not?"

"Succeed at what?" asked someone else.

"At life! At living." Takthan'Tor walked down into the group of Leaders. "At fulfilling our obligation to the Great Spirit. Everything the Protectors told us we must do. We must lead our people into the future of our own making.

"Life goes on. There are pairings to be arranged, new journeys awaiting our young females and males. In time, the happy chatter of even more offling will fill the halls. There are spring plantings to organize, and later, harvests to bring in. We must get on with the busyness of living and stop looking back."

However, Takthan'Tor felt as if he were talking to

an empty room. The blank faces staring back at him reflected no affinity with what he was saying. It was as if they were defeated before they had even started. The Leader unconsciously shook his head.

Then Culrat'Sar spoke again. "It is nearly time to adjourn. We should meet again at the second new moon. I suggest we hold the next meeting at the High Rocks unless anyone has any objection."

The Leaders dispersed to claim those they had brought with them. It took a while for all the items to be gathered and packed in the carrying satchels, but before too long, Takthan'Tor, Vor'Ran, and Wry'Wry were on their way back home.

To break the silence, Vor'Ran struck up a conversation with his daughter. "I am proud of you. You pulled yourself together and made a good impression on the other High Council members. They will remember you when it comes time to select your mate."

Wry'Wry looked up at her father but said nothing.

"And, Adik'Tar, Culrat'Sar's daughter seems to be quite enamored with you." Had Vor'Ran been able to see his daughter's face, he would have noticed her clenched teeth.

"She is a comely and agreeable maiden. I am sure

she will make someone a fine mate," Takthan'Tor answered.

"But not you? You have the right to choose," Vor'Ran answered.

"At the moment, I have more urgent matters at hand."

CHAPTER 4

"Why have you brought me all the way out here?" Useaves' words were short and clipped as she waded through the high green grasses.

"There is something you need to know, and I do not want Laborn seeing us talking alone," said Gard. "He is angry with you."

"That old PetaQ is always angry with me. So what?"

"Yes, but this time he told me to make something happen to you."

"Happen to me? He wants me killed?" Useaves' voice had no alarm in it, only an even sharper edge.

"No. But he wants me to do something that will put you in your place. Scare you."

"What are you going to do?"

"What do you think? Nothing, of course; that is why I am telling you. Just play along and control your insolence for a while. Give him some time to calm down and let him think I did my job," Gard said. Then he added, "You are lucky he came to me and not Kaisak."

Useaves actually looked as if she was thinking about what Gard had said. "Very well, I will not challenge him for a while. But I cannot promise it will last very long. He is a terrible Leader. It should have been you."

Gard stroked the long scar that ran down the side of his face. He was remembering how he had received it after the rebel group had left Kayerm, having been thrown out by Straf'Tor. Still fresh in their minds was the vision of Ridg'Sor's lifeblood flowing in a long red river down the hillside where Straf'Tor's blade had sliced open the rebel Leader's throat. Emotions had been high as the rebel group left Kayerm. Everyone was on edge with no idea where they were going and knowing that Straf'Tor's males were following to make sure they did not turn back.

When they first left, Laborn had assumed leadership. None of the others challenged him, and Gard positioned himself as the Leader's advisor and supporter. After so many were killed in the cave-in at their first location, including Laborn's mate, Shifrin, they moved on to where they had now finally settled. One evening Gard came across Laborn lamenting the loss of his mate. He had never heard the Leader so emotional and knew he had stumbled upon a private moment, yet he could not help himself. He called out in a misguided attempt to offer some consolation. With his privacy invaded and weakness revealed, the Leader was embarrassed and attacked Gard, and they struggled. Laborn had ended the fight by slicing Gard's face with a sharp rock. Useaves treated Gard and started the rumor that he had got the wound when challenging Laborn for leadership. She thought it made Gard sound more formidable. Though Laborn did not like it, he had put up with it rather than have the true story of his emotional breakdown become known.

"Now we need to get back before someone spots us," said Gard. "You saw what he did to me for trying to extend him kindness at a difficult time. What would happen if he knew I had come to you and told him his plans?"

"No doubt he would leave you with worse than that scar on your face. It is obvious he has no respect for you, so neither do any of the others. If you ever expect to lead, you must prove yourself worthy. You should have killed Laborn that night while his guard was down," she lectured him.

"That would have been cowardly."

"That would have made you Leader," Useaves snapped. "If you want to lead, you must be willing to do what it takes."

"So, what do we do next?" Gard asked, tired of her chastisement.

"Just what I said. I will be more orderly, so

Laborn can think you succeeded. That will gain you favor in his eyes while we figure out what to do."

"So what am I to do now?" Gard hated to ask again as he knew he was already getting on Useaves' nerves.

"If you are ever going to overthrow Laborn, you must do something about the Guardian's brother. He must be discredited, shamed somehow. The people are already drawn to him because of his Guardian-like markings. Many of them believe in the Guardian, despite Laborn's trying to influence them otherwise. In Laborn's ignorance, by giving him three females to seed, he has also elevated Dak'Tor's status. The other males are envious but not spiteful, which surprises me."

Gard was surprised. He had never heard Useaves admit she did not know everything.

They carefully parted company, Gard staying after Useaves had left and then taking a longer route back to come into the settlement from a different direction.

Useaves was true to her word and stopped chal-lenging Laborn. Laborn saw the change in her and one night, while they were sitting around the evening fire, gave a slight nod to Gard, acknowledging that he had done as ordered.

Dazal and Dak'Tor returned from their hunting trip with their bounty dressed and preserved, dragged behind them on stretchers. When word reached her that the two males had returned, Iria ran with Isan'Tor on her hip to find Dak'Tor. He smiled at seeing her and dropped the stretcher handles but put his hands up to stop her embrace. "Please. As much as I want to hold you in my arms, this is not the time." Iria took a moment to look him up and down and had to agree. All his silver hair was smudged with sweat and grime. She laughed, and with a glint in her eye, told him to hurry and wash up.

Dazal's sister, Dara, showed up shortly with Vaha and her offling. Soon many surrounded the hunters, and the two showed everyone their kill. Their bounty was impressive.

Dak'Tor invited the other males to take their share for their families, and Dazal agreed, saying that they wanted to do something to help support the community. Even Useaves had to admit it was an impressive bounty.

Laborn resented the congratulations and words of gratitude that he could hear from where he was standing apart from the crowd. Seeing Useaves praising Dak'Tor made Laborn furious. She was too influential. She was too important. He decided then and there that if she was going to openly elevate

Dak'Tor's status with her approval, that she was expendable after all.

That evening, after Dak'Tor had cleaned up and as he was drying off as much as he could next to the evening fire, there was even more talk about the successful hunting trip. Each word cut into Laborn, and it was all he could do not to stand up and explode.

Iria sat next to Dak'Tor, her dark coloring in sharp contrast to his silver-white markings. Their thighs were touching, and they exchanged tender looks. Across the fire, Iria's parents held their grandson, planning on keeping him for the night so the two could have some time alone.

At one point, Dak'Tor leaned over and pulled Iria into him and hugged her in front of everyone, to which the other females smiled. Finally, Dak'Tor said he was tired and stood up, reaching his hand down to Iria, who rose to go with him. There were good-natured remarks made about the rest of their night together after such a long separation.

Dak'Tor had thought about Iria and Isan'Tor the entire time he was gone, wondering how they were doing. He was confident that between his parents,

Dazal's parents, and hers, no harm would come to them. Still, he had been relieved when he saw her hurrying toward him, safe and sound.

"I missed you more than I can say," he told her as they lay on the sleeping mat.

"Tell me, I want to hear it," she smiled.

"You were my first thought on waking and my last thought as I went to sleep. Every day I prayed for the well-being of you both."

"You prayed? As in, to the Great Spirit?" The surprise in her voice was clear.

"Yes, I did. Me. And it felt good. As hard as this journey has been, it has changed me for the better; I know it. I would never have chosen this hardship for myself, but I am grateful for it now."

"Hardship? Being with me is a hardship?" she teased.

"Oh, yes, a terrible burden," he teased her back, softly kissing her face. "Let me show you just what a hardship it is," and he rolled her onto her back. Their lovemating went on throughout the night.

Somehow Laborn managed to control himself until all the others had left. As Gard got up to leave, the Leader told him to sit back down.

He whispered to Gard, "I thought he would fail on the hunting trip. That they would return with a pitiful bounty, which is why I did not stop it. Instead, they come back with a ridiculous haul. Enough for many families. His popularity is growing, and it must be stopped. We must do something— What did you do to get Useaves under control?"

Gard had been prepared for that question for some time. "It is better you do not know, for your own sake."

Laborn nodded. "Well, she stopped challenging me, but tonight she went too far in praising Dak'Tor. I want you to kill Useaves."

Gard's jaw dropped. "You just said Dak'Tor is the problem."

"He is, but so is she. I cannot afford to have her throw in with him against me."

"Why would you think that?" Gard was clearly alarmed.

"You saw her. She gushed all over him and his great success. They both have to go."

"Killing both of them will be too obvious. You are not thinking straight, Adik'Tar," Gard dared to say.

"You give me no credit. Of course, that would be too obvious. So here is what we, or rather you, are going to do. You are going to kill Useaves, but blame it on Dak'Tor. No one will suspect you."

"But how does that get rid of Dak'Tor?"

"Everyone will turn on Dak'Tor for killing Useaves. The community needs her. He will become an outcast."

"Why would he kill Useaves, especially since she

just praised him openly? I do not see how it would work," Gard said.

"I do not know! Think of something. Why do I have to figure everything out? Say they argued. Say— Say that Dak'Tor was angry that she supported me when I wanted to make him mount Dara in front of everyone. And they argued, and in a rage, he killed her. Hit her over the head with a rock."

Gard thought a moment. "Alright. But Dak'Tor will deny it. So you must be there as a witness. They will believe you that he did it."

"Alright. But we need to do it soon. It turns my stomach to see Dak'Tor and Iria so happy together."

As they walked away, Gard's mind was spinning, trying to figure out what to do next. But within a few days, he had come up with a plan.

Laborn sent Gard to bring Dak'Tor and Useaves to him. Kaisak stood at Laborn's side as he often did.

"I congratulate you on your successful hunting trip. I thought you would return empty-handed. Now that you have proven you are a skilled hunter, your use to our community is even greater than it was before. Because of that, I suggest we come to an agreement."

Dak'Tor listened to Laborn cautiously. "What kind of an arrangement?"

"I am not sure. But since it involves all of us, the

Leaders, we should work it out together. But not here. I do not want our conversation overheard. When we have come to an agreement, I will announce it to the rest."

"I want to believe you," Dak'Tor said.

"If you think this is easy for me, it is not," Laborn retorted. "I wish you had never come. But you are here, and it is clear the rest of the community has accepted you. I am not as bad as you think. I can be reasonable. For the sake of everyone here, you at least owe me a chance."

Dak'Tor stared at Laborn before glancing at Useaves, who gave him an almost imperceptible nod. "Alright. When and where?"

"This evening after last meal." Laborn looked meaningfully at Gard. "I will leave it to you to find a place."

"I will do as you ask, Adik'Tar," said Gard. "I will let you know at evening meal where we can go to talk."

Kaisak, having heard the entire exchange, asked, "Adik'Tar, do you not want me to attend to this with you?"

"No. I need you here. I will tell you later what we decided." The Leader ignored the pinched look that came over Kaisak's face.

Dak'Tor went immediately to find Dazal and Iria. "Despite his conciliatory tone, I do not trust Laborn for a moment," said Dazal. "It has to be some kind of trap."

"I agree. He does not accept you; he is up to something. Do not go, please!" Iria pleaded.

"I agree with you both," Dak'Tor said. "I certainly do not trust him. He is up to something. But if I go tonight, at least I might be able to see it coming. If I do not go, then the next time might not be this obvious."

"Shall we follow you from a safe distance?" asked Dazal.

"If we knew ahead of time where it will be, then you could already be stationed there in hiding. But without knowing that, it is too risky. I will be careful. I promise." He did not tell them of Useaves' nod and how she had helped him before. He hoped she was telling him the meeting was safe to agree to, but he knew he could not count on her loyalty.

The evening fire was dying down. Laborn stood up and excused himself. Shortly thereafter, Gard and Useaves also did. Iria looked at Dak'Tor as he, too, slipped away, and she squeezed her eyes shut to hide the concern in them.

Once they were out of sight, Gard offered to lead them there. Useaves fell behind as she could not walk as fast as they did. When they arrived, the males stood waiting for her.

"Hurry up, old female," Laborn said impatiently.

"Come and help me then. Give me your arm," she called out to him.

He snarled, and all three males started to walk back to where she was, Laborn in the lead. As they were almost there, Useaves lost her balance and fell. Laborn got to her first, reached down to help her up, and just as he did, Gard grabbed a nearby rock and smashed it over the back of the Leader's head.

Laborn collapsed into a clump at Useaves' side, blood flowing profusely from where the rock had cut his scalp. He moaned and grabbed the back of his head.

Gard tossed the rock away, then quickly wrapped his arms around Dak'Tor, pinning him in place. "Laborn! Are you alright?"

Dak'Tor struggled desperately in Gard's grasp and managed to break free and stumble away but not before Laborn had seen him in Gard's stronghold.

The Leader struggled to his feet with blood profusely running down the back of his head. He glared at Dak'Tor. "You will pay for this. Dearly!"

By then, Useaves had reached Laborn, and she told him to sit down. She examined him. "It is a deep cut. If you are to survive, I will have to treat you carefully."

"How bad is it?" Laborn tried to reach back to

feel the wound, but Useaves smacked his hand away. "Stop it; you will just infect it."

Dak'Tor called out, "It was Gard. It was Gard who tried to kill you. Not me!"

"Why would I do that?" Gard shouted at Dak'Tor.

"Tell him, Useaves. You were standing there with me. You saw Gard grab that rock and hit Laborn over the back of his head with it!"

Useaves looked at Dak'Tor and said coldly. "Do not ask me to lie for you. It was you who tried to kill Laborn."

A cold bolt shot through Dak'Tor. Useaves had seen it; she knew it was Gard. He felt sick to his stomach.

"Quickly, we must get Laborn back so I can stop the bleeding," Useaves said, shooting Dak'Tor a look.

"What about Dak'Tor?" Laborn asked as he let Gard help him to his feet.

"Do not worry about him. He is in enough trouble as it is. I doubt he will try anything else," Useaves said. "Not if he wants to save his mate and offling."

Slowly the four made it back to camp, Gard supporting Laborn and Useaves and Dak'Tor following. Dak'Tor kept looking at Useaves, trying to catch her eye, trying to understand why she had turned on him.

Finally, unable to ignore his constant looking over at her as they walked, she whispered. "Shut up. Later."

When they got back to the settlement, the others who were still awake raised a commotion on seeing Gard supporting Laborn, who now had blood dripping onto his shoulders. Kaisak was quick to the scene.

As the four approached the group, Laborn called out, "Dak'Tor tried to kill me!" Several males quickly surrounded Dak'Tor.

"I did not!" Dak'Tor shouted. "It was Gard. Gard hit him over the head with a rock. Useaves saw it, but she will not admit it!"

"Enough of this," snapped Useaves. "I need to get Laborn lying down so I can try to stop the bleeding. It is a deep gash. Pray that infection does not set in, or Dak'Tor will have succeeded after all."

By now, Iria had heard, and the males guarding Dak'Tor allowed her to run to his side. She was panicked and clung to him, sobbing. "I did not do it, I swear," he said to her.

"I believe you. Oh, Dak'Tor," she cried, "what will become of us now?"

The crowd stayed up for much of the night discussing what Dak'Tor had done. There had been trouble between Gard and Laborn long ago, but no one believed Gard would try to kill the Leader. He was too afraid of him. And though Useaves had her own problems with Laborn, they did not think she had enough loyalty to Gard to lie if he had done it. Besides, Useaves had just openly praised Dak'Tor on his hunting skills. Why would she do that if she was biased against him? In the end, they decided it had to be Dak'Tor. He was the only one brave enough to try it, after all.

For the time being, guards were placed outside the quarters belonging to Dak'Tor and Iria.

In their quarters, Iria sat holding their son while Dak'Tor sat next to her with his arms around them both. Before too long, the guards allowed Dazal, Zisa, and Dara to join them. The friends listened as Dak'Tor told them what had happened and how Useaves had betrayed him.

"It does not make any sense. Useaves was the one who, in the beginning, kept Laborn from killing you. She convinced him you were useful and three offling is not enough to save the future. Why would she want you blamed for what Gard did?"

Dak'Tor and his friends stayed up late trying to figure out what Useaves' game was. Finally, too tired to think any longer, they turned in. As Dak'Tor lay with his mate cuddled up in front of him, their offling clasped to her chest, he thought what a nightmare it had turned out to be. He knew Laborn would extract a terrible punishment for what he believed had been done, and fear of what that would be turned Dak'Tor's blood cold.

The next morning, the guards stationed outside Dak'Tor's quarters took him away.

CHAPTER 5

Pan was becoming obsessed with the mystery of Irisa. She did not want to ask the Healers for any more information, and Hatos'Mok had not told her much at all other than that the elderly female habitually disappeared from one community and showed up at another. There was something about Irisa that Pan was drawn to, and she wanted to find out from the female herself who or what she might be.

However, it was Irisa who one day sought out the Guardian at the new Healer's cove.

"This is not the same as the Healer's Cove at Kthama."

Surprised, Pan spun around at the sound of her voice.

Irisa continued, "But then, it does not have the history behind it that Kthama Minor does, either."

At the mention of Kthama Minor, Pan could hold back no longer. "Who are you? How do you know of Kthama Minor?"

"Sit down, Guardian. It is time you and I got to know one another."

Pan could hardly take her eyes off the older female but did so long enough to find some rocks not too far away, where both of them could sit comfortably. To maintain their privacy, Pan positioned herself so she could see if anyone else came up the path toward them.

"Alright, I am sitting. Now, how do you know about Kthama Minor?"

"I was there. I was there with Lor Onida, remember?"

"You were there when Lor Onida died and her mate, Oragur, rejected their offling, Liru. So, yes, that is right, you would know of Kthama Minor."

"My friend Lor Onida named it that. Why did it alarm you so much when I mentioned it?"

"I apologize; I overreacted. It is just that, forgive me, I am not sure who you are," Pan said. Then she sighed and added. "I have been asking about you. Hatos'Mok told me that you would visit one of the Mothoc communities and then another, and another, but sometimes with long periods in between."

"I do not stay too long in any one place. Only as long as I am needed. I stayed with Lor Onida longer than with most others," Irisa explained, leaning over and picking a stem of grass to chew on.

"Are you saying that you stay for one person in particular?"

"Yes. I know when someone needs my help. When they no longer need it, or there is nothing more I can do for them, then I move on."

Irisa adjusted her sitting position then added, "I know what people say of me. That I talk to those who have returned to the Great Spirit."

"I have heard that, but people make up things. I am sorry if it hurts you to be talked about like that."

"It would only hurt me if it were not true." Then for the first time that Pan had ever seen, Irisa smiled. "Do not be afraid of me, Pan. I am here to help. Your mother told you to look out for help that would come to you."

"My mother? How do you know—"

"As I said, I talk to people who have returned to the Great Spirit, just as you have done. How peculiar that our people believe in an afterlife, but when someone claims to have first-hand knowledge of it, they are branded as crazy."

Pan did not know what to make of Irisa, though she felt comforted by her presence. "Please, if you are here to help me, just tell me who you are. What you are," she pleaded.

"Did Hatos'Mok not tell you that I was very old?" Irisa asked.

Pan nodded.

"Well, I am. I am older than anyone else here."

"Are you a Guardian?"

"No, I am not a Guardian. If I was, people would have an easier time understanding what I do. I have Guardian blood in me, though; otherwise, I would not be able to come and go as easily, to blend in and stay in the shadows."

Pan said nothing, wanting Irisa to keep talking.

"I have had many names through the thousands and thousands and thousands of years I have been alive. I join the communities for a while, then I reappear later under another name. With so little interaction between the Mothoc communities for so long, it was easy enough to do. Just a female passing through on her way from one community to another, who decided to stay for a while before moving on. But when your father formed the High Council, that made it much more difficult to do because the communities were now interacting. Now, with us all at Lulnomia, my comings and goings will change."

Pan finally thought of an intelligent question to ask. "Is it your Guardian blood that has kept you alive for so long?"

"Yes. I still age—of course, even you will age eventually. And neither of us will live forever; not even a Guardian does that. And now you are wondering how I came to be."

Irisa continued. "Before the mantle was passed to your father, Wrollonan'Tor was the Guardian of Etera. Before your father decreed otherwise, there was little loyalty to any female on the part of any male. But there was one female Wrollonan'Tor favored, who was my mother. It turned out she had Guardian blood somewhere in her background. No one knew that, but she took me to him when she could see I was hardly aging at all. She suspected that was why I was so different, and she wanted me to know."

"But even if you were born when my father was —" Pan asked in a hushed tone.

"You may speak openly with me, daughter of Moc'Tor. There is much about being a Guardian that *you* do not know. Much that was not handed down to you by your father."

"And Wrollonan'Tor died before my father was fully trained. So now that you and I are talking about it, I realize how very young my father was when he died. He was robbed of the vast majority of his Guardian lifespan." Pan dropped her head.

Irisa eased to her feet and gently placed a finger under Pan's chin. She lifted Pan's face up to look at her. "Your father chose to leave. He was not robbed of anything. It was a free choice of his will. It was his soul's intention to leave Etera and pass the Guardianship of Etera to you. You are the last Mothoc Guardian of Etera, Pan. And you must live the full Guardian's lifespan. Yours is not to end early, as was your father's," she added.

"I do not know how you have been able to bear it. The thought of the lifetime that I know is ahead of me is so painful. The idea of losing everyone I love."

"I have lived through many losses. My mother,

my mates. My offling and their offling, and theirs. I have seen everyone I love age, falter, and die. That is part of why I keep moving. I no longer want close ties. I have had enough of grief and loss."

"I am not sure anyone remembers who the Guardian was before your father," Pan said. "I do not remember anyone speaking of it. I am sure your father knew, though it may not have been his father, as Guardianship does not always pass from parent to offling."

Pan did not know how to say what she was thinking. She stared at Irisa. "If you are not a Guardian and you have lived that long, then how long does a Guardian naturally live?" Her heart went cold at the thought of what the answer might be.

"No one really knows, Pan. In truth, our people know very little about the Guardians. How many there have been, who preceded who. The long spans of time between Guardians have erased memories of anything before their time. And your father did not remain on Etera long enough to pass on to you all the knowledge he had about being a Guardian."

Pan could not wrap her mind around Irisa's answer. Did not want to. It was more than she could bear, so she changed the subject. "Where did you go, in between visiting the different settlements?"

"Ah. That is a very good question. And one you will know the answer to someday. But today is not that day." Irisa turned to leave.

"Are we done talking? Please, no, I have so many more questions," Pan objected.

She stood and took a step toward Irisa, who turned back just long enough to reply, "We will talk again. But for now, you have lots to think about. Ponder everything I said."

"But—"

"Hush. You must learn patience, little one. With the eternity of long life stretching before you, patience is one of the most important skills you can develop," Irisa said. "But one thing we must do, and fairly soon, is to find a place for you to discharge your duties as Guardian."

"Enter the Aezaiteran stream."

"And engage in the Order of Functions," Irisa added. "But this is enough for now. Come and find me in a few days."

Pan watched Irisa leave and sat alone for some time. She would do as she had been asked. As for telling Rohm'Mok about her conversation, for now, she would keep it to herself until she had more time to reflect on all Irisa had said.

But her thoughts were troubled; she could not understand how Irisa could be so old. That meant she must have lived through thousands of years of Wrollonan'Tor's lifetime. Pan knew that Guardians lived far longer than any of the other Mothoc, but this was beyond her comprehension. And the idea of living for near eternity made her cold to her stomach.

As time passed, Kyana was starting to feel pressure to reconnect with her family. She turned to her mate for help as they were taking a walk in the brisk winter air.

"I admit I feel guilty for not looking them up yet. But then, they have not sought me out either," she said.

"Was the split between you and your family painful?" he asked as they walked.

"Not as much as for some. We did not vehemently disagree. But they were unhappy that as a young female, I would head out all alone to follow Straf'Tor. So now, as I say that, it seems odd that they have not sought me out. I imagine they are simply as busy as the rest of us trying to adjust to life here."

"Perhaps with your son being the Adik'Tar of Kayerm, following in Straf'Tor's footsteps, they are hesitant to approach you. Perhaps they fear you would reject them."

Kyana had not thought of that. Yes, her son was Adik'Tar, but she did not think of what that might mean to the rest of Lulnomia's inhabitants who were followers of Moc'Tor. She decided she would seek her family out before too long.

Kyana made an effort to look for her family. Her mother and father were gathered together when she found them. The look of surprise on their faces—not smiles—immediately made her even more nervous than she already was.

"Mother, Father, I felt it was time I sought you out. Are you still angry with me for leaving the Great Pines?"

Her mother turned to her father, waiting for him to answer. Ondram'Nul looked Kyana up and down and then said, "You look well. Despite everything."

Kyana frowned, "What does that mean, Father?"

Her mother, Retru, touched his arm, "Please. Do not do this."

"No. It is going to have to be faced sooner or later. We have heard that you were paired to the son of Straf'Tor."

"Yes." Kyana looked at her mother, eyes pleading for an explanation.

"And that this male, Nox'Tor, was it? Was murdered by the male you now share your bed with?"

"No. No. That is not true. I am paired to Wosot, yes. But he did not murder Nox'Tor!"

"The son of Straf'Tor died at the hand of your mate—then are you saying it is not true?" her father pressed her.

Kyana turned to Retru. "What is going on? I do not understand this. Wosot killed Nox'Tor, yes, but he did it in defense of me and another female. Are you saying you believe rumors over the words of your own daughter standing here before you?"

Kyana was close to tears but squeezed them back and hardened herself. "After all this time apart, the first words you say to me are not that you are glad we can be together again, or an apology of any kind for how we parted ways, but you throw up in my face a lie about my life and what happened? A life you know *nothing* about?"

"Kyana—" Then Retru turned to Ondram. "Please apologize to our daughter. Must this rift between us continue now because of a lie someone told you?"

"Can others testify that this was the case?" her father asked.

Kyana's mouth hung open. "You do not believe me? Do you want others to confirm that I am telling the truth? There are many who can, including my son, Norland, who is now Leader of our community."

"He supports your pairing to the male who killed his father?"

Kyana feared she was either going to burst into tears or say something she would regret. She looked at her mother and then at her father. "To find you, I swallowed my pride and my fear. I came to try to make us a family again. And this is the welcome you give me?"

She shook her head and closed her eyes. "I do

not know what to say, so I am going to leave. I want to say I am sorry I came to find you, but at least now I know nothing has changed. You never would listen to me, Father. If you had taken the time to listen to me before, about why I wanted to follow Straf'Tor, the bitter state our relationship ended in might not have taken place."

Kyana turned to her mother. "If you want us to reunite, it is now up to you. I will not bother you again." And she turned and walked away as quickly as she could without breaking into a run.

She pulled herself together as she headed for Kayerm's part of Lulnomia. She needed a safe place to let her feelings and grief out, and that meant going home. Only it did not feel like home yet. She was glad to find Wosot was not there, as she needed privacy to lick her wounds.

Retru turned to her mate. "*How could you*? If it was not enough that we lost all this time with her, now who knows if we will ever talk to her again? Your pride has always been a problem, Ondram. Maybe you do not want her back, but that does not mean I do not."

"What does that mean?" Ondram asked.

"It means that after some time has passed, I am going to find her. The problems between you and

Kyana are not mine. I should have taken this position long ago when the rift opened between us instead of letting her leave on such a hurtful note. If she will listen to me, I will apologize to her for not backing her decision, regardless of how *you* feel about it."

"Are you defying me?"

"I am not defying you. She is my daughter, and I am her mother and whatever problems you insist on keeping alive are between you and her."

It was not long before Wosot returned to their quarters and found Kyana curled into a ball on their sleeping mat.

"What is wrong? Are you ill?" He sat beside her.

Kyana shook her head. "I sought out my parents today. It did not go well." She turned over to look at him. "My father has still not forgiven me for leaving. Only now he has more to use against me. Somehow, he heard a rumor that you murdered Nox'Tor. The implied accusation was that you did it so you could have me."

Wosot fell silent, thinking.

"My mother did not agree with him. Maybe in time, she and I can be mother and daughter again."

Wosot could tell Kyana had been crying. "I know it must be upsetting that he thinks that about me, but we both know it is not true."

"Who would have said such a thing? And how

would it get to my father and mother? Does that mean everyone here has heard that lie? And is repeating it?"

Wosot thought for a moment. "I do not know, but I will find out. In the meantime, rest and try to put it out of your mind. I will be back later with something for you to eat." He leaned over and kissed her.

⟨✿⟩

Wosot did not take long to find who he was looking for.

Lavke startled when she realized he was making a beeline toward her.

"Wosot. What a pleasant surprise. Have you come to apologize?"

"I have nothing to apologize for," Wosot answered.

"You should have come to meet your daughter by now. What kind of a father are you?"

"It is you who needs to apologize. I know what you did. I know you are causing trouble for my mate however you can." He locked eyes with Lavke.

"You do not think that Kyana's parents deserve to know the truth about how you two ended up together?"

"At least you do not deny it. It is not the truth, and you know it. You have not changed a bit; you are still a lying and manipulative female. If you ever wanted to know the reason why I would never pair with you, you have your answer."

Lavke drew back and slapped Wosot across the face. "How dare you? Who do you think you are?"

Wosot did not react and continued to stare at Lavke. "Leave us alone. What happened or did not happen between us is centuries in the past. Let your bitterness go. Make no mistake, it will only backfire on you. You have been warned." He turned to walk away.

"Is that a threat?" she called out after him.

Wosot did not look back.

As he had said he would, Wosot returned later with something for Kyana to eat. He was glad to see she had been sleeping.

She took what he handed her and thanked him for it.

"I found out who told your parents that lie. It was Lavke."

"The female who wanted to pair with you? She insinuated you had a daughter with her—Joquel?"

"Yes. Why she is so bitter, I do not know. It was purely a physical relationship. We both knew that. But she is clearly angry about something."

"She is angry that you paired with someone. As long as you never did, she did not feel less than any of the other females you bedded." Though Kyana could say the words, it still bothered her to think about.

She continued, "It is as if you were a prize catch. As long as you never settled on any one female, perhaps she felt there was still a chance for her with you."

"I do not believe she told anyone that lie except your parents. But for her to hear about what happened, she must have been asking around. That does not speak well for her letting things go. But it is no more important than we make it. Those who know you and know me will not believe it. Try to put it out of your mind. We have our own life to focus on, and soon, our own offling."

Kyana nodded. "I will try. It is not your fault that you are so desirable!" and a little smile crossed her lips.

Wosot grinned. He did not want to stir up trouble, so he decided he would not tell Norland what had happened. Norland was not only their Leader; he was also Kyana's oldest son, but though Wosot felt Norland had a right to know if something was upsetting his own mother, he decided to let it go for the time being.

Despite Wosot's warning to Lavke and his good intentions to let the matter go, Lavke had other plans. Within a few days, Wosot was called to meet with Norland.

"I need to speak with you about something," the Leader said.

Wosot was sure he knew what it would be about.

"You had a previous relationship with a female called Lavke."

Since it was a statement of fact, Wosot did not reply.

"She has alleged that you murdered Nox'Tor in order to pair with Kyana. We know this is not the case; your actions were judged by a tribunal, and you were cleared of fault. But she does not accept that."

"How do you know this?" Wosot asked.

"The female, Lavke, approached me and filed a complaint, citing that you had broken Sacred Law. I told her it has been fairly adjudicated according to Mothoc law, and you were absolved of any wrong-doing."

"But she has not accepted that—or you would not have called me here."

"No. She has not. She has gone to the Overseer and asked for the matter to be looked into."

Wosot ran his hand over his chin. "So what happens next?"

"Hatos'Mok will no doubt ask to speak with me, you, and perhaps some of the other members of the community."

"If he decides it falls to him to re-examine every

situation to which someone has an objection, he is going to be tied up in nonsense for some time."

"I agree," said Norland. "But since it is the first time it has happened, he will most likely hear this as it will set a precedent for all future complaints of this type."

"Let me know when it will take place—and anything else you hear. I hate to upset your mother further, but I must tell her it is coming."

Hatos'Mok, Overseer of Lulnomia's High Council, listened carefully to what the female Lavke was asserting. When she was finished, he said he would consider whether to hear her case against Kayerm's leadership but made no promise.

When all the communities had finally assembled at Lulnomia, Hatos'Mok addressed the High Council and reassured the Leaders that they still had jurisdiction over their people and had lost no authority or power. He announced that if disputes among the Leaders themselves did occur, he would hear the case. But he had not considered someone lodging a complaint against another community's members. This was a new situation, and though he had an opinion about it, in coming to a decision, he did not want to act on his own authority alone. So he called Norland in and explained the issue.

"Situations were bound to arise for which there is

no precedent," Norland said. "In the past, when our communities were divided, this would not have occurred; however, it is possible that someone in a community might have a complaint about how their Leader handled an issue. And in that case, it seems fair that it be heard before the High Council."

Hatos'Mok nodded. "Yes. I agree that would be appropriate, and I will take your suggestion to the other Leaders. In the meantime, there is this situation. For a member of one community to enter a complaint about how the Leader of another community handled a situation feels out of jurisdiction."

Both looked at each other.

"As much as I would like this to go away," said Norland, "I feel you must bring it before the High Council. And not just because I am confident that in killing my father, Wosot did act in self-defense with no ulterior motive. If it is not addressed, I have no doubt this female will continue to stir dissent. I suspect her motives are not as high-minded as she would like them to appear."

"I agree. She has some sort of bitterness toward Wosot, and it will most likely be apparent that this is what is behind her complaint. I will make arrangements for the High Council to come together. Let Wosot know we have spoken, and I will tell you when we will be meeting."

Before very long, it was time. It was a closed session, and only a select few were in attendance. Wosot, Norland, Kyana, and the Mothoc from Kayerm who had been present at the tribunal all stood before the High Council. Lavke was present, as was Tyria, the Healer and Second Rank at the High Rocks. When Hatos'Mok explained to Pan what had happened, Pan felt that because she was Guardian, someone else would need to stand in for the High Rocks.

Hatos'Mok began. "Thank you for coming. A complaint had been entered from Lavke of the House of 'Nil, member of the High Rocks, against Norland of the House of 'Tor, Leader of Kayerm, regarding the actions of Wosot of the House of 'Tar. Before I ask Lavke to speak, I wish to hear the opinions of the other Leaders regarding this situation."

Pnatl'Rar, Leader of the Little River, spoke up, "Were the actions of Wosot not judged by his community? Is that the complaint?"

Norland spoke. "I am the Leader of Kayerm, and as is customary, the incident was judged by a cross-section of our people. The tribunal decreed that Wosot was not guilty of breaking Sacred Law. There was no penalty exacted against him because it was determined that he committed no wrong-doing."

Pnatl'Rar looked at the Overseer. "I do not understand why this was brought before the High Council when it was handled appropriately at Kayerm. The female is not part of Kayerm's community. Is the

High Rocks in accord with this matter being brought to us?"

"I am the Healer at the High Rocks," Tyria replied. "Our Leader, Pan, has authorized me to speak on her behalf. This complaint was not brought to any of the leadership at the High Rocks."

Tres'Sar of the Far High Hills said, "I would like to ask the female, Lavke, some questions if I may."

The Overseer nodded, and Tres'Sar approached her. "You are from the community of the High Rocks. What is your interest in the incident that took place at Kayerm?"

Lavke stammered but could not form an answer, "I— I—"

"Let me ask this a different way. What is your relationship to Wosot of the House of 'Tar?"

"We knew each other at the High Rocks. Before he left to follow Straf'Tor."

"You were acquaintances?"

"Yes. Well, more than that," she answered and looked over at Wosot.

Tres'Sar followed her gaze and turned to look at Wosot himself.

He turned back to Lavke, "What is the 'more'?"

"I bore his offling, a daughter."

"Did you choose him? Did he agree to be your only choice?" Tres'Sar asked.

"No. It did not—it did not go that far."

"Did Wosot seek you out here at Lulnomia? Looking to start up a relationship with you again?"

"No."

"But you did speak with him at some point?"

"Yes."

"What did you speak about?"

Lavke looked at Tyria for help, but Tyria indicated that Lavke should answer the question.

"I asked how he had been. I suggested he might want to know about our daughter."

"Tell us about the conversation, please," Tres'Sar asked.

"I came across him and his mate when I was out walking. I struck up a conversation, trying to be friendly. He was rude and not interested. He did not even care about meeting his daughter."

Tres'Sar turned to Hatos'Mok. "I think it is clear what is going on. This female feels jilted and attempts to take her anger out on Wosot by causing trouble for him over an incident that has nothing to do with her. And which was handled properly."

Hatos'Mok said, "Your point is acknowledged, Adik'Tar 'Sar. Aside from that issue, I would like to know what more there is to this story. Norland, Leader of Kayerm, what do you have to say about this?"

"If you are asking me about the details of the charges against Wosot, I do not see that they are relevant. The issue has been resolved."

"I see you have no fear of my getting involved in the outcome of your tribunal. But I would like to know what took place as it might shed more light on why it is of so much interest to the female, Lavke."

Norland relayed what had happened. How Nox'-Tor, former Leader of Kayerm, had attacked Kyana and Lorgil, two females under the protection of Wosot. And how Wosot had killed Nox'Tor to prevent the Leader from killing them.

When he was finished, the Overseer asked, "And Nox'Tor was your father, correct? And the female, Kyana, is now the mate of Wosot?"

"Yes."

Hatos'Mok looked over at Wosot, Kyana, and the others of the Kayerm community. "Would anyone else from Kayerm wish to speak up about this situation?"

Teirac stepped forward, "I served on the tribunal. Wosot committed no wrongdoing. It was a very difficult time for all of us, and I personally find it abhorrent that someone from another community can raise an issue about an incident that had nothing to do with her in any way whatsoever. I question how she even heard about it and who else she has told. To me, this is clearly a bitter female slandering a male who chose someone other than her."

Wosot stepped over to Teirac and put his hand on the male's shoulder, "Thank you for your support, but the larger issue is, what is the jurisdiction of the High Council in these matters? The complaint has nothing to do with her own community. It is irrelevant to the High Rocks."

Then he looked at Hatos'Mok. "If the High Council decides to entertain such issues, I submit that you will be mired in drama for the rest of your lives."

Voices rose up in agreement.

"This is nothing more than a matter of vindictiveness," Tres'Sar said. "I agree with Wosot. The question is, should members of one community be able to bring charges against another member of another community about an incident that has already been addressed. This female, Lavke, was not involved in any way in what happened. I do not believe her motive has anything to do with a quest for justice, only a quest for revenge."

Hatos'Mok raised a hand for silence. "What is your testimony about this, Wosot? I want to hear it."

Wosot looked at Kyana and then at Lavke. "Lavke and I had a physical relationship. Out of that came a daughter. I did not pair with her, even though she offered many times. When she met Kyana, Lavke was rude to her. I could see she harbored bitterness, but I did not expect anything to come of it. I have since learned that Lavke sought out Kyana's parents and told them I murdered Nox'Tor in order to pair with Kyana. This cannot go unaddressed. Kyana and her family were divided, as were many, over the differences in the philosophies of Straf'Tor and Moc'Tor. Some of the rifts have been healed since we all came to Lulnomia, but the one between Kyana and her family has less of a chance now due to the unfair actions of this female."

The Overseer turned to Lavke. "Is this true? You approached Kyana's parents and told them Wosot had murdered Nox'Tor in order to pair with Kyana?"

Lavke looked down.

A female's voice was raised. "I wish to speak."

All heads turned toward Toniss. Many of the older Leaders who had lived through the great division recognized her as one of Straf'Tor's original females.

"I am Toniss of Kayerm. Many of you remember me from long ago. I am the mother of the former Leader, Nox'Tor, and Norland is my grandson. If anyone has any right to speak about the conditions of my son's death, it is me."

Hatos'Mok waited for her to continue.

"My son, Nox'Tor, became Leader after his father, Straf'Tor, left Kayerm. But Nox'Tor was not ready to lead. And the nature of his father's leaving impacted him more deeply than any of us realized. He was removed from the leadership due to his own actions and choices. It was he who set his mate Kyana aside. He severed their pairing, and later, he tried to kill her and another female. We were lucky—yes, I will say it —that Wosot was there to defend the females, even though it ended in my son's death. So if anyone has a right to be bitter against Wosot, it would be me. But I call him my friend and I look up to him. Wosot is a male of honor, the kind of male I had hoped my son would become. And for some outsider to accuse him of committing murder, with no facts and not even asking those of us who lived through those tragic times, is an insult to Mothoc honor."

Hatos'Mok turned to Lavke and asked her if there was anything else she wished to say. He waited a moment to give her a chance to answer. When she did not, he said, "I think we understand the situation. It is clear that this is a case of vindictiveness.

"Lavke of the House of 'Nil, you have acted dishonorably, not only as a Mothoc but as a female, a giver of life. I order you from now on to hold your tongue about what happened at Kayerm. You are not to continue to stir up trouble with Kyana's parents. Nor are you to tell others your version of what took place. Furthermore, you are to have no contact with Wosot, Kyana, or their families. Do you understand?"

Lavke glanced up briefly at the Overseer and nodded.

Then he turned to the others in the room. "You are not to speak of this outside these walls. The matter needs to die, and talking about it will only keep it alive. What has been said here is private. No good will come of discussing it further. Now, I want everyone to leave except the High Council members."

The others filed out.

When only the High Council was left, Hatos'Mok addressed them. "There were two matters heard today. One was a situation that only took place because of hurt feelings and jealousy. The other matter is whether this is the type of situation that should be heard by the High Council. What are your thoughts?"

The discussion did not take long. In the end, the High Council agreed unanimously that matters should be heard by the leadership of that community and that unless it involved a complaint against a Leader, issues should be handled locally. But for a member of a community to bring a complaint against another community over something in which they were not directly or indirectly involved was not to be sanctioned.

Once Kyana and Wosot were alone in the passage outside the meeting room, she asked, "Do you think Lavke will abide by the Overseer's words?"

"I think she will, certainly for a while. She looked pretty shook up. I am sorry you had to be put through this, Saraste'," he said.

"Are you going to meet your daughter?"

Wosot ran his hand over his face. "I do not know. She is a grown adult. I do not see the point. I do wonder if there was not a male who helped raise her, though. Oddly enough, we know nothing of Lavke's situation."

"And I do not want to. I pray she stays away as

Hatos'Mok ordered. I just want to live our lives in peace."

Wosot drew her into his arms. "I know, I know."

A voice startled them.

It was Kyana's mother. "I heard about the trouble that the female from the High Rocks has caused you. I want to tell you I am sorry."

Kyana released herself from Wosot's embrace. "Mother, this is my mate, Wosot of the House of 'Tar."

Retru looked up at him. "Thank you for taking care of my daughter. I can see you love her."

"Very much. I am committed to her welfare and protection and that of her offling."

Turning back to Kyana, Retru said, "I do not know why I did not consider that you would have offling. May I meet them someday?"

"What about father?" Kyana asked.

"He and I do not see eye to eye on this. He treated you poorly, and you have every right to be angry with him. But I hope that will not stand in the way of us rekindling our relationship."

Then Retru held out her arms and Kyana stepped into her embrace.

"I love you, daughter. I am so sorry we separated in anger. Please forgive me."

Kyana buried her face against her mother's shoulder and answered a muffled, "Oh, Mother, I love you too."

After the Leaders had all dispersed from the High Council meeting, Tyria sought out Lavke. "You have acted poorly, Lavke. I understand why you did not bring this to Pan's attention or that of any other Leaders at the High Rocks. You were not concerned that a wrong had been committed. You were trying to hurt Wosot and his mate Kyana. It was so long ago. Why? Just tell me why?"

"You are not from the High Rocks. You were not there. You do not know. Wosot did care for me. I know it. It was more than he said. There was something special between us. I think he was just afraid of his feelings for me. He and I should be together."

"He does not act as if what you are saying is true. You must follow the Overseer's directions. You must not try to cause any more trouble. We are all together now, Lavke. All the Mothoc. There is no other place for you to go if you ruin your own name and embarrass yourself over this. You have a male in your life who raised your daughter with you. If you are not careful, this will cause you to throw that away; you must hope this does not get back to him! I am trying to advise you. It has been a very, very long time; find a way to heal, to let go of Wosot."

Lavke did not answer.

"Look," said Tyria gently. "I realize emotions cannot just be turned off. But while you are working on healing your pride, you must leave them alone.

You have to control that, at least. The Overseer is not one to be trifled with, and the other High Council Leaders all heard what he told you. If you go against him, it will surface for sure."

"My pride? Is that what you think this is about?" Lavke finally snapped. "I loved Wosot. I did everything I could to win him. But all he wanted from me was to mount me now and then. What did he see in her that made her so special? So special that he would kill another male to—"

"Stop it!" Tyria raised her voice and took Lavke by the shoulders. "You have to stop saying that. It is not true. You heard the testimony of those from Kayerm. Even the mother of the male who was killed. The Leader himself testified to it. Wosot did not murder anyone. And you are contradicting yourself. One moment you say he loved you, and the next that all he wanted was to mount you."

"How can you be so naive!" Lavke shook off Tyria's touch. "Whatever went on there, it was wrong. The male that Wosot killed was Kyana's mate. And he was also the father of the so-called Leader of Kayerm. How convenient for the Leader, Norland, that someone did him the favor of making a way for him to step into leadership. It is all twisted. And no one sees it but me? How can that be?"

Tyria looked Lavke dead in the eyes. "The Adik'Tar Norland only stepped into leadership after Nox'Tor had already been removed. Nox'Tor did not have to die for Norland to become Leader. Norland already was Adik'Tar. There is so much you do not know, and you are twisting what little you have heard."

"Were you there when this happened? No, you had already come to the High Rocks," Lavke snarled.

"No, I was not there, but I know the people there, and they are telling the truth."

"If the people at Kayerm are so great, why did you come to the High Rocks?"

Tyria was stunned for a moment but collected herself, "That is none of your business. I am your Healer, and I do not want animosity between us. For one thing, we do not even know each other particularly well; there is no basis for us to be at odds. The other reason is that as I am your Healer, there may come a time when you need my help. And I do not want you to think that I will not do my best to help you if you ever need it."

"Why will you not answer me? Are you also hiding something?" Lavke narrowed her eyes.

"You have not heard anything anyone has said to you, have you? I do not know what else to say except to heed the Overseer's words. Let it go. Concentrate on your own life. Stop trying to make trouble for others. We are Mothoc. We are the lifeblood of Etera. We must not let problems reduce us to so much less than what we can be."

Lavke let out a long sigh. "I am tired. I will think about what happened today. But I do not believe any of it. Wosot killed Nox'Tor so he could claim Kyana as his own. And nothing anyone says is going to change my mind on that."

"You are making a huge mistake, Lavke. Your thoughts are only going to lead you deeper into bitterness. The more you seek revenge against Wosot for rejecting you, trying to hurt him and Kyana, the worse it is going to be for you in the end."

"You never answered my question; I do not know what you are hiding, but I will find out. Right now, I need to talk to my daughter." Lavke abruptly walked on, leaving Tyria behind.

CHAPTER 6

Useaves made a long process of treating Laborn's injury. She strictly admonished him to keep his hands away from the wound, and since he could not see it, he had to take her word that he was at risk of dying if infection set in. Her plan had worked; Laborn had been reminded anew how important she was to the community, and specifically, to him.

Though Laborn was relieved that his plan to kill Useaves had not worked, he was still waiting for a chance to talk privately to Gard to find out how it had gotten turned around. And there was still the matter of Dak'Tor to deal with.

Kaisak, having been left out of the meeting during which the attack took place, watched Useaves suspiciously. He had never been comfortable with the power the older female had. With Gard seemingly having replaced him as Laborn's right-hand male, Kaisak's resentment had been stirred very deeply.

While Laborn was healing, nothing more had officially been said about Dak'Tor's attempt on the Leader's life. However, the community was abuzz with speculation. The older members were angry and wanted Dak'Tor executed. The younger members, not as sure about Laborn's leadership and not as embittered about the past, were secretly wishing Dak'Tor had succeeded. They were not in agreement with Laborn's plan to annihilate the Akassa and Sassen, and they questioned his sanity and ability to lead.

By now, Dak'Tor's friends had gone over the scenario so many times that they had stopped talking about it. They could only wait for what they knew was coming and fear how severe Dak'Tor's punishment would be.

Dak'Tor could not let go of what Useaves had done. She had betrayed him and let him take the fall for what Gard did. What was her game?

When Useaves declared Laborn sufficiently healed to be able to deal with Dak'Tor's punishment, he called the entire community together and had Gard release Dak'Tor and bring him to the front.

Iria held their son in her arms and stood with Dak'Tor's friends, who were assembled toward the front. It was all she could do not to run to her mate.

Laborn raised his voice, "I have called you here because it is time to declare punishment on Dak'Tor for his attempt on my life. It is no surprise that he denies it, but Useaves and Gard both witnessed him smashing me on the back of my head with a rock."

He walked over to Dak'Tor and said, "You tried to steal my life, so yours is now forfeit."

Iria passed her son to Vaha and ran to Dak'Tor's side. "No! No, you cannot. He did not do it; it was Gard! You have to believe him!"

"Why should I believe him? What possible motive would Useaves and Gard have to lie? It was Useaves who all along has stood up for Dak'Tor. It was she in the beginning who talked me into letting him live. And now look what has come of it. He tried to murder me, and now he will pay for his crime."

Iria raised her voice. "But what about the offling? He has only produced three. Is killing him worth losing your chance to achieve your great goal? Your crusade to rid Etera of the Akassa and the Sassen?"

Laborn looked down into the eyes of Dak'Tor's mate, clearly enjoying her fear. "You are right. He is still of use to us, and I will let him live."

Iria covered her face with her hands in relief.

He turned to Dak'Tor. "But you must forfeit something, regardless. Again, you tried to take my life, so I will take yours."

Laborn stepped around Dak'Tor and grabbed Iria by the arm, jerking her toward him. "Your female is now forfeited to me. That is your punishment."

Iria tried to shrug off his grip, and Dak'Tor immediately lunged forward to push the Leader away, but

Gard and Kaisak quickly stepped in and restrained him.

"No! What do you mean!" Dak'Tor screamed at Laborn. "You cannot harm her!"

"Oh, I will take care of her. Do not worry about that. It has been a long time since I have enjoyed female company," he sneered.

Dak'Tor struggled while his supporters in the crowd raised their voices in protest.

"*Silence!*" Laborn shouted.

"But what about their son? He is too young to be away from his mother!" a female called out.

"This is not right Laborn, why should she be punished?" said another.

The Leader scowled. "So this is what has come of the Guardian's brother living with us. You never questioned me in the past. So be it. I will answer your questions. As for their son, you have a good point. Since the offling is too young to be away from its mother, it will come too."

"No!" cried Iria. "Vaha can care for him; she has just had her own offling. Please, do not do this!"

"I would have thought you would have wanted your offling with you. Very well, Vaha can care for your son. But you belong to me now. You best hope that you find my favor, so it goes easy for you."

Dak'Tor struggled as hard as he could to break away from Gard and Kaisak. "Let me go!" he yelled.

Laborn dragged Iria back to where Useaves was standing. He shoved her at Useaves and then pointed at her as if to say, *if you are smart, you will not move from there.*

Then he went over to Dak'Tor. "The more you argue and fight, the worse it will go for your mate. Is that what you want?"

Dak'Tor's eyes were red with rage. "If you harm her, I swear, I *will* kill you."

"What happens to her is now up to you. If you accept my judgment and do your duty to continue to sire more offling, then she will be treated fairly and kindly. In time, she may even be returned to you. But if you continue to plot against me, or attempt any other attack on me, then I will kill her. After all, she is no use to me; it is your seed I need."

"If any harm comes to her, you can forget about my ever seeding another female," Dak'Tor spat out.

"I would not make such rash statements. After all, you still have a son by your mate. Do you wish his life also to be forfeit?"

The tension in the air was at an all-time high, and the faces of Laborn's supporters were tense and tight. Iria's mother was clutching her mate. Dara turned to Dazal and hid her head against her brother's chest. Not sure what would happen next, no one said a word.

Dak'Tor struggled to control his rage. He knew there was nothing he could do at that moment. For Iria's sake and his offling's, he had to calm himself down. He reached deep within and asked the Great Spirit for help. Suddenly, a feeling of calm came over him. He felt his heart rate coming down and the tension leaving his body.

"Alright, Laborn. You win. I will cooperate. All I ask is that you do not harm Iria. She has done nothing to deserve mistreatment."

"Everybody, leave," snarled the Leader. "Go back to your quarters. Go about your business. Iria, go and gather some of your things. If you are not back before twilight, I will send Kaisak to get you—and your offling."

Iria glanced at Useaves, looking for some comfort or reassurance, but the female's lined face was frozen. Doing as Laborn said, she went to Dak'Tor's side and slid into his embrace. As he hugged her, Dak'Tor stared at Laborn.

Knowing they only had a few hours left together, Dak'Tor and Iria's friends left them their privacy. In the sanctity of their quarters, they shared their love-mating, not knowing when or if they would be together again.

When they were finished and lying together, Dak'Tor held Iria while she cried. "I will not let him hurt you. If he does, I will make him wish he had never been born."

"I will do as he says. I will be obedient. I will not give him any reason to hurt me," she said. Then she looked up at him. "Our son. Isan'Tor."

"You know that Vaha and our friends will look after him. And of course, so will I. I do not think Laborn is so cruel as to never let you spend time with your offling. Now, let us go and get him. I know you want to hold him as long as you can before you have to leave."

Dazal, Dara, and the others were waiting for Dak'Tor and Iria. Not knowing if Laborn would have food for Iria, they had prepared a meal for everyone.

Vaha handed the offling over to his mother, who held him close and showered his little head and face with kisses. Dak'Tor led the others away, giving Iria time with their son.

"This is a travesty," said Dazal. "I wonder if he has not gone too far. Is it possible for his own supporters to question him? If so, this would be the time."

"I saw their faces. There were definitely some who did not approve of what he did," said Zisa.

"Time will tell. Right now, I can think of nothing but Iria," said Dak'Tor, looking over at his mate. "What will her life be like, living with him? He said it has been a long time since he enjoyed female company, but he would not dare take her Without Her Consent. Will he keep her imprisoned, or will he let her go on with her life during the day? He did not say we could not speak with each other. Oh, I know nothing—only that I wish I had been the one to hit him over the head, and I wish he had been killed."

In time, Iria's parents showed up looking for her. Her father's face was tense and drawn, and her mother's eyes were filled with tears as she went over to console her daughter.

Dak'Tor told her father, "I did not try to kill Laborn; this is all a setup, though I do not know why. It was Gard who hit him with the rock. I swear by the Great Spirit, I speak the truth."

"We believe you. But what matters now is that our daughter will be under the control of that madman," Iria's father replied.

"Perhaps she would have been better off if Laborn had just killed me," Dak'Tor said.

"No. She loves you, and she would be lost without you. She is strong; she will survive this. I feel Laborn is losing the support of some of his followers, even the stalwart ones of the early days. They may share his vision of ridding Etera of the Akassa and Sassen, but only because they believe it is the right thing to do. This— This is not right, and any reasonable person can see it. Punishing our daughter is unfair because she is innocent. They can see it is just meant to torture you, but at her expense. Laborn had better tread lightly, I would say."

By the time they had all tried to console each other, and everyone had eaten, the afternoon was drawing to a close. Soon it would be twilight.

"We must go," Dak'Tor said gently. Iria kissed

their offling one more time and handed him over to her mother. Then she embraced her father and her friends one by one.

"I am not going anywhere. I will just not be here among you as usual. We will see how strict he is. If I treat him well, perhaps he will grant me favors and let me return to you sooner rather than later," Iria said. "I love you all."

Then she and Dak'Tor went back to their quarters to gather her things. Dak'Tor watched Iria while she went about the room picking up this and that and stuffing it into a carrying satchel. She was not sure if she would be allowed to return for anything, so she took more than she might have.

"May I have something of yours?" she asked.

Dak'Tor frowned. "Of course." He started looking around. "How about this?" he handed her a small hide toy he had made for their son. "Isan'Tor is too young to miss it, and it represents us both. Hopefully, Laborn will not question it if it is a source of comfort for you."

Iria fell into his arms, and though she had tried not to break down, now she could not help it. Dak'Tor held her close while she let out all the stress of the day.

"I love you so." Her words were muffled.

"I love you too. More than I ever loved anyone."

A few moments later, they were on their way to Laborn's evening fire, escorted by Kaisak, while Dak'Tor carried his mate's satchel.

The fire was just getting started. "You are wise to obey me," Laborn said, getting up from his place. Useaves and Gard remained seated.

"Come, sit next to me," Laborn said to Iria. She did as he said, then looked up at Dak'Tor.

"Be on your way now, Dak'Tor," said the Leader, seeing their eyes caught up together.

Dak'Tor looked at Laborn, then at Useaves and Gard. Then he looked at Iria one last time and left.

In silence, Iria watched her mate walk away. She listened as Laborn, Gard, and Useaves talked about nothing in particular. She used that time to quiet her soul and pray to the Great Spirit for strength. She reached deep within and steeled herself for the days to come.

The fire was dying down, and Laborn announced it was time to turn in. He stood up and reached his hand down to help Iria to her feet. She looked up at him, then down at his hand.

"Take it. I am not the monster you think I am," he said.

Iria cautiously took his hand and let him help her rise.

"Useaves will take you to your sleeping place. We have done what we can to make you comfortable.

Tomorrow, I will tell you what you are to do while you are in my possession."

Iria cringed inwardly at his use of the term but stifled any outward reaction.

She followed Useaves down a long corridor into the part of the cave system that Laborn had taken over for himself. Useaves pointed to an opening on the left, and Iria stepped inside. A fresh sleeping mat had been prepared, and a gourd holding water, a basket of nuts, along with some other items for personal care, were lined up against the walls. Iria looked around and then thanked Useaves.

Finally alone, she lay down on the sleeping mat and pulled the hide up over her, closed her eyes, and pretended she was back in their quarters and that Dak'Tor would come in any moment and cuddle up against her.

Though the first night was uneventful, Iria hardly slept. Laborn's remark about her being his possession had unnerved her. She did not know what that meant. Thinking the worst, she half expected him to come into her room at some time during the night and demand to mount her. Part of her said he would never dare such a thing. The other part was not sure what he was capable of. But one thing she was sure of was that she would not be able to fight him off. Though he was small for a male, he was extremely muscular. If she cried out, would anyone come to her rescue? Finally, she turned to her faith and asked again for strength and wisdom and for the Great Spirit to help her put those frightening *what-if* thoughts out of her mind.

When the first light of dawn broke, Iria heard others stirring in the tunnel outside her doorway. She rose and peeked down the hall. Laborn and Gard were standing talking, and both looked her way when her movement drew their attention.

Neither said a word to her, and they turned back to their conversation. Despite her prayers, Iria felt fear rise. She realized it was the fear of the unknown and that her imaginings were making it worse than it was. She knew she had to learn to focus on the here and now and stop her thoughts from wandering to frightening possibilities. Dak'Tor had not been harmed. Her offling was safe in the care of her mother and Vaha. She had not been banished; she was still in the same community as her family and her mate. In this moment, she was alright. So with that in mind, she went back inside, washed her face, and prepared herself to meet the day.

By the time she came back out, Useaves and Gard had left the tunnel. She found them, along with Laborn, around the fire. Over time, the morning fire had become a habit, a focus point for any gathering, as none of them needed the fire for warmth. They took comfort from the dancing light, and Iria was no exception.

Iria sat down across from Useaves, Gard, and Laborn. Useaves motioned to some strips of meat that had been cooked over the fire. Iria picked up one of the sticks lying around for the purpose and stabbed a piece. She held it suspended in the air, waiting for it to cool.

The silence was awkward. She could feel Laborn looking at her, so she kept her eyes averted. Finally, the meat was cool enough to eat, and she pulled it apart in strings and chewed slowly.

Laborn waited for her to finish eating before saying, "You will spend your time assisting Useaves with whatever work she has for you to do. If she does not have something to keep you busy, then come and find me, and I will direct you. As for the rest of the community, you can socialize with them during the evening group fires."

"Please," Iria said. "May I see my offling?"

"In time, yes. But for now, no. I need to be assured of your obedience before I grant you any favors."

"But if he is there at the evening fire?"

Laborn sighed. "You may look at him but not hold him. This is not to punish you. It is a test of your obedience. Understand?"

It was actually the calmest she had heard Laborn speak to anyone. He almost sounded rational, reasonable. For a brief moment, she almost found herself forgetting the situation she was in. But it came crashing back in the next moment.

"I have been generous in my rules. And I will know if you try to outsmart me, female. Do not even think of it because I promise you the punishment will not be worth whatever small satisfaction you gain in defying me."

Iria turned her attention back to picking at the strip of meat and tried to be nonchalant. She imagined she would now have to wait for Useaves to tell her what she wanted help with today.

Before long, Laborn and Gard got up and left, leaving the females sitting across from each other.

"You had better listen to him, Iria. He can have moments of reason, but they are fleeting and generally followed by an ill-mannered mood. If you hope for any consideration from him, you will only gain it by doing exactly as he says. You are at his mercy now. And mercy is not in his nature."

"What is it you need me to do?"

"I need you to gather some kahari roots for me. It is now difficult for me to get around, and it will be a big help; I will remember you for it someday. You know where to find them. There is a selection of carrying baskets just inside the entrance, stacked up against the wall. Take the biggest one you think you can carry when full. I expect it will take you all morning. When you are finished, you can help me prepare them for storage."

Iria got up, brushed herself off, and went inside to find the baskets. When she came out, Useaves was gone, so Iria went about her task, making her way to where the plants were most abundant.

She did her best to keep her mind off her situation when she heard a voice behind her whisper her name. She turned to see Vaha with Isan'Tor.

Iria quickly turned her head in each direction to see if anyone else was nearby. "Oh, my little son!" she cried out but made no motion toward Vaha. "You must go; if Laborn finds out you are here, it will go hard for me."

"No, do not worry, Useaves sent me here to find you. She told me to bring Isan'Tor to you so you could hold him and nurse him."

Still on edge, Iria looked around again, and finding a spot of tall grasses, sat down and took the offling onto her lap. Vaha then sat next to her. Iria tried to quell her nervousness, but she did not trust Useaves and worried this was just a trap to incite Laborn's anger against her. Though he was small for a male, Laborn was still stronger than any of the females and Iria was justifiably afraid of him.

"I promise you it is alright. Useaves said to tell you not to worry. Laborn is far away, and no one else is around."

Iria looked down at Isan'Tor and thanked the Great Spirit for this kindness. "You cannot stay long. I know what you said, but I do not trust her."

"There is a lot of talk about what happened. People are still divided as to whether Dak'Tor hit

Laborn over the head or not. Others think it possible that Gard did do it, hoping to kill him, and still blame it on Dak'Tor. Then Gard would have become Leader.

Iria waited for Isan'Tor to finish nursing, wiped his little mouth off with her hand, and cuddled him over her shoulder.

"Please give a message to Dak'Tor in private. Tell him how much I love him and that I miss being together as a family."

Vaha nodded, stood up, and waited for Iria to hand the offling to her.

"Be careful no one sees you going back," Iria whispered.

As soon as they were out of sight, she went back to gathering the kahari roots, working more quickly than before to make up time.

When Iria returned to Laborn's fire with Useaves' basket on her hip, she caught the old female watching her. Useaves gave an almost imperceptible nod, which Iria acknowledged only by briefly lowering her eyes.

As the days passed, Iria did everything that Useaves and Gard asked her to do. Usually, Gard's tasks for her were also easy assignments, such as looking for flint and striking stones. In helping Useaves, Iria started to learn about the plants and roots that

Useaves used. It helped pass the time and keep her mind off her captivity.

Then, one afternoon, Laborn came up to where the two females were working and addressed Iria. "Useaves and Gard tell me you have done all they asked you to do without complaint. And so I have decided you deserve a reward. I know you are grieving being with your offling, so he is being brought here to stay with you."

Iria looked at Useaves and then back at Laborn. Her mind was racing. Isan'Tor. As much as she wanted her son, she did not want him here with her.

"Why do you hesitate?" asked the Leader, obviously irritated. "Are you not grateful that I offered to bring him here to you? It has been nearly two moons since you last held him. Surely you are anxious to be with him?"

Iria looked at Useaves, who tilted her head and raised her eyebrows.

"I— I—"

"Stop your stammering," said Laborn. "It is settled. And unless you want this to be the last kindness I bestow, I suggest you show some gratitude."

That evening, Useaves came into the sleeping area.

Iria had been resting after the evening meal but sat up when she heard little Isan'Tor make a noise. She jumped to her feet and quickly took her offling. She closed her eyes and held him close to her, soaking up all his warm offling feel and smell.

Then Iria looked at the older female and said, "Perhaps I should thank you?"

"Not for this. No, not for this," Useaves said as she turned to leave.

Over the next few days, neither Useaves nor Gard assigned her any tasks. She was free to spend her time with her offling and felt the first little bit of joy since being forced away from her home. But her joy was short-lived.

It was late. Iria lay curled around her son, facing away from the door. She was startled when she heard Laborn's voice behind her.

"Wake up."

Iria sat up and picked up Isan'Tor. With him was Useaves, who reached out as if to take the offling.

"No!" Iria exclaimed. "Why?"

"I need to have your full attention. He will not be harmed. Give him to her."

Useaves leaned down and took the tiny bundle from Iria. Then she turned and left. Iria almost let out a cry of despair but stopped herself in time.

"These last few days have been good for you here, yes?" Laborn asked.

Iria nodded, her eyes still flitting to the doorway through which Useaves had disappeared with Isan'Tor.

Laborn's motion brought her back as he came

over and sat down next to her on the sleeping mat. "I gave you something that pleases you. Now you must give me something that pleases me. That is how it works. Give and take." He reached out and grasped a strand of her hair, and started playing with it. Iria turned her face away and twisted around so her back was to him. "No, please. I cannot."

"Quiet," he said. "I can make your life here much harder. You have no idea." And Laborn snaked his arm around her and slipped his hand down to cup her between her legs. Iria scrambled to get away from him, but he caught her hair and snarled into her ear. Her hands went instinctively to his wrist to try to loosen his grasp.

Iria was off-balance, and Laborn easily twisted her around and whipped her down on her back, then moved on top of her. He covered her mouth with one hand and pressed on her throat with the other. "It is up to you now how the rest of this goes. I am going to remove my hand but before you cry out, think of your son. So helpless and vulnerable. I know you would not want anything to happen to him. An accident, maybe. One never knows."

Iria squeezed her eyes shut as hard as she could and armored her soul against what Laborn was about to do to her. She had only ever been with Dak'-Tor; she was a maiden when they paired. The thought of another male taking her was abhorrent, let alone this monster. Now Iria knew why Laborn had brought her offling to her. It was for leverage.

With little Isan'Tor under Laborn's control, he knew he could force her to do nearly anything. And he was right.

She nodded quickly, and he removed his hand.

"That is better," he said.

She opened her eyes just long enough to see him leering down over her and regretted it instantly.

It took all her self-control not to shout out, not to try to push him off. Instead, she focused on her helpless son in the next room under Useaves' care. She had no doubt that if she tried to do harm to Laborn, her offling would pay for it. Every part of her screamed in revolt when he entered her. She wanted to claw his face off, bare her canines and open his throat. But instead, she steeled herself. His groans and huffing and puffing disgusted her, and she prayed he would finish soon, but the sudden thought of his fluids remaining on her made her nauseous.

When he was done, Laborn rolled off and let out a huge sigh of satisfaction. Iria rolled over so her back was to him, and she bit her lip and balled her fists, digging her nails into her palms to keep from screaming. He was sick, twisted. He *was* a monster.

After a moment, Iria felt the sleeping mat shift. She did not move for fear Laborn was still in the room; she did not want to let him see her rage. Then a moment later, she heard her son gurgle and sprang up and took him out of Useaves arms. She did not look at the old female but whisked him back and lay down and curled herself around him. No matter what she had to go through, she would not let anyone harm Isan'Tor.

Iria vowed she would not cry, that she would never cry over what Laborn had done to her. That she would be strong. What would happen now? If Dak'Tor found out what Laborn had done, he would try to kill the Leader. What was Laborn's game? Did he want Dak'Tor to attack him as an excuse to kill him? If he wanted that, Laborn could have killed Dak'Tor long ago, so that could not be it. The more she thought about it, the more she became convinced that the game was the end in itself. Laborn enjoyed hurting others. Enjoyed tormenting Dak'Tor, enjoyed defiling her. And the capacity for that kind of enjoyment made him not only a monster. Laborn was evil.

CHAPTER 7

Though Takthan'Tor had settled back into the routine at Kthama, his duty to honor the Rah-hora was never far from his mind.

"We must move forward with the Brothers, no matter whether any of the other populations decide to do so," he said to Vor'Ran.

"Yes, it is the will of the Ancients," Vor'Ran agreed.

"Not just the Ancients. It is the Rah-hora. We are bound to do so. Let us spend the rest of our return thinking on how this best might be achieved. Our first contact with them must be as innocuous as possible."

"Culrat'Sar once suggested that we arrange a chance meeting with one of our females. Our Healer, perhaps."

"Yes, it was he who suggested it. We should meet with Tensil as soon as possible."

After Takthan'Tor and Vor'Ran had explained to her what they wanted her to do. Tensil agreed to begin wandering closer to the Brothers' territory in hopes of a chance encounter. She and Wry'Wry had talked about different ways to approach the Brothers. Tensil wondered if her presence would immediately be noticed, and Wry'Wry believed it would be.

"What if you left some items. Something that would not be natural," Wry'Wry suggested.

"Not be natural? What do we possibly have that would not be natural?" Tensil smiled.

"Not naturally occurring. Make a pattern of something. Something they will recognize was put there on purpose."

"Like a stack of stones?"

"Maybe. Or a stack of stones with feathers in between? I do not know; I am just trying to come up with ideas," said Wry'Wry. "They must have a Healer of some kind. What could you leave that another Healer would recognize as out of the ordinary if piled together or stacked up?"

Tensil thought for a moment. "Ginseng. I am sure their Healer would use Ginseng. We have a great deal in store from the harvest. Now the question is where?"

"On the ground? On a large rock?" Wry'Wry suggested.

Tensil chuckled, "No, I mean, where on the edge

of our territory. It has to be somewhere they would notice.

"I know. There is a large oak just on the boundary. I remember seeing it when I wandered over that way by mistake. It produces a huge bounty of acorns, and they are already starting to fall. I am sure the Brothers would know of it. I could suspend some Ginseng from a branch. That would certainly not be naturally occurring!"

They smiled at each other, happy with the plan.

That next morning before first light, the two females set out for the oak tree. The crisp fall air was a welcome relief from the summer heat. Wry'Wry kept watch while Tensil quickly scrambled up the tree, the Ginseng tied at the end of a strip of hide and the other end caught between her teeth.

She wanted to climb high enough that it would be spotted but not so high that whoever found it could not get it down. Considering how much smaller they believed the Brothers to be, that meant not very high at all. But it had to be high enough that the deer could not reach it as they would be searching for the acorns and walnuts already scattering the area.

"There!" she proclaimed when she had it secured and dangling from one of the oak branches. She slid down the tree trunk and stood next to Wry'Wry, admiring their handiwork. "We will have to check on it occasionally. Unless a very large animal comes along, it should be safe."

In his shelter, Chief Chunta was also enjoying the cooler fall weather with his mate, Muna. Their Medicine Woman Sitka passed by, singing softly, which made the chief realize their lazy awakening needed to end.

Sitka had a clear and lilting voice, and her songs blessed everyone who heard them. Those in the village often stopped to listen to her singing.

"She is in a good mood today," Muna remarked to her mate.

"Yes, today must be a good day. Her mind must be off the heartache of losing her beloved. What will you do today?" he asked. The chief's wrinkled skin and grey hair matched the years of wisdom he had gained.

Muna flipped their blanket back and rose to meet the day. "I promised to keep Sitka company while she did some weaving." A broad grin broke out on her face. "She is teaching me a new pattern. It is already morning; I had better hurry as I do not want to keep her waiting."

Chief Chunta cherished his mate, and seeing her happy promised a good day for him too.

Sitka and Muna sat together, Muna watching and listening closely to what the Medicine Woman was showing her. Muna was fascinated by the new pattern and new colors Sitka had mixed. Before too long, a collection of young girls had also gathered. Sitka smiled at them, happy to see their interest.

As they were sitting there, Tocho, one of the younger boys, came up and tugged on the hair of one of the littler girls. "Come and hunt for acorns with me, Tiva," he said.

"Nooooo," Tiva said, brushing her brother's hand away. "I am busy here. Go on by yourself."

"You said you would come with me," he reminded her. "I will let you pick the best ones if you come?"

Tiva twisted her head around and looked up at her brother. "Really? You mean it?"

Tocho nodded quickly, seeing the chance of getting his way. He loved his sister, and he was happiest when she was with him.

"Alright," she said. She got up from her squatting position, took the carrying baskets from her brother's hand, and off they went.

"Where are we going?" she asked.

"Up to the big oak. I told Momma I would see what the squirrels left us."

"You said I could have the best ones."

"You can. What will you do with them?" he asked.

"Bury them by the riverbank, so they turn dark and sweet!" she beamed. "And then surprise Momma with them later."

The longer they walked, the more Tiva became uncomfortable. "Tocho, did you mean the big oak at the edge of our territory? I did not think you meant that one."

"It is the best one because no one else goes there. We might even be able to fill our carrying baskets," he exclaimed.

"Hardly anyone goes there because it is too close to *their* area."

He knew his sister meant Oh'Mah, the master of the forest. Tocho had seen two while out bow-hunting with his father. Though he had been scared at the time, he was no longer afraid of them. In fact, he hoped to see one again. "There is no reason to be afraid. We are told to stay away out of respect for their territory. But just this one time will not hurt. Remember, it was only by accident that I ran into the two I did. They do not want to have anything to do with us. And all our people's stories tell us they are peaceful."

Not quite convinced, Tiva continued on with her brother.

Finally, the large oak tree Tocho was looking for came into view. It was a massive tree, its branches stretching out across the blue sky behind it. Birds hopped from branch to branch, and squirrels chattered at them as they approached. A meadow filled with tall grasses stretched before them.

As they got closer, Tiva stopped.

"What is that?" she asked, pointing.

"What?"

"That!" she said, drawing a circle in the air with her finger.

Tocho squinted to see what she was pointing at. Something was dangling from one of the tree branches, swaying gently in the morning breeze.

Excited, the two started running through the tall grass that covered what was left of the distance between them and the towering oak.

When they reached the tree, they looked up at what was dangling from an upper branch. They stared at it for a moment and then looked at each other.

"Someone put that there," said Tocho.

"*Who* someone?" asked Tiva, staring over at her brother, her eyes now wide. "I am scared. I want to go back."

"Shhh," he said, handing her his carrying basket and starting toward the trunk of the oak.

"What are you doing!" she called after him.

"Be quiet!" he replied. Tocho readied himself and then started climbing the tree. He was very careful to watch his footing, only looking up briefly to make sure he was headed toward the prize.

He dodged the branches, carefully pushing the

smaller ones away with one hand while making sure he did not lose his balance. Finally, he reached the branch he needed. His fingers worked quickly to undo the knot holding the piece of hide from which the bag was dangling. Once it was loose, he called down, "Careful. Watch it does not hit you on the head!"

Tiva stepped back and waited for it to drop. With its binding loosened, the bag tumbled to the ground among the soft grasses below.

Tocho scrambled down as fast as he could and ran over to his sister, who was staring at the little bag on the ground in front of her.

"Are you not going to pick it up?" he asked.

"No."

Tocho looked at his sister as if she had a point. Until then, too caught up in the adventure, he had not felt any need for caution.

"Do you think *they* put it there?" his sister asked.

Everyone in their village knew that Tocho had been blessed to see not just one but two of the Oh-Mah. As their father had instructed, he had done his best not to let his new status make him think he was different or special.

He thought for a moment. "Maybe. But the branch it was hanging from is too thin to support the weight of the Oh'Mah I saw."

"What if it were a younger one, like us?"

"Perhaps. I do not know any more about them

than what the stories say. I am not an expert just because I saw them."

Tiva knelt down to look more closely at the little bundle, then picked up a nearby stick and poked at it. "I smell ginseng," she proclaimed. She looked up at her brother, "It is ginseng."

"It is a gift," Tocho decided.

"How do you know?"

"It has to be. Why would it be hanging there in plain sight? If someone was going to come back for it, they would have hidden it. But why leave it at all? It is small, not difficult to carry. It was put there for us to find!" His voice rose with the excitement of what this could mean. Oh'Mah was reaching out!

"What should we do with it? It seems ungrateful to leave it here," said Tiva.

"I am going to take it back to the Chief. He will know what to do!" Tocho picked up the bundle of ginseng and started off.

"What about the acorns?" his sister called after him.

"I think this is more important. We can come back tomorrow for the acorns. Come on."

Chief Chunta and Sitka were at the main fire pit when the two youngsters came hurriedly into sight. The two adults waited silently for the brother and sister to reach them.

"Chief. It is I, Tocho. My sister and I went out to gather acorns and found this hanging from the regal oak at the far end of our territory." Tocho stretched out his hand with the bundle of ginseng in it, the hide cord from which it had dangled still attached to it.

Sitka and the chief peered closely at what Tocho was holding out.

"You found this?" Sitka asked.

"It was hanging off one of the branches," Tiva explained. "My brother crawled up and loosened it."

The Chief nodded his head and then asked, "Did you see who left this?"

Tocho shook his head.

Respectfully, the two waited for the Chief and the Medicine Woman to say something more. Tocho was waiting for an admonishment about going to the oak so close to the edge of their territory. Moments went by, and neither child moved.

Finally, Chief Chunta said to Sitka, "This is a good gift. This is a gift of good medicine."

"We must leave something in return," the Medicine Woman replied. "Something of equal value."

"You must decide what is to be left in return."

Sitka let out a long sigh. This was no small task.

Though neither said it aloud, both Chief Chunta and Sitka believed this was a gift left by Oh'Mah and was a way of making contact. Despite being sure that the Oh'Mah still walked Etera, no one other than Tocho had ever seen one in a very long time.

"I must consider this carefully," Sitka said. "I will decide by nightfall."

"May we go?" Tocho finally dared to ask. The

Chief waved his hand to dismiss them, and the children scurried off in relief to tell their mother and father their exciting news.

Before long, all of the village was talking about the gift from Oh'Mah and wondering what it portended.

🐾

Sitka returned to her shelter to seek guidance from the Great Spirit about what to leave in return. She wanted it to be something of value to Oh'Mah. But not knowing anything about them, other than that they served the Great Spirit, she did not want to make this decision based on her assumptions.

Clearly, Oh'Mah did not need blankets, and any food Sitka could give would be in too small a quantity to have any impact. Even a personal carved item or piece of jewelry seemed senseless. She wanted to give them something they would value, just as they had given the highly-esteemed ginseng to her community. Seeking to still her mind, Sitka started singing praise to the Great Spirit and set her problem aside.

Eventually, she had her answer and knew what to do.

That evening she told Chief Chunta her plan, and he smiled at her wisdom.

🐾

Wry'Wry and Tensil could not wait to check on the bag they had hung from the oak. After a day or so, they set out very early for the tree at the edge of their territory. As they approached, they heard a beautiful noise. Not one they had ever heard before.

"What is making that sound?" Wry'Wry whispered to Tensil. They stopped to listen.

"It is coming from next to the oak tree," Tensil answered.

The two females got as close to the area as they could while staying hidden. Around the base of the giant tree, a lone female Brother was moving gracefully about and making the lovely noise they had heard. Tensil and Wry'Wry waited for some time until the female had finished. They could see from where they were that the ginseng they had suspended was missing. Since the hide cord holding it was also gone, they surmised that one of the Brothers had found the gift.

But why was the female Brother acting so?

"What was she doing?" Wry'Wry asked.

"I think I know," said Tensil. "She is giving us a gift in return. The gift of beauty, of praise to the Great Spirit, in the way that they must express it.

"It is beautiful. A gift only she could give," Tensil added in a soft voice.

"What do we do now?" asked Wry'Wry.

"We must acknowledge in return that we have accepted her gift. Come on, we must find a way to signify that the exchange between us is complete."

Tensil could not think of any way to let the female know that they had heard her that would not frighten her but would get her attention. Then Wry'Wry picked up a large stick and thunked it against a nearby trunk.

The female turned to look in the direction of the sound and then stood perfectly still. Then, arms outstretched, she turned around in a circle, apparently letting them know she realized it was a signal.

Wry'Wry grabbed Tensil's arm and kind of hopped up and down a little. "It worked! It worked! She knows we were thanking her back!"

Tensil smiled and said, "Shhh! Well, she is acknowledging *something*. We must wait here quietly until she leaves." Inside, Tensil felt a warm satisfaction that they had made contact. Her seventh sense told her this was a good move. She was anxious to return and tell their Leader what had happened.

Takthan'Tor, Vor'Ran, and First Guard Anthram listened attentively.

"You did well," Takthan'Tor said, looking first at Tensil and then at Wry'Wry. "The question is, what happens next? How do we continue this conversation in a way that keeps it going and gains in significance?"

"At some point, we will need to meet face-to-face," Tensil said.

"And at that point, they will wonder what in the name of the Great Spirit we are," said Vor'Ran.

"We are more like them than the Ancients!" said Wry'Wry.

"This is true. But while we are more similar to them in appearance than were the Ancients, more so at a distance, we are considerably larger. And at some point, we will have to explain who we are," Takthan'Tor said.

"And how we came to be?" asked Anthram. "That will be the end of that, no doubt."

"We cannot allow it to be," replied Takthan'Tor. "We have to succeed in befriending them. We must avoid answering that until they get to know us well and see that we mean them no harm. Meet with me this same time tomorrow and give me your thoughts."

With that, the Leader dismissed them, but as Tensil started to leave, he asked her to stay.

When they were alone together, he asked her, "How are we going to prevent them from discovering our origin?"

"We do not even know if the males ever talked about the dreams. The dreams that the Protectors used to take their seed from them to create us. If they did not, then there might never be any need to explain."

"Is that possible?" Takthan'Tor paced as he spoke. "That in the thousands of years since our people were created, none of the Others'—the Brothers'—

males ever broke their silence? I cannot believe it, even as taboo as the dream was."

"If they did talk about the dream, there is nothing tying it to our existence," Tensil said.

"That is probably true, but is that to be the basis of our relationship with them? A lie?"

Tensil wiped her hand over her face and shook her head. "I know. It is wrong. Somehow, we must tell them the truth of who we are; we owe them that. But I do not know that we should tell them how it was accomplished. That, we were not given the right to disclose. It is the shame of the Ancients. Would we not be betraying them by revealing the wrongs of Wrak-Wavara?"

"Perhaps you are right. But at least they must know we share their blood. But not until we have established our good intentions. We must stall as long as possible because otherwise, First Guard Anthram is right. It will be a short-lived relationship. For now, we will see what Wry'Wry and the others come up with. Now that contact is in play, we must continue the conversation."

Sitka returned and told the Chief what had happened, that she had gone to the oak every morning since the gift was found, dancing and singing praise to the Great Spirit in the hopes that Oh'Mah would notice.

"Your gift was honorable. You did well," the Chief said.

"What does it mean, that it happened, that Oh'Mah has reached out to us in such a clear manner?"

"It means that Oh'Mah either requires something of us or has come to deliver a message from the Great Spirit. We must prepare ourselves."

The Brothers' Chief gathered the Elders together, and in ceremony, sought wisdom for what they believed was coming. For Oh'Mah intentionally to make contact with them was of great significance. Oh'Mah was the spiritual protector of the forests, rivers, and mountains. He was more powerful than any other creature on Etera. But he kept to himself, elusive, rarely sighted. Other stories remained of a silver-white Oh'Mah, but as with all the others, it had not been seen for thousands of years, either.

"Since Oh'Mah has thanked Sitka for her gift, she should be the one to continue to reach out," Chief Chunta said. "It is fitting as she is our Medicine Woman and spiritual guide. If Oh'Mah is willing, perhaps in time, others will be invited in."

With that decided, Sitka set about making small gifts she hoped would be appreciated. Since she could not think of anything of use to Oh'Mah, she decided that perhaps items of beauty or craftsmanship would be pleasing to him.

Many of the other women in the village sat around Sitka, watching her weave a brightly colored basket. She was striving to make it as large as possible and very sturdy. It was not that she thought Oh'Mah would use it, but she wanted something to put the other gifts in, and she knew the basket would stand out among the natural backdrop and be noticed. As she wove it, she sang, which made for a sweet experience for her and her friends.

At the back sat Tocho and his sister.

"Will we get to go again?" asked Tiva.

"I do not know. That is up to the Chief. And our parents. I am hoping so since we were the ones who found the first gift," Tocho said wistfully.

"You should definitely go. Remember that it was you who Oh'Mah first showed himself to," Tiva said.

"Well, I stumbled on them; it was not on purpose. The smaller one was as surprised as I was. So they did not choose to show themselves to me."

When Sitka was finally ready, she gathered the large basket and the items to go in it. Others wanted to offer gifts too, so there was a varied collection. There were carvings of deer, eagles, and wolves, as well as medicinal herbs and roots. Just as Sitka was about to leave to deliver the basket, Tiva came up and reached out her hand to the Medicine Woman.

"What is it?" Sitka asked as she peered down into

Tiva's little open palm. "Oh. A beautiful red jasper stone. Is it yours?"

Tiva nodded. "Yes. It is my favorite thing. And I want Oh'Mah to have it."

"That is generous and kind of you, little one. A great sacrifice speaks of a great heart," Sitka said.

Tiva smiled and lowered her eyes.

Many of the villagers watched as Sitka hoisted the large basket onto her shoulder and left for the oak tree. As she was nearly out of sight, she turned around and called out to Tocho and Tiva. They looked over at their parents, who both waved them on, and the two siblings took off as fast as they could to catch up with her, kicking leaves and sticks in front of them as they ran.

When they got to the oak tree, Sitka picked out a location not far from the trunk to leave the basket. Then she and the children cleared a large circular area of the fallen leaves and danced around in joy and celebration. With the circle tamped down, and satisfied that it would easily be seen, Sitka placed the basket in the center. Before they left, she asked for a blessing from the Great Spirit. Tocho and Tiva were so excited that they danced much of the way home.

As they went, Tiva asked, "What will happen now, Sitka?"

"We will go back in a few days and see if it is still there. If it is not, then I will believe that Oh'Mah came and found it worthy. If it is only moved about, then I suspect an animal would have disturbed it.

Perhaps, if we are truly blessed, the basket will be gone and something left in its place!"

"Oh! How exciting!" Tiva exclaimed.

That evening, around the main fire, Sitka and the children told the story of how they had delivered the basket and how they made a clearing so it would be noticed. There were smiles and much laughter at the gleeful way Tocho and Tiva demonstrated their stomping about. Everyone considered this a sign that something wonderful was about to happen and that Tocho would play a big part since he was the one who first saw the two Sasquatch not that long ago.

CHAPTER 8

Iria busied herself with tasks for Useaves and tried to keep her mind off nightfall. Her sleep was fitful as she expected Laborn to come to her as he had the first time. But days passed, and he did not. Eventually, she thought perhaps having violated her once, he was satisfied. But she was wrong.

That same night, Iria had a sense of dread come over her. And it was not long before Laborn entered the room with Useaves behind him. She knew that Useaves had come to take Isan'Tor and what was going to happen next.

This time, Laborn took her from behind, savagely ramming himself into her as hard as he could. She squeezed her eyes shut and clenched her jaw tight. When he had finally emptied himself into her, he let out a moan that turned her stomach. More than almost anything, she wanted to rush to the banks of the river and wash him off her, but she knew Useaves would be bringing her son back soon and instead had to wait for her precious offling to be returned.

"You are enjoying it, I can tell," he taunted her.

"You are insane. You disgust me. I hate every moment of it, and you know it. That is what you want, is it not? For me to feel humiliated and defiled?"

"On the contrary. You should see it as the honor it is. I have not mounted anyone since—" His voice trailed off.

"It is not an honor. It is an abomination," Iria sneered, glaring at him.

"Be careful. You are under my protection here," Laborn threatened.

At that moment, Iria was beyond caring about the consequences. "You disgrace Shikrin's memory by taking me Without My Consent."

The moment she said the words, she knew she had gone too far.

"You ungrateful— You need to remember your place!" Laborn jumped to his feet and stormed into the hallway, calling for Useaves.

Within a moment, Useaves showed up carrying Isan'Tor.

"Get up," he barked at Iria. *"Get Up!"*

Iria stumbled to her feet, a cold knot starting to twist in her stomach. She had gone too far, and she knew it.

"No, please. I— I—" she stammered.

"It is too late for that. It is time you learned your place here." Laborn grabbed her by the arm and dragged her from the room.

"Kaisak!" he called out.

Kaisak appeared looking as if he had just woken up.

"Take the offling," Laborn ordered, "Useaves is too slow to come with us." And he briskly led them outside. "Useaves you wait by the fire for our return."

Iria's heart started pounding faster as she watched Kaisak take her son from Useaves.

The evening sky was lit with stars. The full moon cast a faint glow over everything, so Iria could see where Laborn was taking her. He still had a tight grip on her arm and was practically dragging her along. She kept trying to twist around to see if Kaisak was carrying Isan'Tor properly. She prayed fervently to the Great Spirit for protection; she was terrified of what Laborn might be going to do.

They ended up quite a way from the settlement. Laborn had taken them into a large cleared area with tall grasses. Not far was the edge of the woodland. He took Iria over to Kaisak, shoved her to the ground, and said, "Make sure she does not go anywhere."

Then to Iria's horror, he took Isan'Tor from Kaisak and walked out into the large meadow toward the wooded area. She tried to rise, but Kaisak pushed her back down into the damp leaves.

Laborn then laid the tiny offling down and

walked away, leaving him there, helpless and unprotected.

"No, what are you doing?" Iria called out. "You cannot leave him there!" As she spoke, she could hear coyotes yipping close by. She could see little Isan'Tor waving his little arms and legs under his wrap. *Stop moving, please,* she begged silently.

Laborn went over and grabbed Iria hard by the upper arm. He dragged her to her feet and pulled her a good distance away from where he had left her son.

"No, please," she begged; the farther away they went, the greater the danger to her son.

"Shut up. You are about to get a lesson in gratitude."

Laborn brutally shoved her back onto the ground. Iria raised herself up and looked around to try to see the place where he had left Isan'Tor. "I have learned my lesson; I understand, I will be grateful. Please, let me have my son. You cannot leave him there. The coyotes—"

"You should have thought of your offling's welfare before you talked back to me," Laborn chided her. "Yes, you are apologizing now, but how long will your regret last this time?"

Iria turned abruptly when she heard rustling a distance off. Then more, and soon the brown shapes of the coyotes appeared at the edge of the woods, moving back and forth. Her heart stopped when Isan'Tor started to wail.

"Stop. Stop it," she cried out. "Stop it, or I will tell

everyone what you did to me! They will turn on you when they find out you took me Without My Consent!"

"Are you sure of that? It will be your word against mine! You forget you are just a female. No one will believe you over me, their Leader."

Slowly, one of the coyotes started to venture toward where her son was lying. It lifted its nose and sniffed the air before moving closer while the others waited in the background. By now, Iria was nearly hysterical. She shouted and screamed in an effort to scare them off.

"Make her shut up!" Laborn barked.

Kaisak quickly squatted down behind her and placed his hand roughly over her mouth. He wrapped his free arm around her and grabbed her by the throat.

The lead coyote stopped when it heard Iria screaming, but the noise was such a distance off that it gave the coyote only a moment's pause. Then it started, head down, toward the offling.

Laborn squatted down in front of Iria, taking a piece of her hair in his hand as he had before. "We are running out of time. Or should I say, your son is." Then he leaned in so she could feel his breath on her neck and asked, "Once and for all. Do I have your obedience?" Iria fiercely nodded her head, tears of fear streaming down her cheeks.

Just then, the coyote bolted toward the precious bundle lying unprotected in the open. As it was opening its mouth to snatch Isan'Tor up in its jaws, Laborn was at its side. He kicked the coyote out of the way at the very last moment. It yelped and ran off, looking back as it disappeared into the tree line.

Laborn picked Isan'Tor up and carried him over to Iria. She took him in her arms, and sobbing, curled her entire body over him.

"You will obey me. You will say nothing to anyone ever about anything that has gone on while you are under my *protection*. Anything. Do you understand?"

Still curled protectively around her son, Iria frantically nodded her head.

"That is good. Because we were lucky tonight. I got to your son in time. The next time, I might not be as fast."

Then he told Kaisak, "Get her up."

Kaisak pulled Iria to her feet and steadied her as she found her balance. Then Laborn walked off, leaving them to follow him back to the settlement.

Useaves was still sitting by the embers, waiting, wondering what Laborn was up to by taking Iria and the offling off into the night without her. She was relieved when she saw the three figures coming back and could see Iria carrying her offling. Though she had not seen what had happened, she sensed in Iria terrible panic followed by total exhaustion. Whatever Laborn had done, it seemed as if it had broken her.

Dak'Tor had been in a state ever since Laborn took his mate. Then, when Kaisak came to claim their son, it had taken Dazal and several other males to restrain him. They told Dak'Tor that perhaps it was best for Iria to have her offling with her. But he was not convinced as he knew Iria had felt Isan'Tor was safer in Vaha's care.

He spent his days off with Dazal as much as possible, training and building up his physical strength. The only way he could manage his anger was to exhaust himself every day. Not knowing what was happening to Iria—and now his son—was destroying him.

Then one morning, Gard intercepted them just before they left to go outside.

"What do you want?" Dak'Tor asked.

"Come with me," Gard said.

"No. Why should I?" He was almost shouting. "You lied and said I tried to kill Useaves when it was you. Whatever you want, forget it. It is not happening."

"Useaves needs to speak with you."

"Hmmph! Why should I listen to her? You are both liars."

"It is about your mate and your offling."

Dak'Tor shuddered involuntarily. He swallowed hard, "Alright."

He followed Gard a long way, back down to the riverbank where Useaves had found him once before, and his heart sank when he realized she was alone. He had been hoping that perhaps Iria and Isan'Tor would be with her.

"Sit down," she said as Dak'Tor approached. "You may leave us," she directed Gard.

"I do not wish to sit," growled Dak'Tor.

"Sit anyway." Her voice was stern.

"My days of listening to you are over," he snapped back.

"And yet you are here."

"Say what you have to say. I grow tired of these games. I am only here because Gard said this was about my family."

"Your mate and offling are safe. For the moment. But each day they stay minimizes the chance of their return to you."

"If you have a suggestion, then tell me what it is," Dak'Tor answered curtly.

"You must have something of value to Laborn? Something you could trade in return for your loved ones?"

Dak'Tor's mind went immediately to the crystal. Could Useaves know about it? If she did, why not just search his quarters. No, she was just fishing. But why was she helping him?

"Why are you helping me? You know it was Gard who hit Laborn with the rock, not me. Yet you and he framed me."

Useaves picked up a twig and drew something in the dirt. Then she said, "Laborn wanted Gard to kill me and blame it on you. I was the target, not Laborn.

But Gard told me about Laborn's plan, and we turned it back on him."

"You mean, you turned it back on Iria and me. And why would Laborn want you dead? He needs you."

"For the same reason he wants you dead; we stand up to him. Oh, I often have before, but now that there are two of us challenging him, it poses too much of a threat. And you could lead the community against him. But he cannot just kill you; he needs your seed, and in addition, killing you would make you a martyr. And martyrs can become powerful inspirations. He wanted you discredited by killing me, both of us out of the way. But I could not have that."

Then she added, "Besides, he fears the Guardian, no matter what he says. And you *are* her brother."

"But if you have that much control over Gard, why did you not just have him kill Laborn? You could still have blamed it on me. Same outcome. I am discredited."

"The community needs a strong hand to lead them, or they will splinter. There is already dissension. Laborn does not realize it, but not everyone agrees with his plan to kill the Akassa and the Sarnnon. At least, not the younger ones. And it is they on whose strength we must most rely. Laborn is starting to lose favor. If you had killed him, or rather, Gard had, you might have become a hero, and Gard would have been in charge. But Gard is not ready to lead and is certainly not prepared to do so in opposition to someone as charismatic as you, so I could not have let that happen."

Useaves tossed away the twig. "Now you are discredited. Laborn realizes he needs me and will have no further thoughts of doing me in because he would not have recovered without me. And there is still time to prepare Gard to take over."

"I am already blamed for trying to kill Laborn. Why do I not just kill you right now? You cost me my family. My mate and offling are being held captive by a madman."

"Yes, but they are alive. Laborn knows he needs me. What will happen to them if you kill me now? A while ago, he would have been glad if you had killed me. But a few months ago, you had no reason to, did you? Remember, if it were not for me, you would have been publicly humiliated for being unable to seed Dara."

"You are as insane as he is with these sick twisted games you play!"

Useaves struggled to her feet, and leaning on her walking stick, stood directly in front of Dak'Tor. "And are you so different? Tell me, what was the real reason you had to leave Kthama? I know your kind. Pampered, elite, living a life of leisure. Nothing but time on your hands to manipulate others. If it had not been for me, Laborn would have killed you the day you came. I convinced him you were valuable. Aside from your relationship to the Guardian, the only value you have to Laborn is that seed pack dangling between your legs. And as I already pointed out, if it had not been for my help, he would have learned of your performance problem, which, if you recall, I helped you with. You owe me for your life here."

"That may be so, but it is your fault I am in this situation. So how do I get my mate and son back? Tell me!"

Useaves turned and slowly lowered herself to sit on the bank. "Calm down. You are useless when your emotions run wild like that. Surely you have something of value to Laborn? Some bit of information about Kthama? Something that will help him annihilate the Akassa and Sassen? Do you have nothing you can trade for your mate and son to be returned to you?"

Once again, Dak'Tor thought about the crystal. But he had vowed he would never tell them about it or that the Mothoc had left Kthama and Kayerm. So what now? Then Dak'Tor remembered Useaves saying that Laborn did fear the Guardian.

"Take me to him. I know what to do," Dak'Tor said.

"No. I cannot take the chance of being seen with you. Wait a few days, then go to him and have your say."

Useaves sat watching Iria cleaning some roots for the store of medicines. Iria had been very quiet and withdrawn for some time now. As she squatted down to work, her hide wrap pulling tight around her hips and waist, Useaves stopped cold.

"Iria. Iria."

Finally, Iria looked over at her.

"You are seeded."

Iria's eyes grew wide. "Yes," she said quietly.

"Does Laborn know?"

"If he has noticed, he has not said anything. I do not know what to do."

"Oh, Iria," It was one of the few moments Useaves had shown any kindness or concern toward Iria. "You must go to the community and tell them what he has done," she said.

"I cannot. He told me not to say a word about anything that has taken place." Then Iria told Useaves what Laborn had done to Isan'Tor, with the coyotes, to gain her silence.

"If he finds out you are seeded, he will kill you to cover up what he has done. You must know that. Your only hope is to tell everyone what he did before he can hurt you."

"If Dak'Tor finds out what Laborn did, he will try to kill Laborn. And then Kaisak and Gard will step in and kill Dak'Tor first."

Useaves shuffled over and pointed to the cutting blade that Iria had been using on the roots. "Keep that with you. I will not say it is missing. Tuck it under your sleeping mat. You will not have the strength to kill him, but you can wound him and prove you tried to fight him off."

"Prove I tried to fight him off? Of course I did! How could anyone think otherwise?"

"They might think you traded yourself for your son's protection. You cannot hide forever that you are seeded."

"Attacking him will just make him angrier! He might kill me or my offling."

"You have no choice," replied Useaves. "Once he realizes you are seeded, he will kill you. Or have someone else do it for him. If the community finds out that he took you Without Your Consent, it will not go well for him. And that may protect your mate."

Iria's head was reeling. It was overwhelming. She knew Useaves was right. It was a matter of time before Laborn—and others—would notice her swelling midsection.

But Laborn had already noticed. He caught Useaves alone. "Iria is seeded. You must do something about it. I cannot have others knowing that I mounted her."

"You should have thought of that before you violated her," Useaves said.

"I am old. I did not think my seed would take

root. You must have some way to make the offling leave her body."

"No." Useaves turned to face Laborn. "I will not. I will not kill her offling. Enough. There has to be a line somewhere that you will not cross. Iria told me what you and Kaisak did to her with the coyotes. What do you think will happen when that comes out? Dak'Tor will kill you for sure."

"Then I will kill him first!" Laborn roared.

"And then what happens. What happens when the Guardian finds out you murdered her brother?" Useaves shouted back. "Do you think she will never return here? Perhaps when the Promised One arrives, she will bring him here. Who knows?"

"Ahhhhh!" Laborn grabbed his head with his hands and stormed about the room.

"You got yourself into this; you get yourself out," Useaves shouted again before leaving him to his misery.

Laborn was panicking. It had not occurred to him that Iria could become seeded. He was so caught up in the sick pleasure of defiling her that he had not considered it. He had to make this go away, and there was only one way he could think of.

Iria had carefully tucked the cutting blade under her wrap and pressed it into place with the basket of roots she carried. She made her way to her quarters, and when assured she was alone, dug a shallow hole under the sleeping mat and tucked the blade into it. Then she delivered the basket to Useaves' living space. It worried her to have the blade as she knew that if Laborn discovered it, there would be no end to his fury. But Iria knew Useaves was right and that she had to protect herself against him. She just prayed that when Laborn made his move, her offling would be in Useaves' care.

She did not have to wait long.

Around the usual time, Laborn and Useaves entered. Being used to Laborn's visits, Iria quickly handed her son over to Useaves. She avoided looking at the old female for fear Laborn might see something pass between them. When Useaves had left, Iria looked at Laborn, waiting.

"Useaves said you were slow today. That she had to wait on you to finish your chores," Laborn said.

"What? No. That is not true!" Iria defended herself.

"Are you calling Useaves a liar?"

"No. No. But that is not true. I did not tarry at all!"

"Then you are calling me a liar?" he said.

"You are twisting my words," she said.

"I am not at all. Either you are calling Useaves a liar, or you are calling me a liar? Which is it?"

It then occurred to Iria that Laborn was trying to

pick a fight with her. Why? So he could justify killing her? That did not make sense; no matter how much she might argue with him, it would not justify his taking her life.

"You need to be punished," he said and started toward her.

She braced herself to be taken Without Her Consent but was unprepared when, instead of hitting her in the face as he had done before, he grabbed her forearms and raised her up, then threw her down hard, intentionally forcing her to land on her stomach.

She curled up with a long groan. The realization hit her that he knew she was seeded and was trying to kill her offling while making it look like a deserved punishment for an insolent female.

"Get up. I am not done!" he shouted at her. He apparently did not care if others heard them arguing.

"I cannot. I cannot!" she cried out.

He roared and bent over to lift her up again. Still in pain, Iria scrambled to get away from him. He grabbed her by the hips and started to pull her closer. She managed to roll over enough to kick him, but her defense only enraged him more.

"Stop it! You are hurting me; stop it!" she called out as she continued to kick and scream. One of her feet landed solidly in his belly, and it stopped him for a moment. While he was gasping for breath, she crawled over to the sleeping mat. With her body shielding from view what she was doing, Iria started clawing feverishly under the mat, and her hand closed around the handle of the blade. She flipped over just as Laborn came flying at her intending to slam his body on top of hers. Almost too late, she managed to get both her feet up between them in time to divert his fall from landing directly on her belly, but he still landed on top of her upper torso. And directly on the blade.

Blood gushed everywhere. Laborn screamed out in anguish. Iria pushed him partially off, enough to get away from him, and started calling for help.

"Help, please. He tried to kill me. Help me please!" she screamed at the top of her lungs. Within moments, in rushed Kaisak and Gard.

Kaisak went immediately over to Iria while Gard went to Laborn. A red river was flowing from the Leader's midsection, the handle of the cutting tool sticking out of his flesh.

"He tried to kill me. You have to believe me," she said, still clutching her belly and rocking back and forth. "Did you not hear me screaming? Why did you not come to my aid sooner?"

"A female screaming is not something to be alarmed out," said Gard. "Not when she is in the Adik'Tar's protection."

"*Protection*? He tried to kill me, and you waited to see if my screaming was serious enough for you to come and see what was going on?"

"What happened?" Useaves came rushing in, holding Isan'Tor.

"She said Laborn tried to kill her. Yet he is the one dead," said Gard.

Useaves looked at Laborn's limp body lying to the side, a red river of blood seeping out from his core.

"I believe her," said Useaves.

"You do?" asked Kaisak, at Iria's side.

"Yes. Just this afternoon, Laborn asked me for something to give her to kill her offling. When I refused, he apparently decided to take care of it himself," Useaves said.

"It is true. He picked me up and threw me on the ground. Then he lunged at me as if to bring all his weight against my belly," Iria said.

"Her offling?" Kaisak asked. "The female is seeded?"

"He took me Without My Consent. Many times," Iria said.

"Tend to the female," Kaisak told Useaves. "Gard, help me with the Leader."

By now, Laborn was nearly lifeless. The floor of the living quarter was slick with his blood, and it was clear there was nothing to do to save him. Kaisak leaned down and pulled the blade out, wiped it on his thigh, and held it up to Iria.

"How did you get this?" he asked.

Before Iria could answer, Useaves said, "I gave it to her. When I realized Laborn was going to kill her, I gave it to her for self-defense."

"I did not mean to kill him. It was the way he

came at me. I only meant to stop him from harming me further," Iria said.

Kaisak ignored her and turned to Useaves, "Why did you not instead come to Gard or me and tell us about this?"

"Would you have believed me? A female accusing the Adik'Tar of a plot to kill another female? What level of importance would you have given it?"

"Had you told one of us about this, it might not have come to this," Kaisak said.

"What would you have done? Gone to Laborn and told him what I said? Taken the female back to her mate to protect her? You would have done none of it," Useaves said.

Neither Kaisak nor Gard said anything. Instead, Kaisak went over and hoisted Laborn's now lifeless body up over his shoulders and carried it out of the room.

With the males gone, Iria rushed over to take Isan'Tor from Useaves' arms but the elderly female held onto him. "You are covered in blood. Go and clean up first."

Iria found some clean rags and water and hurriedly wiped as much of Laborn's blood off her as she could. "What will happen now? I have killed the Adik'Tar."

"Now you must do as I said. You must tell everyone what happened here tonight and what happened before with your offling and the coyotes. They must face the fact that Laborn had become truly evil. No matter what your mate's crimes are, only his staunchest supporters will condone what Laborn did to you. And tried to do to your offling."

"I hope you are right. Otherwise, they will call for my death in return for his!"

"I will help you. It will be alright," Useaves reassured her as she handed Isan'Tor over.

Kaisak laid the body down and prepared to light the evening fire. By now, it was clear Laborn had returned to the Great Spirit. Once the fire was lit, Kaisak sent Gard to call the community together as they needed to know what had happened.

Dak'Tor was with Dazal and his friends when they heard Gard calling out to everyone. They were trapped in the middle of the procession that made its way to the central meeting place at the fires. As they approached, the firelight illuminated the two females and Kaisak standing over what looked like a body. As they got close enough to see who it was, a clamor arose among the crowd.

"Is that Laborn? Is the Adik'Tar dead?" someone asked.

"Silence. When you are all quiet, I will tell you what happened," Kaisak announced. While they were waiting for everyone to assemble and settle down, Dak'Tor and his friends pushed their way to the front.

"Iria!" Dak'Tor called out. He forced his way through the others and ran up to her. She handed Isan'Tor to Useaves just in time as Dak'Tor caught her up in his arms. "Are you alright? And Isan'Tor? What happened?"

"Isan'Tor is fine, but be strong, my love," Iria whispered in his ear as he held her tight. "Please. No matter what happens, you must control yourself. I am begging you, for all our sakes."

Dak'Tor set her down just as Kaisak began to address the crowd.

All eyes went from watching Dak'Tor and his family reunite to watching Kaisak.

"The Adik'Tar is dead, as you can see. According to the female Useaves and Iria, the mate of Dak'Tor, Laborn attacked the female Iria with an intent to harm her. In protecting her life, she killed him."

"Ah—" Iria started to say something.

"Hush female. Your time to speak is not now," Kaisak barked at her.

Useaves frowned at Iria and shook her head. Useaves did not know what was going on any more than Iria did, but she was adept at moves and counter moves and knew when one was being played out.

"How did she kill him?" someone called out. "How could she? He is twice her size and far more powerful."

"Laborn told Useaves earlier today that he meant harm to Iria, to cause her to lose the offling he seeded in her Without Her Consent," Kaisak said. "In the belief that Laborn meant what he said, Useaves gave Iria a cutting blade to use to defend herself. There was no intention to kill him; it was ultimately an accident."

"So she claims!" a supporter of Laborn shouted.

Iria's family turned to each other in horror.

Dak'Tor burst out in a rage. "How dare any of you doubt her. You know her. You have known her all her life. How can you defend any male who takes a female Without Her Consent! That PetaQ! I will fight anyone who dares to say he did not deserve to die!"

He turned to Iria and placed his hands on her shoulders so she would have to look at him. Then he whispered, "I am so sorry. If he were alive, I would kill him slowly with my bare hands. Please do not worry. It is your offling, and it is part of you. I will love and protect it as if it were mine."

For one of the few times in his life, Dak'Tor thought only of someone other than himself. He pulled her into his embrace and held her gently.

"She had the right to defend herself! Our laws proclaim it!" It was Iria's mother, calling out from the crowd.

"What if she is lying?" a male voice called out. "After all, her mate tried to kill Laborn himself; perhaps she was just finishing the task!"

Dak'Tor released Iria from his brace and started menacingly toward the male, his canines bared.

Useaves stepped in front of him, held her hands

up, and shouted, "Dak'Tor did not try to kill Laborn. It was Gard!"

Gard was standing next to Useaves. His head snapped toward her, and his mouth dropped open.

Kaisak also turned to her. "Gard! Why would Gard try to kill Laborn?"

"No, he was not meant to kill Laborn, just hit him over the head with the rock and make it look like Dak'Tor had tried to kill him. Laborn ordered Gard to do it. It was a set-up to frame Dak'Tor. Laborn made us go along with it. He wanted to discredit the Guardian's brother as he feared Dak'Tor's influence over you all," Useaves shouted.

Isan'Tor, still in her arms, started to cry. Iria rushed over to take him.

A voice rose from the crowd. "Why would you go along with it, knowing it was a lie!"

"He said if we did not, he would be forced to kill Dak'Tor, and then when the Guardian found out what we had done, she would kill us all," Useaves said. "He only meant to discredit Dak'Tor, as I said."

Dak'Tor knew that there was no way his sister would destroy them all even if they had killed him. The fact that the crowd believed this about Pan told him how much their minds had been poisoned and how little they knew about their own kind. Or the Guardian.

He stared blankly at Useaves. *Such deceit. Manipulation.* At that moment, Dak'Tor realized why he had been brought here. Not only to understand real love.

Coming here was what he had needed to discover just how lost he was. He saw his old self in Useaves now, spinning this or that to get his own way. He might have been smoother, more polished, his intentions not grave or evil to this extent, but in the end, it was the same intention. Deceit, misleading, and twisting of words—doing whatever it took. He had not progressed to her level, oh, but he had been on the path there. And as hard as the more recent part of his journey had been, he now counted every challenge and every hardship he had been through as gain.

"Who is Adik'Tar now?" someone asked from the gathering. Kaisak glanced at Useaves and then Gard. He stood up taller and announced, "I am."

Gard started to object, but Useaves caught his arm. He looked down at her restraining hand, and in silence, glared at her.

Dak'Tor made his own announcement. "I am taking my mate and offling home. The injustice that has been done to them and to me is unwarranted. I did not come here willingly. I did not come here wanting to make trouble. But trouble everywhere is all we have found."

Then he looked at his circle of friends and family and added, "*Almost* everywhere."

And Dak'Tor put his arm protectively around Iria, who was still holding Isan'Tor, and led them home. Their friends and family followed them.

As Useaves talked, Gard had watched her in

bewilderment. *Why?* Though she had recovered the story enough so that no one would be angry with either of them, he felt betrayed. His allegiance with her felt broken.

⟨⟩

Before they went inside, Dak'Tor turned to address his friends and Iria's parents. "Whatever happens in the upcoming days, do not drop your guard. Time will tell if Kaisak will continue Laborn's reign of terror. Does anyone know what his position is on the Akassa and Sassen?"

Iria's father answered, "He is in agreement with Laborn that they should all be destroyed."

Dak'Tor nodded.

"It is a shame it is not Gard; he is not as strong as Kaisak. We would have had a better chance of you overthrowing *his* leadership," Zisa added.

Dak'Tor knew that in time there would be another conversation with Useaves, but he was confident he already knew why she supported Kaisak as Adik'Tar and had not made a case for Gard. But right now, his concern was for Iria and their son.

⟨⟩

Iria nursed Isan'Tor and then tucked him into his nest. Dak'Tor waited patiently until her attention was free, then led her to their sleeping mat.

He smoothed the hair from her face, "Look at me. I meant what I said. I will not think any differently about this offling than I do Isan'Tor. He or she is part of you and so part of me also. What Laborn did to you was not your fault; do not think that for a moment I would blame you. No male should ever touch a female Without Her Consent. I love you as I have never loved anyone, and I regret that I cannot avenge you by killing him myself."

When Iria had finished telling him about what Laborn had done with the coyotes, Dak'Tor was beside himself with anger. "I should never have left you there; this is my fault. I should have killed him and brought you home!"

"No. That was the last thing I would have wanted. Gard and Kaisak would never have let you get that close to Laborn, and once they saw you coming, they would have killed you first. We are safe now. We must let it all go and try to move forward."

Dak'Tor calmed himself down. Useaves' admonishment about how he let his feelings take over was playing in his mind's ear. "How did you survive it?"

"I kept thinking about you and our life together. And Useaves helped me several times. She gave me easy work to do, and I even learned some things about healing practices. She defended us tonight. She made sure they understood how evil Laborn was, and she confessed the truth about Gard hitting Laborn over the head and not you. Maybe she is not as bad as we thought."

Dak'Tor did not want to contradict his mate, but he did not agree. He knew now that everything Useaves did was formulated to serve her own purposes only. If that meant betraying someone, so be it. If it meant appearing to befriend and help them, she was capable of doing that too.

"You are right. We are together, and we will get through this together." Then Dak'Tor gathered her in his arms and held her for a very long time.

⟨⁊⟩

The crowd remained for quite some while. Some continued to argue that Laborn deserved to die. Others still supported him, and despite Useaves' announcement, questioned Iria's motives. Over-hearing the comments, Useaves mingled with others in the community and told a few key members in detail what Laborn had done with Iria's offling and the coyotes. She would make sure that no one would blame Iria for killing Laborn.

Gard waited patiently for Useaves to leave the gathering and followed her as she went. "I need to talk to you."

Useaves first led him to a more secluded area. "What?"

"You supported Kaisak as Adik'Tar. The plan was for me to take over, not him!"

"You are not ready. It is unfortunate timing that Laborn was killed. In time, you could have grown strong enough, but I could not advocate for you as Adik'Tar. They would have wondered since the obvious choice *is* Kaisak."

"I am tired of this!" Gard said. "Kaisak is young and strong; he will be Adik'Tar for centuries to come. I will never be Leader now!"

"You do not know what the future holds, and we need balance. You cannot command the respect that Kaisak can. The Guardian's brother is revered by many of the younger ones, and maybe by some of the others as well now that people realize he is innocent of trying to kill Laborn. People are drawn to him. Only Kaisak can compete, and it is balance we need."

"You dishonored me by telling them that it was I who injured Laborn, and you freed Dak'Tor from condemnation at the same time. How could you do that, *Mother*?"

Useaves drew her hand back and slapped Gard hard. "Never ever call me that. You know better than that; I am not your mother."

Gard's hand went to his face where her slap still burned. "You birthed me. No, you did not raise or care for me; you left that to your sister while you went off with that PetaQ! But like it or not, you are my mother."

"You know better than to speak of it. No one knows this about us. If you mention it again out loud anywhere—" her voice trailed off.

"What? What else are you to do to me? You already made me look like a weak fool in front of everyone. How much more lost can the cause of my becoming Adik'Tar be?"

"You trusted me all along. What has changed now?" She stared at him, her mouth tense.

"I just told you. You betrayed me. You sealed Kaisak's position as Adik'Tar by speaking up for him."

"And I told you why. You cannot compete with Dak'Tor! In time, Dak'Tor and Kaisak will come up against each other, and by then, you will hopefully have grown in status and stature in the eyes of the others. *That* is what you need to focus on now. Then, we will worry about taking on whoever is left after the inevitable battle between Dak'Tor and Kaisak."

Gard stared at Useaves. Her rationale seemed sound, but he was even less convinced that her intentions toward him were true.

Despite the shameful reasons leading to Laborn's return to the Great Spirit, the Good Journey ritual was held the next day. After it was over, Kaisak addressed the community.

"As your Adik'Tar, I command that any animosity against the Guardian's brother and his family be released. Useaves has explained what truly happened in the assault against Laborn and what took place while Dak'Tor's mate and offling were in his possession. Despite the suffering they have endured, the plan for Dak'Tor to continue seeding females will continue." He briefly glanced at Dak'Tor. "Nothing has changed. We need unrelated offling to mate with our current ones. In time, I will let you know what my decisions are in other matters."

Dak'Tor knew why Kaisak had said this and was expecting it. Kaisak needed him, just as Laborn had. Kaisak also intended the annihilation of the Akassa and Sassen, and he could not achieve that objective without a much larger force of Mothoc than currently existed. For now, Dak'Tor served a purpose. Whether Kaisak was afraid of the Guardian as Laborn had been, Dak'Tor did not know. In time he would learn for himself.

CHAPTER 9

Too much time had passed. Pan needed to engage the Aezaiteran stream and enter the Order of Functions. It was weighing on her mind, countered by her reluctance to be reminded of her father trapped in the vortex.

As she was visiting the Healer's Cove, Pan felt Irisa come up behind her. She turned around to face the elderly female.

"I have a place to suggest," Irisa said.

"I am ready now if you have time," Pan answered, not questioning now how Irisa knew she was once more worrying about having neglected her duty this long.

She followed Irisa on a fairly long walk through a particularly beautiful area fringed with tall pines and stately oaks. As they walked, wildlife unhurriedly crossed their path. Eventually, the pair arrived at a high lookout that offered a breathtaking view of the fall-painted mountains cradling Lulnomia.

Pan took a deep breath of the clear mountain air. As she exhaled, she reaffirmed her intention to serve as Guardian of Etera.

At the High Rocks, guards had always stood watch while Pan and her father entered the Aezaiteran stream and Order of Functions.

"You will stay with me?" Pan asked, glad for Irisa's company. Knowing that the elderly female had special insight into the role of the Guardian made her feel less lonely.

"Of course. I will rest over here until you are finished."

Pan looked up a moment at the crystal-clear sky overhead and then closed her eyes and sent her awareness down through her body and entered the Aezaiteran stream. As always, becoming one with the creative life force of the Great Spirit bathed her in pure joy and love. She let the union with the Three-Who-Are-One overtake her, gladly giving way to the bliss, surrendering to time until she sensed the moment to disengage. When she opened her eyes, daytime had been replaced by twilight. Time passed quickly on Etera compared to the time spent in the Aezaiteran stream.

She looked over to find Irisa, who was still waiting patiently. "I am sorry. You have been waiting a long time."

"Do not apologize, Guardian; I have learned

patience through the ages. You are not yet done, however."

Pan knew she had to engage the Order of Functions, and once again, experience the devastation of sensing her father trapped in the vortex. The only condolence was that she hoped he was aware of her presence there, however slight, just as she was of his.

Once again, she sent her awareness down into the vortex, this time into the Order of Functions. And as always, she felt as if she was being torn apart, stretched beyond endurance across the threads of eternity. Though she had built up her ability to withstand the nearly unbearable fragmenting of her being, she was relieved when she felt herself reassemble and knew that it was nearly over. As she felt her consciousness re-forming and leaving the Order of Functions, she reached out to touch her father's consciousness even though it was so vague and seemingly so far distant.

As she had been taught, she reengaged with the Aezaitera, and the unbearable fragmentation was replaced with indescribable peace, belonging, and joy.

Irisa was still waiting when Pan returned to herself. Though it had felt like an eternity in the Order of Functions, the rising moon indicated she had not been engaged there very long. But long enough.

Irisa rose and approached Pan. "Come; you need to eat. Then you must tell your mate and the Overseer that after first meal tomorrow morning, you are going away for a while but will return safely."

"Where are we going?" Pan asked.

"Patience," Irisa answered.

Pan sighed, and they made their way back to Lulnomia.

Rohm'Mok was used to not seeing his mate off and on. He simply picked up the reins and attended to the needs of the High Rocks community and their daughter Tala. He was just finishing putting Tala to bed when Pan came home.

She kissed Tala good night and turned to her mate.

He wrapped his arms around her and hugged her tightly, leaning his head against hers. "You look tired."

"Yes, I am. I entered the Order of Functions."

Rohm'Mok knew this meant she had also once again been faced with her father's entrapment in the vortex. He hoped his embrace would comfort her at least a bit.

"Rohm," Pan said, looking up. "I need to be gone for a little while."

"We will be here waiting for you when you return."

"Thank you for being so understanding." And she once more relaxed into his chest.

"I knew that being the mate of the Guardian would require sacrifices. Do what you must and know that my love goes with you wherever you are off to and whatever it is you have to do."

"You never ask; you just wait for me to tell you—or not."

"You tell me what you feel you can, or should, or need to. I would never want you to divulge any aspect of being a Guardian that you do not wish to. You are my life, Saraste'. Nothing you ask of me is too large a price to pay for your loving me," he answered.

At first light, Pan went to eat while she waited for Irisa. To her surprise, Irisa had already eaten, and as soon as the Guardian had finished, she followed Irisa outside.

"How long will I be gone?" Pan asked. "And where am I going?"

"We will be gone as long as it takes. As for where we are going, you will see."

Irisa preceded Pan down the main path from Lulnomia back to level ground. The Guardian looked back at the magnificence of their new home, admiring how the tall pines and fall-covered trees surrounded not only the entrance but wrapped themselves around the mountainside.

Irisa patiently waited for her.

"I am ready," Pan said, turning her attention back to the moment.

Irisa led the way in silence. They had not seemed to go far when Pan felt a shift of some type. For a moment, she was dizzy and had to close her eyes and shake her head to clear her vision. When she looked again, everything was as it had been and yet different. The greens were greener, the golds were more golden, and the sky was a little bluer. It reminded her of the Corridor though it was nowhere as vibrant and alive as that.

"Irisa—"

"You felt the shift. It will be explained in time. Come." And Irisa continued on.

Not very long after, they reached a high wall of rock. Irisa followed the wall around to where a portion jutted out. As they walked around the abutment, Pan saw an opening. It was not very large but generous enough that they could easily fit through.

Pan's eyes quickly adjusted to the low light as she followed Irisa through the winding tunnel. The walls seemed different from Lulnomia. They were smoother as if something had honed them down. The air held the scent of dust and dirt that had been little disturbed for some time. Pan realized that they seemed to be traveling up a slight incline, and after making a turn, they entered a larger chamber. Not as large as Lulnomia's entrance with its towering ceiling, but stately in its own way.

· · ·

They stepped into the center of the cavern, their feet leaving prints in the soft sand that covered the floor.

"Why have you brought me here?" Pan finally asked, having looked around the room. She could see nothing out of the ordinary other than the same vibrance as everything else here.

Just then, a large figure appeared to step out of nowhere. Pan gasped, startled in spite of herself. Whoever this was, he or she was larger than anyone she had ever seen. Her eyes moved rapidly over the form, not quite believing what she was looking at. The torso was thick and muscular, with a chest so broad it took her breath away. The entire body was covered with a silver-white coat, slightly more white than silver, and it was simply, unbelievably huge. Her gaze slowly traveled up to the face, and when their eyes met, it felt as if a door opened, and for a moment, she lost herself. It was as if she was not looking at this towering behemoth but looking through it to the beginning of time. Deep in her soul, a sense washed through her of things ancient, as old even as the dust of Etera. She blinked and stepped back, then looked over to Irisa, who was standing calm and composed.

"This is my father. Wrollonan'Tor," Irisa said.

Pan shook her head, frowning. "No. No. How can this be?" She looked at Irisa in confusion, then back up at the figure before her. The figure of the Guardian who had served Etera further back than memory existed.

The behemoth took a step forward, and she involuntarily stepped back. "No." Pan turned her head away as she tried to compose herself.

A rich, resonant voice filled the chamber. "It is true, Pan, daughter of Moc'Tor and Guardian of Etera." It was as if time had stopped, and even the rock walls were captivated, listening to this voice.

"Yes, it is I, Wrollonan'Tor." The voice seemed to roll through her consciousness like the deep rumble of thunder through a stormy sky.

"But how can this be? Are you still alive? If what we were taught is true, then you must be older than—"

To her surprise, Wrollonan'Tor smiled. "Older than time itself? Almost. Almost. Though some days I feel that perhaps I am."

"But you died!"

"Ah. Yes, that. Well, that is what people surmised. But as you can see, it is not true."

"That is what I was taught. What my father believed. What everyone believes."

"Not everything everyone believes is true, even if appearances seem to support it. Would you like to sit down?" Wrollonan'Tor offered.

"No. No, thank you. I prefer to stand for the moment. But if that is not true, why were we allowed to believe it—a lie?"

"It is a misconception. I knew I had to turn over

the Guardianship to your father, and when I disappeared, people assumed I had died."

"A misconception?"

"I can see this troubles you, Pan. So before we go any further, let me ask you this. If the food stores were dangerously low at Lulnomia, would you share that information with the offling? Or if there was dissension in the community, would you let the offling know? Of course not. In the case of offling, exposing them to worries that they are not equipped to handle and have no ability to cope with only harms them. In the same way, information is allowed to be given to adults only when they are mature enough of mind to be able to handle it."

Pan's head was reeling. A thousand questions vied for her attention at once. Before her stood a legend, the Guardian who had served Etera for longer than memory held. Had there been another Guardian before Wrollonan'Tor? No one knew, except that here was the one who could answer that question. And probably a hundred other questions she could not formulate nor would dare ask.

"I can feel your confusion. For now, it is enough for you to accept that I exist. This is a shock to you as it would be to anyone in your situation."

"Irisa is your daughter."

"Yes. She has told you the story—at least enough of it for you to understand."

"Wait." Pan put her hand up and then froze. "You have been alive all this time. You were alive when my father sacrificed himself to the vortex in the belief that the burdens to come would be too much for me to bear. He did not have to do that. You could have revealed your existence to him. You could have helped him!" Pan was close to tears, and only her sudden anger kept them at bay. "You let my father sacrifice himself *needlessly*!"

"Pan," Wrollonan'Tor took a step toward her, and Pan stepped back accordingly.

For a moment, she squeezed her eyes shut.

"No! I do not care who you are. If you are a Guardian, as you say, then you can enter the Aezaiteran stream. You can enter the Order of Functions. He did not have to die to save me from a burden *you* could have lifted. A burden he did not believe I could bear."

"You loved your father dearly and still do, just as he still loves you. But you see through an offling's eyes. Your father was riddled with guilt over his decisions, and the impending loss of your mother, along with his feelings of failure, was too much to bear. He could not live with himself and what he had done. It was his choice, his recompense for the wrongs he felt he had committed and condoned. Without his sacrifice of himself—for you, for our people—his soul would have been in anguish the rest of his life. And perhaps for all eternity."

Pan listened silently to Wrollonan'Tor's words.

"Daughter," Wrollonan'Tor turned to Irisa. "Take

the Guardian home. This is enough of a shock for now. When she asks to return, bring her then."

Iria put her hand on Pan's arm.

"Go home to your family," Wrollonan'Tor said gently. "Cherish your moments with them, for to love and be loved is the greatest blessing in creation."

Irisa put her arm up around Pan's shoulder and led her away. Pan walked stoically, not turning back to bid the Ancient Guardian farewell. They made their way back down the tunnel and out into the light of day.

A small red squirrel hopped across their path, shaking Pan out of her stupor. "Where are we? We did not travel far. How can he live here so close to Lulnomia and no one know it? Is he going to reveal himself to the rest of us?"

"No, Pan. This is for only you to know. You will understand more later. For now, do as my father said. Go home to your mate and your daughter and give yourself time to assimilate this new information. It is a shock, to be sure."

Pan said nothing the rest of the way back, only letting out a gasp as she felt the shift again. "What—"

"Later. Trust me and trust the Order of Functions. All will be revealed in time."

The moment they stepped back into Lulnomia, Pan was on her way to find Rohm'Mok and Tala. She flew into her mate's arms, and then, after a quick embrace, scooped Tala up and twirled her around, making the offling laugh with glee before gently setting her down. "I love you both so much."

"Is there something you need to talk about?" Rohm'Mok asked, searching her face.

"Yes, but I cannot. I am sorry."

"I understand. You look tired. It is early, but my duties are complete for the day. Come and lie down with us, and I will tell you a story that my mother used to tell me at sleep time."

Pan, Rohm'Mok, and Tala all piled onto the generous sleeping mat, little Tala tucked in between her parents. Then Rohm'Mok told them a sweet story about a young Guardian and a little owl who wanted to use some of the Guardian's silver-white hair for her nest. Pan smiled; this was a story her own mother had told her, and she knew it was a story from her father's youth. Rohm'Mok's voice was comforting, and before the story was over, both Pan and her daughter were sleeping peacefully.

Sometime later, in the deep of night, Pan awoke. She gently eased herself away from her mate and her daughter and quietly made her way out through the halls of Lulnomia and into the rich night air.

The faint twinkling of the stars overhead greeted Pan. Peace lay like a blanket over all of Lulnomia, and she thought of her people, sleeping safely inside the generous, stalwart halls. Night creatures stirring rustled the leaves on the ground. An owl called to her from overhead, and for a moment, though knowing it was unlikely, she wondered if the visitor might be one of the descendants of the little owl in Rohm'Mok's story.

Pan stretched her arms out to the sky and leaned her head back. Then she let her tears fall. Tears for her father, for her mother, tears for her lost brother, Dak'Tor. Tears of confusion and fatigue, and despair. The longer she lived, the more uncertain life became. When she thought she had gained solid ground, it shifted under her feet. Getting a glimpse of just how much of her father's life he had sacrificed, how long he could have lived, was too much to bear. Learning that Wrollonan'Tor still lived had snapped the last piece of trust she had in what she thought she knew.

Pan straightened herself back up and covered her face with her hands. *It is what it is*, she thought. And nothing she could do would change what was past. She desperately prayed to the Great Spirit to guide her steps and for strength to face whatever was to come.

Pan avoided Irisa for the next few days. Above all, she wanted to calm down and appear her normal self so as not to alarm others. She considered Hatos'Mok's request for the Leaders to find a means to unify the community, and she was still not prepared to reveal that Lor Onida's scroll still existed. A check in her soul told her this was not the time. But she was out of ideas other than that everyone at Lulnomia should come together to celebrate good news or happy outcomes—in the way that the communities within themselves had in the past.

To her surprise, Hatos'Mok was highly pleased with her idea and chagrined that he had not thought of it himself. He said he would propose it at the next High Council meeting. Then he paused. "Forgive me, Guardian, but you seem distracted?"

"I am. For one thing, the issue with Lavke accusing Wosot of breaking Sacred Law in dispatching Nox'Tor disturbs me deeply. Despite your admonishment and your prohibition against her meddling again in Wosot and Kyana's lives, I do not believe she will obey. There is some deep disturbance in her over this."

"I feel that too, even with my seventh sense being limited compared to yours."

"I must talk to Tyria. As the Healer at the High Rocks and our representative in the matter, perhaps she has some insight that will help us figure out how to deal with it."

"We are both anticipating further trouble from the female, I am afraid," Hatos'Mok admitted.

Pan found Tyria, who relayed her conversation

with Lavke after the Overseer's decree that she leave Wosot and Kyana and their family alone.

"I have to agree with you, Guardian," she said, "I do not believe she will stop her troublemaking."

"I understand what it is like to love a male so much," Pan said wistfully.

"I am not sure it is love. My impression is it is more a feeling of possession, entitlement. Perhaps you should meet with her yourself? A visit from her Leader, and Etera's Guardian, might be what she needs to realize she cannot continue this behavior with impunity."

That was it. That was the quandary troubling Pan. What would the penalty be if Lavke continued to meddle? Though the repercussions for Wosot and Kyana would be painful and cause them stress and strife, was it a serious enough crime to warrant banishment? They had no other form of punishment other than the Jhorralax, which was seldom used. And that was too brutal a sentence for the deed. Causing trouble for another was not a hard-and-fast crime. It was not something you could point to and say, *Here are the repercussions.* The effects were obscure, elusive, yet no one would deny that harm existed. How did you quantify the effects of slander? And how did you stop it?

Rohm'Mok noticed his mate's despondency. He had seen her go through ups and downs during their pairing, and she always came out of it eventually, but this time it felt different to him. As much as she anguished over her father's death and her brother's betrayal, this felt even darker. He had noticed her on and off spending time with Irisa and thought perhaps the old female might know what was going on.

So, one day, he approached her. "You are Irisa."

She nodded. "I am."

"I will get to the point. I am concerned about my mate, the Guardian. I know something has happened that has her deeply disturbed. Do you know what that is?"

"If she has not shared it with you, then I will not."

"You do know, then. Please, do whatever you can to help her. More than anything, she needs people she can count on. I do not pretend to know the burdens of a Guardian, but I think perhaps you are the one who might be able to help her."

"I will go to her," agreed Irisa. Then she added, "You must be strong for her. The burdens she has shouldered are nothing compared to those that are to come."

Rohm'Mok felt a chill run up his back, and he watched her walk away, the effect of her ominous words still hanging over him. He wanted to follow Irisa, stop her, and make her tell him what she meant. He loved Pan more than he had thought he could love anyone, and the idea of her suffering broke his heart and sent an arrow of despair through his soul. But he had always understood that becoming the mate of a Guardian would bring unforeseen challenges. He had willingly taken them on, but to see Pan in anguish was different and almost more than he could bear.

CHAPTER 10

Within a few days, Sitka and the children had returned to the oak tree and found that the basket had been opened. The contents were gone but placed inside were several large gourds, hollowed out to hold water or other items. At the bottom, wrapped in hide, were several oversized cutting stones. They were expertly honed, large enough to be made into hatchets. The three were so excited they could hardly wait to get back to show their chief and the others what had happened. So they took the basket with its contents and headed home.

On the way, they talked about what to do next. And what would come of this? Would Oh'Mah at some point reveal himself? They were enthralled with the mystery unfolding in front of them and knew everyone in the village would share their excitement.

They went directly to the Chief's shelter. Sitka was invited inside and laid out the gifts. The Chief looked at them carefully and then, asking Sitka to stay, called the other Elders to meet with him. Tocho and Tiva waited patiently outside with their parents.

Chief Chunta welcomed the Elders as they arrived and explained what lay before them. He waited a while as they examined the gifts that had been left in the basket.

"This is a great event," said one. Another agreed, then a third.

"What you have said is true," said Chief Chunta. "Only, I am led to ponder the answer to one question—"

Everyone was still, waiting for his next words.

"What need does Oh'Mah have to learn to hone such precise cutting stones?"

Stunned silence hung in the air.

The Chief was right. Oh'Mah was extremely powerful. The ancient stories were that he could rip trees up by their trucks, their root ball intact. He could heave boulders far into the middle of the rivers. He had nails strong enough to strip the bark off trees and to claw marks into solid rock. What use could he have for these, and what dexterity would he have to fashion such intricate implements?

The Elders sitting in the shelter said nothing. The truth of what Chief Chunta had said was self-evident and needed no debate. But the question hung in the air. If it was not Oh'Mah they were communicating with, then who—or what—was it?

Dismissed, Sitka left the shelter quietly with her head down. She was embarrassed that she had not thought it herself, that Oh'Mah would have no need of cutting tools. And without a need, a skill did not develop, certainly not to the extent evidenced by the quality of the cutting stones. Tiva and Tocho were waiting and ran after the Medicine Woman. Their parents followed at a distance.

"What did Chief Chunta say?" asked Tocho. "Is everyone as excited as I am?"

"Me! I am!" exclaimed little Tiva.

"Children, you have done well. Now, off with you; go with your parents. We will talk about this tomorrow," and she shooed them toward their mother and father, who ushered them home.

It was not yet evening. There was still much daylight left, but Sitka did not know what to do with herself. Beyond her embarrassment, she was overcome by the Chief's question. If it was not Oh'Mah they were communicating with, then who was it? Clearly not an animal. But who? Was there another tribe in the area? But if so, why so secretive? Others traveled through their territory, and there was no need for such an exchange as this. Sitka decided to spend the rest of what was left of the day in ritual, seeking wisdom from the Great Spirit about what it meant and what it portended.

Back at Kthama, Tensil and Wry'Wry were sitting together in the Healer's Quarters, planning their next move. They were filled with curiosity about whether the gifts in the basket had been discovered but wanted to figure out what to do next before they went back to the oak.

Takthan'Tor announced himself and waited for the Healer's welcome before he walked in on their discussion. Both the females started to rise to their feet when he entered, but he raised his palm, indicating that they should remain seated.

"I came to tell you that when Vor'Ran was making his rounds, he went out of his way to check on the basket at the oak tree. You might be interested to hear it is gone."

The females clasped each other's hands in delight, which made Takthan'Tor smile.

"Oh, Adik'Tar," said Tensil. "What should we do next? We are running out of ideas of things to leave."

"I do not think you need to leave anything else. Instead, I believe it is time to reveal yourselves to this maiden of the Brothers. At least one of you."

Tensil looked at Wry'Wry, and Wry'Wry looked at Tensil.

Finally, Wry'Wry said, "It should be you. You are the Healer. We both decided the female who came to interact with us is their spiritual Leader. It is appropriate for you to do it."

Tensil could imagine Wry'Wry was disappointed not to be going but that she also understood two of them would be overwhelming.

"Alright. I will be the one to meet her."

"Healer," Takthan'Tor put in. "They are expecting to meet one of the Protectors. You must think this through and prepare yourself before you make contact."

"I know. I am hoping the cutting stones we left will have prepared them, in a way."

"It was a good plan and has been well-executed. Let us pray the rest of it goes as well," he said. "I will leave you to the rest of your planning. Check in with me, as you have been doing, before you make your next move."

"I am afraid it will frighten her. What we are. There is no way she can be prepared to meet us— me. There is no doubt that we look far more like them than do the Protectors. But there are likely no stories about us in their history. I cannot imagine what it will be like for her."

"You are both seekers of the Great Spirit. The One-Who-Is-Three will make a way."

Over the next few days, Tensil made many trips to the oak tree, hoping to see the female Brother there. Each time she went, she left a stone in the center of the tamped-down area where the basket had been. She brought stones that would not normally be in the area. Soon there were one, two, three stones signifying three separate visits. She only hoped that the female would figure out that she was leaving a stone each time she came and realize she was coming every day hoping to meet her.

Finally, on the sixth day, Tensil saw that a new stone had appeared. It was lined up next to the first one that she had left, and she knew it meant the female had returned that day. Now she knew that eventually, they would meet, though the problem was at what time of day the female Brother would come. She decided to try to draw a sunrise and scraped out a clear area of dirt. She took a stick and drew a horizon and then a half-circle. She did not know at first how to depict that it was sunrise and not sunset until she got the idea to draw a half-circle that arced to the far right as if to denote the path of the sun as it traveled to nightfall. Tensil did several versions until she thought it was as clear as she could make it. She planned to come at sunrise for the next few days to see if her message was clear enough.

The next morning, Tensil arrived, but there was no sign of the Medicine Woman. They returned to the High Rocks, and later in that afternoon, one of the watchers assigned to that area told her another rock had appeared.

"That means she came after we left!" Tensil exclaimed. "She placed a stone to show she came. Oh, I am excited. If she has figured it out, she will be there tomorrow morning at daybreak!"

❀

Back at the Brothers' camp, Sitka could not contain her excitement, but she was also a tiny bit afraid. Knowing that whoever was out there was not Oh'Mah meant there was another sort of tribe living near the oak tree. Chief Chunta asked if she wanted others to go with her, but she declined. It was her path to walk, and though she was nervous, she had no real fear about meeting whoever it was she had been communicating with.

She set out quite a bit before daybreak the next morning to be sure she was not late. Tocho and his sister wanted to come with her, but their parents had said no, and Sitka agreed. There were too many unknowns. And it was best that she was not distracted by having the two children along.

Sitka made her way through the woods and then into the meadow, walking reverently toward the oak tree. Her eyes darted back and forth, scanning the area for any movement or anything out of the ordinary.

When she came to the center of the circle, she stood for a few moments. Then, realizing it could be a while, she sat down and made herself comfortable. A very short time later, an object bounced onto the grass and rolled toward her. Sitka looked around quickly but saw nothing. She leaned forward to pick it up and discovered it to be a very large, perfect pinecone.

Holding it up in the air, she said, "Thank you!"

Suddenly there was rustling in the brush beyond the oak tree. Her palms began to sweat, but she swallowed hard and pushed down her inclination to run away. She had come this far; she had to be brave enough to face whatever was out there.

Slowly, a hand reached through the tall grass and parted it ever so slightly.

Sitka narrowed her eyes to see more clearly. Something was not right. It was a hand and appeared to be almost the same as hers, nearly the same color as her skin, but it was so much bigger. And the nails were very long and rough.

"I welcome you, in the name of the Great Spirit," she called out, her voice shaking.

A voice said something back, something unintelligible. Sitka was relieved that it was a female voice.

Very slowly, a figure stood up behind the oak tree. Sitka could see it was a female. There was a definitive waist and hips, and despite the loose wrap, Sitka could see she had breasts. Something was different about the structure of the mouth, but she could not tell why, and the hair was very long and somewhat wavy, a dark brown that was almost black. There was also something soft about the figure that made the outline a little blurred. Though Sitka had no way of realizing, it was the soft coat left over from the Akassa's Mothoc blood, not clearly visible from a distance.

Sitka had to push down her fear as the female stood up, far larger than the Medicine Woman or any of her people.

Finally, the creature reached her full height and started to talk, but Sitka did not understand. However, the voice was soothing, not at all harsh. The female reached out her hand and pointed to the stones, then at Sitka, and then herself and nodded. Then she smiled, revealing sharp canines. Sitka could not help but gasp and realized this was what made the female's mouth look a little different.

For a while, the two females looked at each other. Despite her intense curiosity, Sitka was glad that the other female stayed where she was.

The large female chattered some more, and Sitka said back, "I am sorry, I cannot understand you. But you cannot understand me either," and in spite of herself, she chuckled a little.

The strange female spoke again. Then she raised her palm as if she had an idea and started slowly to walk forward.

Sitka clamped down on her reaction as her body

wanted very much to get up and leave. But she used her will to control her fear and let the large female come closer. Finally, the female crouched down and picked up a rock. She lifted the rock in one hand and made a gesture with the other. Then she motioned for Sitka to try it. Sitka made the same gesture, and the other female smiled and nodded.

Next, the large female pointed back over her shoulder to the oak tree and made another movement. *Is it some kind of hand language?* Sitka repeated the motion and pointed to another tree not far away. The female nodded again.

As the sun climbed and made its journey overhead, Sitka stayed while the other female continued to teach her different signs for different objects. Every few signs, she would stop and review what they had just covered. Sitka knew she had to get back to the village before they came looking for her, so she pointed to herself and then back in the direction from which she came and said, "I have to go; I am sorry."

The female simply looked at her. Sitka took a stick and pointed at the drawing in the sand that showed the sun and its arc across the sky. She pointed to the circle representing the sun, then pointed at herself and again to the ground. The female seemed to understand she should return in the morning, but Sitka would not really know until then.

Sitka got up and brushed herself off, but the

female stayed crouched down. The Medicine
Woman said goodbye and turned and walked back
toward her village, though she stopped several times
to see if the female was still there. The third time she
looked, the female had gone. Sitka was still close
enough to have heard something and marveled at
how quietly the female could move—especially
being so large.

She was lost in thought on her way back home.
What would she tell the Chief? She wondered if she
would have believed someone who came back with
this story of an incredibly large stranger who
communicated with gestures.

For a short while, Tensil watched the female
Brother walk away before turning and leaving too.
She was very satisfied with how the day had gone.
She was also glad the other female had come alone.
It had been draining enough as it was trying to
communicate with one of them, and Tensil was
grateful not to have had the distraction of another.
Seeing the female Brother that close, it had struck
Tensil how small they were. They were built simi-
larly to her own people but just so very small. She
could not help but make the comparison in her
mind that as small as the female Brother seemed
was perhaps how small the Akassa had appeared to
the Protectors. Tensil could not imagine how large

one of the Protectors would have appeared to the Brothers.

When she got back, Wry'Wry was waiting anxiously. "What happened? You have been gone nearly all day. Oh, please tell me something happened, and you have not just been away all day leaving me waiting!"

"It was amazing; I met a female Brother. Oh. She is so small. So fragile. I wonder how they survive the harsh winters. They have no hair, not even a fine coat. The tools we left must have been huge to them. It just occurred to me now that the basket she first brought must have been one of their largest ever. Yet to us, it seemed quite small."

"Were you able to communicate?" Wry'Wry asked.

Tensil told her friend all about the interaction she had with the female and about teaching her Handspeak. "It was the only thing I could think of. But we ran out of objects. So tomorrow—"

"Tomorrow! You are going to meet her tomorrow?" Wry'Wry exclaimed.

"Yes," Tensil laughed. "But you must help me now. Help me gather items I can use to keep teaching her Handspeak. If she can learn the names of these items, then we can move on to more abstract ideas."

"Like how in the world the Akassa came to exist—"

"Oh. I hope that does not come up for a long,

long time! We have made a good start, and I would hate to see our connection destroyed so early on."

"You think it will upset them," Wry'Wry said.

"It is hard to tell. But we have to prepare for the worst. Let us hope we have enough good will established between us before that truth comes out—if it must come out," Tensil answered.

They spent the rest of the day together thinking of items that Tensil could take with her. When they ran out of portable things, they talked into the night, trying to figure out how to teach the female more abstract ideas.

Sitka told the Chief and the Elders all about her visit with the strange female. They listened quietly, though they did glance at one another as her story unfolded. When she was done, Chief Chunta said only that she should continue her work with this stranger and continue to report back to him after each visit.

In her heart, Sitka was a little disappointed they had not seemed as excited as she was about the meeting. To her, it had been a life-changing event. Who were these people, and where did they come from? How many were there? What did the males look like? Where did they live? Her mind was filled with questions and frustration as she knew it would take a long time to learn the hand language the female used. And now Sitka wanted to know everything.

As she had been told by the Chief, she did not share her experience with anyone else.

Tocho and Tiva were very disappointed that the Medicine Woman would not talk about what had happened.

"This is Sitka's work, and you should be grateful when the time comes that she shares it with you," their mother admonished them. "And until then, you are to act respectfully at all times."

When Chief Chunta and the Elders were alone, one of the Elders asked the Chief what he thought of Sitka's story.

"Sitka is wise," he replied. "My concern is that with a female as large as the one Sitka described, one must wonder about the size of the males. Let us pray to the Great Spirit that they are friendly and that we may have good relations with them."

"Perhaps she exaggerated," the same Elder suggested.

"Sitka is not prone to imagination,' pointed out the Chief. "I find no reason to doubt her even though these people are unknown to us. There is nothing in our stories or legends about them. Have they simply appeared on Etera by the hand of the Great Spirit? And if so, to what purpose? We must seek wisdom more than we seek answers. Wisdom will show us the way, and answers only spur the mind to create more questions."

The other Elders nodded, and again all lapsed deep into thought.

🦊

Sitka spent the evening gathering items she thought might help her and the other female communicate further. She carefully stacked them inside her shelter and turned in to try and sleep.

The next morning, she was at the oak tree before daybreak. She was surprised when she heard some rustling as she had thought she would surely have been the first to arrive. As she waited, she realized that the rustling was for her benefit. As quietly as the large female had disappeared the day before, Sitka knew that making the grasses move was just a way not to startle her by appearing as if from nowhere.

The Medicine Woman had braced herself in preparation for the other female's size so it would not rattle her. The previous day they had kept some distance between them. Today, Sitka decided to decrease that.

The large female appeared, and Sitka smiled and motioned for her to come closer and sit down. Within a few moments, they were almost within touching distance of each other. This close, Sitka had to calm herself again about the size difference. And for the first time, she could see a fine down covering all over the female. She tried not to stare but stole glances as often as she could.

"I cannot keep calling you *the female*; I think we need names at least," Sitka said.

Her counterpart stared and tilted her head as if trying to understand.

Sitka pointed to herself. "Sitka." She repeated it then pointed to the female.

"Ten-sil," the other said.

"Ten-sil," Sitka repeated, and the other female smiled and nodded.

It was a small thing, but it felt like great progress to Sitka. They spent the rest of the morning pointing to things and saying the name, but it was not too long before Sitka realized that though it was interesting to hear Tensil's names for physical objects, it did not really convey enough.

As if she understood, Tensil stood up and made a gesture. She sat back down. Then she stood up again and made the same gesture. *Ahhhhh,* thought Sitka. *Standing up.* Sitka copied her twice, mimicking the same gesture the other had used. Then Tensil stood up, making the gesture for standing up, and then sat down, making another gesture. Sitka copied her, now knowing the sign that meant to sit down. They continued on in this way for some time, focusing on everyday movements and activities both with signs and with spoken words. By the end of the day, they had a small vocabulary, and small though it was, it was encouraging. They made plans to meet again by scratching the drawing of the sun and the horizon and placing two stones to indicate two days' time.

As they stood to go their separate ways, Sitka was overcome with elation and threw her arms up in a circle and laughed.

Tensil smiled broadly and laughed too.

The noise startled Sitka, and she stopped and glanced up at Tensil. She froze—for the first time, she saw the sharp canines very clearly, and in that moment, where up until now she had been focused on their similarities, their differences hit her with force. The huge height. The advanced musculature. The coat of fine hair, the sharp, almost claw-like nails. And the animalistic front teeth.

Motionless, Sitka stared at the stranger and frowned. Then she shook her head. *How do I ask this?* She took a step toward Tensil. She pointed at herself and ran her hand down her arm, meaning to show it was smooth. Then she pointed to the other's arm. Sitka then raised her hand above her head to indicate her own height and raised it as high as she could before pointing to Tensil. Lastly, she pointed at her own small canines, one on each side of her mouth and then at Tensil's. She raised her open palms up and shrugged a little, asking the question as best she could. *Who are you? What are you?*

Until then, Tensil had been quite happy with the progress she and this female named Sitka were making. But her happiness disappeared when she realized what Sitka was asking her. Tensil had hoped to put off for some time the question of what the Akassa were; she wanted to establish a solid relationship before facing that topic. But Sitka was standing there looking at her, waiting for an answer.

Tensil closed her eyes for a moment and then accepted that she had to do her best to explain who she was. Who they all were. She squatted down, and by pulling up the grass and weeds by the roots, cleared out a larger area. Then she smoothed the newly exposed dirt until she had enough room to draw in and got up to find a sharp stick. On the right side, she drew a figure of Sitka as best she could. She pointed to it and then to Sitka and then made a circle in the air to denote a larger group. Sitka nodded as if understanding that meant her people. Then to the side, she drew a much larger bulky figure with a jagged outline which she meant to represent a hairy coat. She made it with wide shoulders, a broad chest, and long arms. Tensil looked at Sitka to see if there was any understanding of what she was drawing. She saw Sitka look at the figure, then up at her, and then back down. Her eyes were wide, and Tensil believed she understood that this figure represented the Mothoc.

Tensil paused, and then, below and between the two figures—one representing the Brothers, Sitka's people, and one representing the Protectors—she drew a female figure of a size that fell between the two. Then she pointed to herself, then made the same circle in the air with her finger meaning a larger group of her kind.

Sitka blinked. Then she frowned, stared down at the drawing, and looked back up at Tensil. Then she shook her head as if to say, *That cannot be.*

Tensil silently prayed to the Great Spirit for help because she could feel the female's fear rising.

Sitka scooted back and then stumbled to her feet. She looked at Tensil again and shook her head.

The Healer stood up and immediately knew it was the wrong thing to do. She was close enough to Sitka that her height was now menacing. Her heart sank when Sitka put her palms up as if to say not to come any closer, then turned and ran. Tensil watched as the small figure fled through the meadow, her wrappings flapping behind her. Calling after her made no difference. Sitka kept going.

Sitting down with a thump, Tensil put her head in her hands. All her high hopes had just been destroyed. She had known it was too soon to explain who the Akassa were. But if she had not answered the question, it would have damaged the trust anyway. Now what?

Tensil got up and used her foot to scratch out the drawing she had made. She waited a little while longer, though knowing that Sitka was not coming back. With a heavy heart, she returned to the High

Rocks to tell the Adik'Tar and Wry'Wry that she had failed.

When Tensil got back, she did not even get to share what had happened as a devastated Wry'Wry headed toward her with news of her own.

"What is the matter?"

"Oh, Tensil, they have found a mate for me. I am to be paired," Wry'Wry sobbed.

Tensil put her arms out and drew her friend close. "Your father knows you do not want this. And your mother too. Who is it? Who told you this?"

"My father is the one who gave me the message. It is someone from the small community up from here. He took over the record-keeping from Varos when the Protectors left. Kant is his name, of the House of Dran."

"Have you ever met him?"

"He has been at the Far High Hills, but if I met him, I do not remember. At least, we were not introduced."

"Come and sit down," Tensil said.

"It is almost time for the High Council meeting again. That means that if they have made other matches, I could be paired soon. What am I to do?" Wry'Wry sounded frantic.

"I wish I knew how to help you. You are of pairing age, but it seems that you should have a choice in it. This was your parent's decision, not yours, right?"

"Yes. And how is this different from Never Without Consent? If I do not wish to pair, why should I have to?"

Tensil thought for a moment. "You are absolutely correct. It is no different. I think you should go to your parents and in that context explain your feelings. If a female cannot be mated against her will, how is that different from being paired against her will?"

Wry'Wry smiled for the first time since she had greeted Tensil. "I am going to do just that. Now, tell me about your visit with the Brothers' Healer!"

Tensil's face fell. "It started out fine. I taught her the signs for common movements, objects, animals. I cannot remember everything we covered. But then, when it came time to go, she asked what we were. Are."

"Oh, no."

"Yes. I thought about not answering, but if I did not, that might be worse, for it could turn her away. So I explained. I drew one of her people, one of the Protectors, and then basically my figure from those two."

"Did she understand?" Wry'Wry asked.

"She ran off. From the look on her face, she was frightened."

"Oh, no! So now what?"

"I will give a report to Takthan'Tor and the High

Protector and then seek from the Great Spirit what to do next. But I fear we now have a serious setback in creating a relationship with them."

"I will pray with you," Wry'Wry said. "I am going to go talk to my parents now, but I will find you later."

Wry'Wry found her mother and made her case. Tlanik listened carefully, then sat next to her daughter and took one of her hands.

"I have never told you this, daughter, but I did not want to be paired either. When my time came, I had the same conversation with my mother as you are having with me. I wanted to be free; I did not want to compromise what I had in order to accommodate a mate. But as time went on, I realized my mother only wanted what was best for me. And that is what your father and I want for you. Sometimes in guiding our offling, it can feel like we are pushing them, but this is only meant to be in your best interests."

Wry'Wry shifted uncomfortably but continued to hold her mother's hand.

"As you get older, you realize the benefit of a partnership with another," Tlanik explained. "It is good to have someone to share life's pleasure with as well as life's challenges. Then you have offling together, and you share in the joy of watching them grow and develop. Discovering who they become. It ties both of you together in a way that nothing else does. You help him, and he helps you. If love is not there to begin with, it can still blossom."

"Did you not love Father when you and he were paired?"

Her mother laughed, "Oh, gracious no. I thought he was overbearing and bossy. We had many arguments at first. But then I came to realize that though his delivery was gruff, he only meant well for me. And it is the same for you. He is not the most well-spoken of males. But his heart is good, and he is a great provider and protector. He would do anything for any of us. You do know that."

"Yes, I know that. But I also do not know what to do."

"We have not talked about this directly, but I am going to ask you now. Is it about the Adik'Tar?" her mother asked.

Wry'Wry's voice was small as she replied, "I thought we might be together someday."

"I thought so, too," said Tlanik, "and so did your father. It seemed you were becoming close and that you enjoyed each other's company. But then it changed."

"When he became Adik'Tar. When the Protectors started training him to take over—I mean really take over. When they said they were going to leave. After that, something shifted," Wry'Wry said.

"Have you talked to him? Asked him what happened? I think you have a right at least to ask."

"No. It is clear he has no more interest in me. He knows I am to be paired. If he cared for me in that way, he would speak up." Wry'Wry was looking down at her hand clasped in her mother's. Then she looked up again. "I guess I need to move on. If I stay here, I will long for him, and in time, he will take a mate, and then what? Am I to live out my days here watching them together? No. I could not bear it. You and father are right, after all."

Wry'Wry's mother's heart was breaking for her daughter. Responsibility could change people, and as far as she could understand, it was responsibility that had altered the path Takthan'Tor and Wry'Wry had seemed to be walking. "I am sorry. We both just want you to be happy."

"I know that," Wry'Wry said. "I know that. I will spend the next month preparing myself to leave the High Rocks. At least I will not be so far away; it is only a short trip up the Mother Stream. I just pray he is kind and in time will grow to care for me, as you said."

She stood up, leaned over, and kissed her mother on the cheek. "I love you, Mama. Thank you for always being here for me. I will prepare myself to be paired at the next High Council meeting if it is to happen then. I only hope they tell me for sure ahead of time."

"I will talk to the Adik'Tar and make sure they do."

Tlanik went immediately to find Takthan'Tor.

He was speaking with his First Guard, Anthram. When he saw Wry'Wry's mother approaching, he wrapped up his conversation and excused himself to speak with her.

"Tlanik, it is good to see you. What can I help you with?"

"My mate has informed me that Wry'Wry is to be paired."

"I see. Does she know?"

"Yes," Tlanik replied. "She is going to prepare her tools and personal items just in case it takes place at the next High Council meeting. So it seems it will not be long."

Wry'Wry's mother's words made Takthan'Tor's heart sink. *So she is willing.* "Whatever I can do to help, please let me know."

"I am surprised that you did not know, Adik'Tar, since as Overseer, it will fall to you to declare Ashwea Awhidi over her."

Takthan'Tor could see that Tlanik was watching him closely, so he forced a chuckle. "Leaders are often the last to know what is going on. That is why we rely on people like you and your mate."

"Forgive my imprudence, but you yourself should be thinking of taking a mate. It is not good for a male to be alone. Nor anyone, I suppose."

"So I have been told," he replied. "Thank you for reminding me. I wish Wry'Wry every happiness."

Tlanik watched Takthan'Tor walk away. She had been looking for any sign that it bothered him that her daughter was to be paired. He had not even asked to whom, or which community Wry'Wry would be joining, and she decided that either he was very self-controlled, or her daughter was right—whatever they had all thought was blossoming between Wry'Wry and the Adik'Tar was in their imaginations or had since died.

Takthan'Tor made a beeline for the Great Entrance. He passed Vor'Ran and Anthram talking together and stopped long enough to tell them he would be gone a while.

He started climbing, working his way up to the tallest lookout around Kthama. His muscles strained and pulled. He scraped his knuckles, arms, and legs as he hoisted himself up over each boulder and overhang. When he reached the summit, he looked around at the land sprawling out in front of him. The high fir-covered peaks, the Great River snaking through the valleys below. Fall had touched the landscape with her signature colors. Blue skies and bright white clouds embraced the expanse, and as far as the eye could see, there was beauty in everything. He deeply inhaled the fresh, crisp air, taking it as deeply into his lungs as he could. Scattered out there were the communities of his people. The small community whose name was forbidden to be spoken. The Far High Hills. The Deep Valley. The Little River. The High Red Rocks.

Because he was alone, he could speak aloud the words of his heart. "In all of this, how can it be that there is only one female I desire? Surely that is not true. Surely I am not doomed to pine for this female the rest of my days? Tell me, oh, Great Spirit. Tell me there is mercy for me and that I will love another this deeply someday?" He waited in silence, knowing the answer already. His heart had answered the moment he spoke the words. There was no other. And there never would be. Not as he felt for Wry'Wry.

Takthan'Tor dropped to his knees, and stones cut into his skin. He leaned forward and pressed his forearms on the coolness of the rock beneath him. He sent his awareness deep into it, pulling strength from its hardness. He slipped into the silence that connects with That-Which-Is and allowed himself to notice the aliveness around him. A small, winged insect landed on his outstretched arm, and he turned to marvel at its delicate yet complex design. Everything around him spoke of the intricate functioning of creation. He prayed for guidance on the path that lay ahead. He prayed for wisdom to be the best

Leader possible. For courage, for perseverance, for his continued commitment to the people of the High Rocks and all the Akassa communities. He prayed to be worthy of the trust placed in him. Lastly, he prayed for Wry'Wry. That though she would never be his, she would find the love she so richly deserved.

CHAPTER 11

The days following Laborn's death were filled with gossip and speculation. The community was divided between those feeling his death was justified and others who felt it was not. There was a small faction that was undecided, and they were beset by others badgering them to see it their particular way. Dak'Tor and his friends and family kept to themselves and stayed as far away from the mix as possible.

Kaisak wondered why Laborn had not just killed Dak'Tor—or had him killed—but surmised it was partly for fear of the possibility that Dak'Tor's sister might come as had been foretold. Despite his reluctance to admit it, Kaisak carried the same fears. Unlike Laborn, Kaisak did hold reverence for the Guardian of Etera, though not enough to keep him from destroying the Akassa and the Sassen as he saw no conflict in wanting them annihilated. Like

Laborn, he considered it an act in accord with the wishes of the Great Spirit. They were an abomination that could never naturally have occurred, and therefore, should be eradicated.

As time passed, the talk switched to Iria's growing belly. It had not gone unnoticed by Kaisak, either, and he did not doubt that Laborn had taken Iria Without Her Consent. Kaisak knew that taking Iria was not about mating. It had been about dominating her, violating her, a slap in the face of her mate, Dak'Tor.

Kaisak did not try to hide his interest in Iria's belly. He saw her discomfort at his stares but did nothing to alleviate it. What was on his mind was her offling. He wondered if it had occurred to others that Laborn's offling, if born a male, would be the rightful heir to the leadership of their community. Yes, it would take years for him to grow into the position, but it meant an eventual end to Kaisak's rule. And Kaisak was not sure he was willing to relinquish the position. In fact, he was pretty sure he was not.

But he would not make the same mistake as Laborn. Should some unfortunate accident cause Iria to lose her offling, it would indeed be a chance occurrence. And Kaisak would make sure it could never be tied back to him.

Isan'Tor was lying on the rock floor in front of Iria and Vaha. Vaha's offling, Altka, was next to him. The two mothers were enjoying watching their offling rolling about and exploring their budding mobility.

True to his promise, Dak'Tor provided for Vaha and her daughter, though only he, Iria, and Dazal knew that her offling was really Dazal's. Iria had noticed how Dazal looked at Vaha when he thought no one was watching. It occurred to her that perhaps Dazal had feelings for the mother of his offling.

"Dazal is a good male, is he not?" In her fingers, Iria twirled the stem of a particularly beautifully colored leaf.

"Yes, he is. He has been kind to me, and I appreciate it."

"I hope you do not mind me saying, but I think he likes you."

Vaha looked up. "You think so? Why do you say that?"

"He watches you. When you are not looking."

"Males are always watching females. They just like to look," she chuckled.

"No, this is different. He is not leering. He is watching as if he cares about what you are doing. He smiles when you smile."

Vaha looked as if she was considering what her friend was telling her. "That would be nice if it were true," she said wistfully. "But what of Zisa? Laborn ordered Dazal to seed her."

"Zisa wants nothing to do with Dazal. At least not

in that manner. Now that Laborn is gone, perhaps that will fall to the wayside. But even if Dazal were to seed her, it has nothing to do with you and him. Trust me, I am not imagining it. I think you should arrange to spend some time with him. Just the two of you. I would be glad to watch Altka. The Great Spirit knows I certainly owe you for taking care of Isan'Tor while I was trapped with that monster."

"Maybe I will."

Useaves had been biding her time, waiting for the day-to-day activities to resume their place. For some type of order to be restored. So far, Kaisak was not a highly visible Leader. He did frequently meet with Gard and Krac. To Useaves' disappointment, he did not include her in the meetings as Laborn often had. But she was about to change all that.

"A word with you, Adik'Tar?" She interrupted his morning conversation by the crackling fire.

"Speak, old female," he answered. He nonchalantly reached back and picked up a pile of leaves and tossed them on the fire. The flames licking skyward were a beautiful sight against the backdrop of the fall colors.

"Alone."

"There is nothing you cannot say in front of my males here," he retorted.

"Very well." She drew herself to as much height

as she could muster while still braced by her walking stick. "I am wondering what your plans are for the Guardian's brother. You mentioned assigning him other females to seed."

"I intend to. I do not see how that is any of your business."

"You ought to make it my business. I would think the Adik'Tar would want to make the best decisions possible for our people here. For the future."

"What do you mean?" He spat out what remained of the dried meat he had been working, having reduced it to a piece of gristle.

"No one else knows more about the families and the others who followed Laborn here. I would think you would want my counsel on which female would be best to mate with Dak'Tor to provide the most benefit for future generations."

"It is true," Gard said unexpectedly. "Laborn relied heavily on Useaves' guidance. She has the experience of helping to birth the offling, so she has the most knowledge of who was seeded by which male. The wrong choice might make the offling unsuitable for the future."

Kaisak curled his lip but said, "Very well then. When it is time, I will seek your counsel."

"In case you do not know, our community is divided. Best not wait too long, as sympathy for Dak'Tor and his mate grows along with her expanding belly. When she delivers Laborn's offling, you will lose favor if you press him to seed another any time soon after that."

Without permission to leave, Useaves turned and hobbled off. She could feel Kaisak's anger rising at her criticism of his answer. It did not matter to her. She had handled stronger Leaders than Kaisak. And more insane ones too. What did surprise her was that Gard had supported her. She had thought the rift between them was growing, not lessening. Perhaps her words had taken root, and he realized that in time, Kaisak and the Guardian's brother would come to blows. And then there would be only one charismatic male left to handle.

Useaves' comments left Kaisak in a foul mood. He stood up, kicked some of the nearby sticks and leaves into the flames, and barked at Gard and Krac. "Do you not have anything better to do than to sit here all day? Get up! Get on with your duties."

The two males rose immediately, and Kaisak was left to his own thoughts. He realized now that he needed someone to talk things over with. But it could not be Gard; that male was virtually useless and why he enjoyed Useaves' apparent favor was beyond him. Kaisak considered Gard a blunt instrument at best, known more for his physical attributes than anything. As for Krac, Kaisak was not sure about him, either. He did not doubt Krac's loyalty, but he was uncertain of the male's mental acuity. For now, Kaisak would have to keep his own counsel and not rely on others—except for reluctantly having to turn to Useaves for guidance about which female next to order the Guardian's brother to seed.

Was Useaves right? Was favor turning to Dak'Tor because of sympathy for his mate? If so, then Kaisak would have to carefully reconsider his plan that Iria never deliver that offling. If some were sympathetic to them now, who knew what losing the offling would do. Perhaps it would be best if something were to happen to it later on when it was a little older. Less suspicious. He did not want to make a misstep this early in his leadership. A serious mistake would open the door for either Gard or Krac—or another— to challenge him. Still, harming an offling did not sit well, not even if it would turn out to be the best strategic move for him.

It took days for Kaisak to swallow his pride and seek out Useaves. "I am here for your opinion on who next to carry Dak'Tor's seed."

"Sit," Useaves said. "I cannot stand for long, and your towering over me makes me irritable." She motioned with her stick to the ground across from her. "So you have considered my advice on not waiting for the offling to be born."

"I considered it, yes. And I believe you have a

point," Kaisak said as he squatted across from the elderly female.

Useaves could not help but let out a "Hmmph" that sounded very much like a smirk would look. She realized now that she did not like Kaisak. She had not minded his position with Laborn in the past because he rarely had input and mostly did as Laborn ordered. But getting to know his personality lately, she decided she would very much like to see him humiliated, even if it meant it would be Dak'Tor who Gard would have to go up against in the future.

"So, who do you suggest?" he got right to the point.

"Visha."

"Krac's daughter? Why her?" Kaisak immediately regretted the interest that came through his question.

"Three reasons. One, she is Krac's daughter, and Krac will be grateful for the elevation in her status, and that will increase Krac's loyalty to you. Two, she is a safe choice as she has no 'Tor in her background."

"You said there were three."

"Thirdly, she and Iria do not get along."

"—And forcing Dak'Tor to seed her will create enmity within his tidy group of followers," Kaisak said, nodding.

"Within that generation, yes, though they are not all in Dak'Tor's circle. But in case you have not noticed, his circle is increasing. He started out with a small group of friends, but now others are being drawn to his charisma. You need to create dissension within that group. For one thing, Laborn ordered Dazal to seed Zisa, yet there is no evidence of any success. Iria has shown that she does not take Dak'Tor mating other females lightly. And the fact that Iria and Visha do not get along should create some problems."

Useaves struggled to her feet. "And while you are taking care of this, stop worrying about Iria's offling."

"What?" He frowned.

"You underestimate me, Kaisak. I am old. I have years of studying people and understanding what is behind their behavior. I have seen you staring at Iria's belly. No doubt you are concerned about what the existence of Laborn's offling might do to your leadership, if it is a male, of course. You have greater worries than that. If this manifests at all, it is far off in the future."

Useaves turned to leave, but Kaisak moved quickly in front of her. "Stop. I have not dismissed you, and this discussion is not over. What do you know about Laborn's offling?"

"You doubt my worth, Kaisak. You wonder why Laborn turned to me for counsel. Alright. I will prove to you why right now. The offling is not Laborn's."

Kaisak stared at her. "How can you possibly know that? She was seeded by Laborn by force."

"Not true. Oh, he took her by force. Many times. But she was already seeded by then."

"Again, how do you know this—and your answer had better not be some old Healer-gibberish."

"It was I who looked after Iria. I did not assign cleaning of her area to anyone else because that was the only way I could legitimately be in her living quarters. Iria has not yet figured it out because she has been under duress. But if her mind would quiet, she would realize she did not have her issue in the time before Laborn assaulted her, so she was already seeded before then. The offling is not Laborn's. It is Dak'Tor's."

"You would bet your life on this?" Kaisak snarled.

"Yes."

"Good. Because you just did. If you are wrong about this, Healer or not, you will pay for misleading me." Kaisak turned and stalked off, hoping his words had rattled the old female as much as he intended.

Useaves smiled to herself. These males were so easy to control, overcome by their drives to dominate others. In time, she would control Kaisak just as she had Laborn. Poor Laborn. Had he taken a moment to think about it, he would at least have considered that the offling Iria carried might not be his. Had he questioned it, it would not have been so easy to point him down the path she wanted him to take, but he had gone off in anger and tried to kill Iria.

Useaves had been a step ahead of Laborn. She

had not only led him to think the offling was his but also that he had to take matters into his own hands when she refused to give Iria something to get rid of it. So it had been easy enough to see what was coming and give Iria the cutting blade ahead of time to thwart his attack. While Useaves was hoping for Iria to wound Laborn, the fact that his life had ended suited her all the better.

In a way, Useaves was disappointed that Kaisak did not seem to be turning out to be any more challenging an adversary than Laborn. And Gard certainly was not. But that made Gard the best match for the leadership. He presented no challenge and would be the easiest of all to manipulate. As for Dak'Tor, she was still undecided about him, but time would tell. Time would always tell.

Kaisak hated to admit it, but Useaves was right. Visha was the perfect choice. It was no secret that the two females did not get along. Dak'Tor would have no choice but to mount Visha, and that would no doubt anger Iria. As for Iria's offling, Kaisak did believe Useaves that it was Dak'Tor's and not Laborn's; she was not one to be wrong about such things. Kaisak was starting to realize why Laborn had depended on her so, but he was also starting to fear her. As clever as she was, the true question was whether Useaves would be more of a liability or an asset.

Kaisak did not waste any time calling Dak'Tor and Visha to see him. He sent Gard to fetch them and did not allow any others to come along.

"Visha, you are to be seeded by Dak'Tor and bear his offling."

Visha raised her eyebrows. "Is this true?" She looked to Dak'Tor for confirmation.

"It is the first I have heard about it," Dak'Tor answered, looking from Visha to Kaisak.

"You are surprised? I told you I would continue the plan Laborn put in motion. Vaha has a new offling; she is not ready to be bred again. Iria is carrying Laborn's offling. It is time for you to seed another."

Visha chuckled.

Dak'Tor looked at her. "What is so funny?"

"You do not know?"

"I do not know *what*?" Dak'Tor was losing patience.

"Adik'Tar, may I please be present when Iria finds out about this?"

Kaisak glanced at Visha and shouted for Krac. "Fetch Dak'Tor's mate and bring her here. Immediately."

It was not long before Krac returned with Iria in tow. She stood next to Dak'Tor, looking at him and then at Kaisak, waiting for an explanation.

"Visha here thought you should be the first to know that she is to be seeded by your mate," Kaisak said.

Iria's eyes narrowed. "Why *her*?" She could not contain her irritation.

"She is the best choice. She is young and fertile, as you are. And strong. She will bear him many offling."

Iria frowned. Of all the females, Visha would have been Iria's last choice.

"You are busy with your offling, and you are seeded. This should not concern you," Kaisak said.

"And yet you call me here to tell me anyway. I am tired of you Leaders deciding for us what is and is not to be," Iria spoke up. "I hoped you would have more compassion than your predecessor, but I see that is not the case."

"Like my predecessor, as you call him, it falls to me to look out for our future. And we cannot eliminate the Akassa and Sassen without increasing our numbers. Be glad your mate has a purpose; otherwise, we would have no need for him.

"Now be off, all of you. Make arrangements. I expect Visha to be seeded before long."

Iria had tried to ignore Visha throughout the exchange but could not help but glance at her as she and Dak'Tor went to leave. She regretted it instantly when she saw the smugness gloating on Visha's face.

Iria held herself together until she and Dak'Tor were back home. The moment they were inside, she said,

"Kaisak is as evil as Laborn. He had to know that Visha and I do not get along. There was no worse female to pick. He wants to upset me."

"You know it will mean nothing to me. It is only you I love." Dak'Tor held his arms out, but Iria spun away, refusing his embrace.

"I hate being here. Oh, can we not leave? Could we not go to where you came from? Kthama? Or some other community? Would they not accept us?"

Dak'Tor hung his head. "It is not possible." He had not told Iria the rest of the story, how he had been banished for lying and letting everyone believe that their father had chosen Pan to lead the High Rocks.

"I know," Iria said. "They would have us followed, and it would lead them right to Kthama."

Dak'Tor felt guilt rising. He should tell her the rest of the story, but he loved her, and the thought of her thinking less of him was too much. So he said nothing and let her think she had come up with the reason on her own.

"Perhaps when your sister comes with the Promised One," Iria said, "our troubles will end. She will have the power to defeat Kaisak and his followers. Until then, we must make the best of our lives. I only pray that time will come soon."

Dak'Tor could only hope that when the time came, Pan would have forgiven him for how he had wronged her.

Iria had resigned herself to the fact of her mate having to mount other females. She consoled her broken heart by thinking about it as if it were his duty and remembering it was what kept him alive. She knew there would be others after Visha, but she also realized that at some point, there would be no other appropriate females to seed. And then what would happen to Dak'Tor? Between now and that time, they had to increase his popularity or increase as much as they could the fear of retribution from the Guardian if Dak'Tor were harmed.

As her belly grew, she noticed Kaisak still staring at her. It was becoming so frequent that it was impossible to miss. The other females were mostly as kind to her as they would be to any seeded female. Only a small circle who were militantly loyal to Laborn avoided her.

As for Visha, she paraded proudly around the settlement basking in the honor of being the next female to carry Dak'Tor's seed. While Dak'Tor did his best to keep Iria from knowing when he mounted Visha, she did just the opposite, making remarks about having been with him and smirking at Iria in plain sight.

One day, not getting the reaction she wanted, Visha took a more direct approach. She tracked Iria down in the center of the gathering area as Iria was speaking with her mother. "Your mate is a dedicated lover. He makes sure I enjoy it as much as he does. He does this for you too, I assume?"

"Excuse me, you were not invited to join us," Iria's mother said.

"As someone who Iria's mate mounts regularly, I should not need an invitation."

Iria clenched her teeth, vowing not to let Visha get to her.

"So, does he? You did not answer my question."

"I know you are lying, Visha, so what you say has no power over me. Dak'Tor mounts you because it is his obligation to do so—nothing more. On the other hand, he mounts me willingly. And frequently."

By now, word had spread, and a small group had gathered, watching the verbal sparring match.

"You are lying. He cannot possibly perform with you at the frequency he is visiting me!"

"It is you who are lying," Iria said. "Dak'Tor tells me each time he discharges his duty to you. And that is all it is. Oh, and I misspoke. Dak'Tor does not mount me. He lovemates me. Big difference. Only, you would not know that, never having had a male care for you as he does me."

"How do you know what it is like between us!" Visha raised her voice. "You have no idea."

"I know exactly how it is between you because he tells me. How you try to cajole him into staying longer after he has finished. How you try to ply him with treats to get him to spend the night with you. You are the only one you are fooling. The rest of us are well aware that if Kaisak had not ordered him to, Dak'Tor would never touch you, let alone mount you."

That did it. Visha came at Iria with her nails extended and canines flashing. Iria put her hands up to defend herself, but Visha's forward movement knocked them both to the ground.

"Stop it! Stop it!" Iria's mother was shouting loudly. "She is seeded! You will hurt her offling!"

The two females rolled around, stirring up a cloud of debris. Visha eventually ended up on top of Iria, spitting and snapping, feverishly trying to bite Iria's neck, but Iria sank her teeth deep into the fleshy part of her opponent's hand. Visha screamed, and just then, Dak'Tor, Gard, and Kaisak appeared and pulled the two snarling females apart.

Dak'Tor helped Iria to her feet and immediately looked her over. "Are you alright?"

She nodded, wiping Visha's blood from her mouth with the back of her wrist.

Visha howled in pain as the other males helped her to her feet. "I will kill you for this!" she screamed.

"For what? Standing up to you?" Iria shouted back.

Dak'Tor stepped in front of his mate to keep her from advancing toward Visha, who was held in place by Gard's strong arms encircling her waist.

"Let me go!" Visha snarled over her shoulder at Gard.

"Shut up!" Kaisak bellowed. "Both of you! What is going on here? Someone tell me!"

Iria's mother stepped forward, pointing at Visha. "She started it. She clearly wanted to incite a fight. She kept goading my daughter about Dak'Tor mounting her. Saying things intentionally to upset Iria." She turned to Visha, "You should be ashamed of yourself. You had better hope the offling is unharmed."

Kaisak towered over Visha, who was still under Gard's control, and glared at her through slitted lids. It was true he had chosen Visha to irritate Iria, but he did not want more sympathy created for Dak'Tor's mate. "I bestow an honor on you, and this is how you repay me?"

Visha stammered unintelligibly.

"It was my fault too," Iria called out. "I was the one who went after her first. Until then, it was only words."

Kaisak turned to Iria. "You admit fault in this, female?"

Iria raised her chin and looked him directly in the eye. "I do."

"Very well. Since you are both at fault, then you are both equally to blame."

Iria stiffened, waiting for his punishment. She risked a fleeting glance and saw Visha doing the same.

"Gard. Bring her over here."

Gard brought Visha over to stand next to Iria.

Dak'Tor took a few steps forward.

"Stay where you are," Kaisak snapped at him and turned to the females.

"Since you are both at fault, the matter is settled. But I strongly advise you that there be no further outbursts of this type. The female, Iria, carries the offling of Laborn. If it is a male, by rights, it is heir to the leadership here."

Some of the group gasped as this had not yet occurred to them.

"Now, go about your day. Quickly!"

Useaves had watched nearly the whole thing from some distance away. She smiled. She knew now that Kaisak believed Iria was already seeded by the time Laborn had taken her Without Her Consent; he would never publicly have acknowledged the offling's right to leadership if he really thought it was Laborn's. This way, when the offling was clearly Dak'Tor's, Kaisak would be remembered as being just, fair, and willing to honor the old ways. Perhaps Kaisak would turn out to be a worthy adversary after all.

Of course, there was always the possibility she was wrong about who the father was. Iria could have missed her monthly issue because she was still nursing her son. It was a gamble on Useaves' part, but a calculated one, as was every move she made.

CHAPTER 12

Pan had avoided Irisa for some time now, but her curiosity about Wrollonan'Tor could not be denied. Feeling she had re-grounded herself, Pan approached her.

"You are ready to go back?"

Pan should have expected that Irisa would know why she was there, but it still unnerved her that the older female could apparently read her mind.

"Yes."

"This time, you will be gone a few days, Guardian. You had better let others know so they do not worry."

Pan nodded and made the arrangements. True to his nature, Rohm'Mok said little and wanted only to make whatever was going on as easy as possible.

When all was set, she and Irisa set off again. At about the same point in the journey, Pan again felt the shift. It was as if she had stepped sideways yet remained in the same spot. And as before, everything became a little clearer, a little deeper. The color in the leaves was that much more vibrant, the oranges brighter, the yellow more intense, and the damp smell of fall that much richer. This time, she would seek an answer.

Once inside the inner chamber, they did not have to wait long for Wrollonan'Tor to appear. "Are you ready to start your training, Pan?"

"My training, Guardian?" she asked.

"Yes. That is why you are here. You need my help to deepen your understanding of your role as the Guardian of Etera and to learn how to fully utilize your abilities. Abilities you do not even know you have."

"So this is how I will be able to teach the An'Kru," she said.

"The Promised One. Yes."

"May I ask you something, Guardian?"

Wrollonan'Tor nodded the slightest amount.

"Both times on our way here, we seemed to pass a threshold. I paid attention this time, and it happened in about the same area when everything became more vibrant and alive. Have we entered the Corridor?"

"It is a good question, Pan. No, this is not the Corridor. But it is similar in the way that it exists on a different level than the rest of Etera. Here." He pointed to a large sharp boulder jutting out from the side of the chamber. "Look closely at that protrusion."

He waited a moment, then said, "Now step sideways and look at it again and tell me what you see."

Pan did as he said. "I see the same thing I did a moment before."

"Yes. It is the same boulder. It has not changed, nor have you. But you are looking at it from a slightly different angle now, are you not? In a similar way, we are still on Etera, but we have, so to speak, stepped sideways into a different view. One that only the three of us currently share. One that separates us from everyone else's."

"But I saw animals on the way here. A small red squirrel. How are they here if this is a different vibration?"

"Because I wish them to be."

Pan's eyes widened. "You are controlling this? You are creating this—change in vibration?"

"It is not so different as when you or the others cloak themselves. You know how to do it, but you do not understand what you are doing. You are shifting yourselves into a mildly higher vibration. And at that frequency, everything else remains because it is not that powerful a shift. Only the person being cloaked becomes invisible, so to speak. What I have done here is basically the same."

Wrollonan'Tor chuckled. "All that I do, you will do too. And more."

Despite herself, Pan placed her hands on both sides of her head and looked for a place to sit. "I do not know if I can understand all this."

He pointed to a nearby boulder. "Sit. It is not for you to understand. I explained it only to satisfy your mind's desire to know. But what is required of you is not to understand but to accept that it is."

Irisa sat next to Pan, placing an arm around her shoulder. It was an unexpected gesture of kindness and caught Pan off guard.

"Do you live here with your father?" she asked Irisa. "Is this where you came when you left for those long periods of time?"

"Yes. I spend time here."

"But how do you survive? Or do you not need to sleep or eat?"

"My daughter has need of all those things. What you experience here is only the entrance to the world we live in. There is far more for you to discover, and you will when the time is right. Your faithfulness to do what must be done will set in motion all that must happen to usher in the Age of Shadows."

"The Promised One will free my father."

"Many pieces must fall into place before that can happen, Pan. If we succeed, your father will be freed from the Order of Functions, but it will come at a great price. For now, you must focus on the moment at hand."

"Come at a great price? Why is it that every time I find my faith again in the Great Spirit and the Order of Functions, something happens to push me back down again?" Pan realized she had raised her voice and was immediately ashamed.

But it did not seem to faze the Ancient Guardian of Etera. "That is the nature of life in our realm. We cannot move forward by standing still. Each time our faith grows, it moves us forward, but we reach a plateau. And so it must be challenged again for it to deepen further."

"But what about you, Wrollonan'Tor? How do you survive here? Do you hunt? Store food for the winter times?" Pan realized these must seem mundane questions compared to what they had been talking about.

"I no longer have need of any of that."

"But you still enter the Aezaiteran stream and the Order of Functions?"

"That is now up to you as the current Guardian of Etera."

"Guardians are only *almost* immortal. If you do not eat, you will eventually die."

"That is my hope," he answered. "Do not look shocked. You have no idea how long I have lived. In fact, your mind could not comprehend it. You will discover for yourself, Pan, eternity is a lonely place."

"But you are not alone; you have your daughter. And now I am here."

"The Guardian's body can live practically forever;

however, the soul cannot bear it. I have witnessed too much sadness and loss. Needless suffering. It is my hope that when the Promised One comes, I will be freed and allowed to return to the Great Spirit."

"Knowing what you know then, you offer me little joy for my future," Pan lamented. "Everyone we love will age and die, and now you say it is your wish to die too."

"A Guardian's burdens are great, Pan. And yours will become even heavier in time. You will be the greatest Guardian of Etera ever to live. It was no mistake that you are female. Through you, the Great Spirit will birth an entirely new world of peace and light. But until then, you must set the highest standards for yourself. You must have the deepest faith. Others look to you for leadership, guidance, inspiration."

"I do not know if I can do all that."

"At present, no. But life makes a way. Struggles on your path prepare you to face the struggles ahead. That is how we grow. And the more you connect with the Aezaiteran Stream and the Order of Functions, the greater your wisdom will become and the deeper your faith will grow in the benevolence of the Three-That-Are-One."

Irisa, still sitting with her arm around Pan, looked up at her father. "I think we should let her rest. It is much to take in. You can start her training tomorrow?"

Wrollonan'Tor agreed, and Irisa rose and reached

her hand out to Pan. "Come with me. Your journey here has just begun."

Irisa led Pan out of the main chamber and down one of the dark tunnels. It seemed they walked a fair distance before Pan noticed the tunnel becoming lighter. Finally, she could see what looked like sunshine. The exit.

Pan squinted while her eyes adapted as they stepped into the outdoors. In the distance was a waterfall, the spray creating humidity but also having a cooling effect. Where around Lulnomia, the season had been well into fall, here it looked like spring. Bright green leaves adorned the branches. Flowers had sprung up everywhere, and butterflies flitted from one bloom to another. Off to her right was a row of blossoming fruit trees, as well as raspberry bushes and grapevines. They walked farther in and came alongside a small stream of crystal-clear water in which Pan could see fish swimming lazily. Her eye followed the bend of the stream, and it seemed to disappear into the horizon. How could this be Etera? This seemed like some kind of paradise.

"Where are we?' she asked Irisa. "Your father said we were still on Etera, but it is not spring there."

"It is spring here because my father wishes it."

It was the same answer as that to her question

about the squirrels and other creatures they had passed on the way in. "Your father has creative power?"

Irisa smiled. Pan had never seen her smile until today, when she had smiled twice. Irisa was much happier here, Pan surmised.

"The Aezaitera is the creative power of the Great Spirit. My father has spent ages connecting with it. As a result, he has the ability to mold this level as he wishes."

"It is as if we are in another world, if such things are possible," Pan mused aloud.

"Not another world, but closer to the perfection Etera is meant to be. We were created for this beauty and for so much more than this. We were created to love and be loved."

"And yet your father is not happy here."

"My father has lost too many loved ones through the ages. Even though I am still with him, he has now shut down that capacity in himself. He has closed off a great deal of himself even to me, so he is truly alone."

Pan remembered the timeless feeling that had come over her, reached down through her soul and out of the other side when she first looked into Wrollonan'Tor's eyes. Ancientness on a scale her mind could not comprehend. The smell and feel of dust as old as time itself. She suddenly felt great compassion for him and could not imagine the heartbreak of his path. Yet, despite all his heartache and loneliness, he remained faithful to the Great Spirit.

"Come." And Irisa led Pan a little distance to where a woven enclosure stood.

It was made up of thick vines and covered in vibrant green leaves and velvety blossoms. "Oh, this is beautiful! What is it?" Pan said, peeking into the domed structure. The scent of the wildflowers filled the space, and a warm breeze stirred the air in a pleasurable way.

"This is your home while you are here."

"Did you make this? Did your father?" Pan asked, impressed by its beauty.

Irisa chuckled. "No, Pan, you did. Your training here has already begun."

Pan looked at Irisa incredulously. "I did not create this!"

"Not consciously. But your longing for peace, comfort, and beauty did. In time you will learn to control the creative matter intentionally."

"Will I be able to do these things back on our own level?"

"On the level that Etera now exists, no. Not to this extent. But some of what you learn to do here will serve you there in other ways, just not quite so remarkably obvious as this."

Pan suddenly realized how tired she was. "I would like to sleep now."

"Go ahead. I will not be far away."

Pan ducked to enter the woven enclosure. Inside

it was a deep covering of green moss that gave under her feet. She lowered herself down and stretched out her full length. The softness seemed to mold to support her body. It was the perfect cocoon of peace, comfort, and beauty. The thick vines were woven tightly enough together to create a bit of darkness once inside. She was grateful for the solitude and privacy as she needed time to mull over what had just taken place. However, in spite of herself, she fell fast asleep.

When Pan awoke, it took her a moment to figure out where she was. The first thing she noticed was the sweet smell of the air, then the lilting bird song. She rolled up on one elbow and wiped tears from her eyes, but she could not remember crying.

She stooped over to leave the enclosure, and everything came back to her. Not seeing Irisa, Pan walked over to the stream, lay down on the bank, and scooped the clear water up with her hands to wash her face. Then she took a long, satisfying drink. She knelt back and noticed a small lizard within reach watching her from the rocks along the stream's edge. Pan thought about scooping it up and eating it as she was very hungry, but it seemed wrong. She got up, and still not seeing Irisa anywhere, followed the edge of the stream. Then to her right, just inside the edge of a forest beside her, she spotted a huge berry patch.

After having her fill of early juicy plump berries, she went back to the stream to continue her journey.

The horizon looked the same as it did on Etera. The primary difference was how alive everything seemed, though not quite to the extent of the Corridor. And there was the fact that it was clearly spring here, yet at home—if that was the word—the leaves were adorned in their fall colors.

Hundreds of questions were burning in her mind. Was this place only a construct of Wrollonan'-Tor's mind, or did some version of it actually exist somewhere on the far side of Lulnomia? Had they walked far enough for that to be true? If Wrollonan'Tor died, would all of this cease to exist? Though she was not a Guardian, had Wrollonan'Tor been able to reach Irisa to do this? Were these even important questions to ask?

Pan kept walking until, off in the distance, the figures of Wrollonan'Tor and Irisa appeared. She picked up her pace, realizing she was truly happy to see them.

Irisa held her hand out, and Pan wondered why she was so much friendlier here than she was at Lulnomia. She was softer, kinder, not as distant. Pan felt closer to her and was grateful for that.

"It is so beautiful here; how far does it go?" Pan asked.

"As you walk, it extends in front of you. So it is limitless," Irisa answered. "I know, I have tried to outwalk it, but there is no end to this place."

Pan thought about that and decided it was the same everywhere on Etera and wondered why she had even asked it. "Of course. I guess I am not thinking straight," she confessed.

"During this visit, I want you only to get accustomed to being here," Wrollonan'Tor said. "We have ages in which to train you, so there is no need to rush."

The concept of the number of centuries, the thousands and thousands of years she would live, hit Pan all over again. "Rohm'Mok, Tala," she said.

"It is of no benefit for you to think about it," Wrollonan'Tor said. "Do not waste your time thinking of the years to come. Enjoy every day you have with them because, in time, all you will have is memories,"

"Ohhhh," Pan moaned as a great sadness filled her, and she realized she was picking it up from the Ancient Guardian. She tried to strengthen her boundaries as the grief was nearly unbearable. "Ohhhh," she said again.

Then looking into his eyes, she asked, "How do you bear it?"

"With great difficulty. People say they wish they could live forever, but they do not consider the reality of it. What they mean is that they wish their present pleasant circumstances would never end."

A moment later, Pan's distress was gone. She realized Wrollonan'Tor must have done something to shield her from his emotions.

"We will leave you now," he said. "Explore. Discover. Seek answers to your questions and not just those pertaining to how this is created and sustained. Irisa will find you tomorrow morning and take you back to Lulnomia."

"First, please tell me, was it by coincidence that B'Hit and Asolp found Lulnomia? No, you do not need to answer. I know the answer. The Order of Functions," she said.

Wrollonan'Tor raised his hand as if to say good-bye, and he and Irisa turned and walked back the way Pan had come.

She watched them for a while, not sure what to do with herself. But she was still hungry and so went farther along the stream. She passed a grove of fruit trees. Too bad it was only spring and too early for them to bear fruit. Then before her eyes, nearly as soon as she thought it, the colorful blossoms curled inward and transformed into buds, which grew and formed ripe, fragrant fruit. She helped herself, delighting in the depth of taste, how crisp and sweet, how the experience practically burst into her mouth when she bit into the fruit. A little farther on, she found a large oak with acorns everywhere under its wide-spread branches. A little farther and a bounty of hazelnuts. Irisa was right; everything that one could want was provided. Except that which the soul longed for most—love, companionship, belonging. Purpose? What of purpose? How long could a soul survive without a purpose, Pan wondered.

Wrollonan'Tor had said she would be the greatest Guardian ever. *But how can that be?* He had lived practically forever. How could her abilities surpass his? Who were the Guardians before him? All she had was questions, but he had told her to seek her answers here.

As Pan walked farther, the soft grasses under her feet gave way to a rocky bank. Beside her, the current became stronger until the water was no longer a small stream but a river. In the distance, the sky seemed darker, as if storm clouds were forming. She thought of turning back but was too enthralled to stop. Heavy humidity filled the air, and she could smell the rain that was coming.

As she continued on, the wind got stronger. The leaves on the trees started turning up, and all the birds that had been darting through the sky were now returning to shelter. The wind was becoming so strong that even Pan was having trouble walking, and she raised her forearm to shield her eyes from the small leaves and debris being thrown at her. A flash of lightning startled her, and all of a sudden, the heavens let loose with a torrential downpour. So dense was the deluge that Pan was soon soaked to the skin, the cold outburst stinging her. Thunder clapped overhead, so loud that she had to cover her ears. The sky was nearly dark now, with angry clouds overhead and the harsh wind chilling her. But Pan kept on, struggling not to fall over. A loosened branch flew by, striking the forearm she was still using to shield her eyes, and she cried out involuntarily. The river's waters were so high that they crested the banks, and Pan was losing her footing on the slick rocks. She stumbled several times, cutting her palms on some of the rougher stones as she caught herself. More than once, she lost her purchase and slipped into the waters up to her knees. Sopping wet and cold, she fought her way back to land.

It was now as dark as night. Despite her night vision, Pan could barely see in front of her as the rain was coming down at such an angle and with such force. She pressed on, still protecting her eyes. There was so much water in her coat that she found it hard to keep moving from the extra weight she was carrying. She had never been this wet before. She was getting chilled from the biting cold air. Finally, unable to see where she was going and fearing she would fall into the angry current, she had to stop. She dropped to her knees and curled into a ball, trying to retain as much body warmth as she could. After what seemed like a very long time, she suddenly realized that the pelting rain and the roaring sound of the wind had stopped. She could feel the warmth of the sun on her back. She opened her eyes and squinted at the bright sunlight.

Then Pan slowly rose and ran her hands all over her torso, her limbs, everywhere she could reach, pressing the water out of her coat with downward strokes. The warm rays seemed to caress her, bringing her core temperature back up. She checked her palms and saw that the wounds were already starting to heal even faster than they would on Etera with her Guardian's remarkable healing abilities.

The horizon was now clear. White puffy clouds dotted the perfect blue sky. Birds reclaimed their flight. She turned and looked back the way she had come, expecting to see the water starting to abate. But the river was already nearly still, gently moving downstream.

In the next instant, Pan realized she was dry. Not knowing what else to do, she turned and went back, looking forward to the comfort of the vine hut and the soft mossy bed that awaited her.

The return trip seemed short. Before long, she could see the little welcoming shelter with Irisa standing beside it as if waiting for her. Pan waved, and Irisa waved back.

When they were within hailing distance Irisa called out, "Did you find your answers?"

Pan drew closer. "I ran into a terrible storm! I kept going as long as I could, but eventually, I had to stop and wait it out."

She realized that the greatest question on her mind all along had been whether she could do what was required of her. The great challenges that Wrol-lonan'Tor had foretold had frightened her. Suddenly, Pan understood. "So the storm was not an accident," she said. "It came to show me I could persevere even when I thought I could not."

"But you stopped at one point?" Irisa asked.

"Yes. At the point where I realized it was foolish to try to continue on."

"What were you thinking when you finally stopped?"

"That the storm could not last forever. Eventually, it would let up."

Then Wrollonan'Tor appeared as if from nowhere.

"Reflect on your experiences here, Pan. The storms of life will come to us all. There is a time to press on, no matter what the odds. And then there is a time to stop. To know the difference, when to do which, you must listen to yourself. You must trust that you will find within yourself the wisdom to know when to use your will to press forward and when it is time to surrender. Listen to the counsel of others, yes. But ultimately, the answer must come from within you.

"Are you ready to go home?" he asked.

"Yes," Pan said.

He turned to his daughter, "Please take Pan home now."

As they went, Pan thought longingly of the little shelter and regretted she would not get to rest there again before they left. But she was also anxious to see her daughter and her mate. "Irisa, may I tell Rohm'Mok about this?"

"That is up to you. This is your path, Pan. You

must start following your own guidance. That is the only way you will grow in wisdom and confidence."

must start following your own guidance. That is the only way you will grow in wisdom and confidence."

Pan so wanted to tell Rohm'Mok about Wrollonan'Tor and Irisa, but a check within her spirit kept her from doing so. She wanted someone else to share it with so she could mull it over out loud, just as she had told him about E'ranale and the Corridor. But she knew this was hers alone to bear. The longer she lived, the more she understood the burden her father had carried. More than simply being Etera's Guardian, there were decisions he had made, the consequences of which he would never know. He'd had to face opposition from his brother, his people. Even himself.

Wrollonan'Tor's words haunted her. If she was to be the greatest Guardian ever, did that mean she would also be called on to make decisions of the magnitude her father had faced? Pan could not conceive of it.

Their reunion was a happy one. Pan delighted anew in their daughter and her life with Rohm'Mok, partially spurred on by not being able to get Wrollonan'Tor's loneliness off her mind. Rohm'Mok did not press Pan to tell him where she had been but instead focused on what had happened over the two days for which she had been gone.

The cooler weather spurred on more outside

activities, coaxing her people out of the shelter of the cave system. Those who had stepped forward to represent their communities had agreed on the distribution of the rich resources around Lulnomia so there would be no disputes about which area was to be worked and harvested by whom. The allocation of the land also provided an opportunity for one community to trade with another, should one have a more bountiful crop of something than they could use. In short, the community was accepting the new life at Lulnomia. The only thing missing was what Hatos'Mok had asked for; something that would unite them as one people.

It was not that Pan had not tried to come up with the perfect suggestion, but she had put the scroll hidden in the Leader's staff out of consideration. Some part of her knew the power of the scroll was not to be used in this way. Something told her it would come into play at some point and was to be held back for when that time came. And after meeting Wrollonan'Tor, she was now convinced that this time would come and that she would know when it had.

CHAPTER 13

Tlanik busied herself with her tasks, trying to keep her mind off her daughter's upcoming pairing. She was happy that Wry'Wry had relented and agreed to be paired. She was also glad that the male the High Council had chosen for her was from the community closest to them, so there would not have to be long stretches in between seeing her daughter—and in time, her daughter's offling. As for Wry'Wry and Takthan'Tor, Tlanik had done all she could. Whatever might have been between them had apparently died.

The colder weather would make for a more enjoyable journey, and before long, it was time to go to the Far High Hills where the Ashwea Awhidi would be held. Takthan'Tor and Vor'Ran went on ahead, wanting to meet with Culrat'Sar before the activities started.

Tlanik and Wry'Wry were the last to arrive

because Tlanik had let her daughter stall their leaving. The friendly daughter she had once known now seemed to be forcing herself to be sociable, and Tlanik could only hope that in time Wry'Wry would grow to care for the male the High Council had paired her with.

None of them would meet Kant before the actual ceremony. Tlanik was racking her brain, trying to remember him, but she could not. She wondered if Wry'Wry was doing the same, but based on her daughter's aura of resignation, decided that Wry'Wry was probably not.

The High Council meetings ended, and everyone was gathered in the main chamber for the Ashwea Awhidi. Wry'Wry waited as other pairs were called to the front first. Finally, it was her turn. She had been scanning the crowd trying to recognize the record keeper. She wondered if perhaps he was doing the same. The one she avoided looking at was Takthan'-Tor. She did not want to acknowledge him any sooner than she had to. It would be hard enough to stand there in front of him, next to this other male, and hear Takthan'Tor proclaim them paired. He was the Overseer; it fell to him.

Wry'Wry's name was called, and she walked to the front. Takthan'Tor was waiting for her approach; she could feel him watching her. She kept her eyes averted as she did not trust her self-control if she were to look at him. At the front, in relief, she turned to face the crowd.

Kant was called forward. Wry'Wry looked for movement and then finally saw him stand up. He was quite tall, as tall as Takthan'Tor. He had light brown coloring, and his hair was straighter than most of the Akassa. Wry'Wry clenched her teeth, fighting for the control needed to force a smile at the male who was coming toward her. The male who would mount her that night and whose offling she would carry and raise.

Kant was all too soon standing in front of her. She dared a fleeting glance up at him, then quickly searched the front row for her mother and father. They were standing there stalwartly. *This is for the best*, she told herself and tried not to think about what was happening.

"Wry'Wry." Someone said her name.

"Oh—what?" she turned and looked directly into Takthan'Tor's eyes. Her heart stopped.

"You are paired now. You may leave with your mate."

Wry'Wry felt her lower lip start to quiver, and she turned away quickly. She grabbed her new mate's hand and urged him forward into the crowd, where everyone smiled and nodded their congratulations.

As she walked past her parents, her mother mouthed, *we love you*. Others said their congratulations as the two walked out.

Once they were out of the main chamber, Kant stopped and said to Wry'Wry, "Do not worry, relax; we have time to get to know one another. Yes, I am looking forward to mounting you, but I will not rush you. We must get to know each other and become a strong team. My hope is that we will have solidified our relationship before the offling come."

After the shameful history of abuse of the females, the culture had turned itself around. Females were held in high esteem. Males were taught to respect them and to subjugate their own desires, focusing instead on wooing the female into coming to them.

Wry'Wry heard him but felt like she was far away. That this had happened seemed like a dream. Was she really paired to this male and not to Takthan'Tor? How could it be? Everything in her heart and soul told her she belonged with him, not this stranger standing in front of her.

She forced herself to speak. "I have heard of your renowned skill in record keeping. I look forward to learning more about it."

Kant chuckled a bit. "Oh, I doubt you will find it interesting. I find it boring, myself."

Wry'Wry tilted her head, not expecting such candor. "Then why do you do it?"

"I have a knack for it. And it is my contribution to our people, just as your toolmaking is yours."

"But I love what I do," she said.

Kant started walking and turned back for her.

"Then you are doubly blessed. To be skilled at something you love is a great blessing."

Before too long, they stood in front of an open door. He motioned for her to go inside. The quarters were not very large, but she also knew that this was just where they were staying until the rest of the ceremony and High Council meeting was over. She would then return with him to his community.

"I thought you might want to spend some time together before we rejoin the others."

"Yes, thank you," she said. "I was feeling overwhelmed in there. After we rest a bit, I will be ready to face them."

"Face them?" Kant asked. He found a gourd and brought her some water.

"Thank you," she said as she took it.

"I do not know why I put it like that. I suppose I do not enjoy large gatherings."

"Well then, you will like my community," Kant said. "We are very small. And we are not far from the High Rocks. So you will be able to visit your parents as often as you wish."

Wry'Wry was taken aback at how kind he was being. She had expected him to be in a hurry to mount her right away. She felt this was a good sign and hoped that as they got to know each other, there would be other pleasant surprises. Perhaps her mother was right. Perhaps in time, she could learn to love him.

Takthan'Tor could not bear to watch Wry'Wry and
Kant walk out together, so he quickly turned to
Persica, who was helping with the events, and asked
for the next couple waiting to be paired. There was a
surprisingly large number, several of them from the
small unnamed community that Wry'Wry would be
living in with Kant.

After Takthan'Tor declared the last of them
paired, he busied himself with conversation for the
rest of the evening. It was not difficult as there were
many people there. And there were always the other
Leaders to speak with when he became bored of chit-
chat.

It was not long before Wry'Wry's parents found
him. Takthan'Tor did not want to talk to them. Did
not want anything to bring him back to reality. It was
all he could do to maintain a stately presence as it
was. But here they came, and he could see no way to
avoid them.

"I am happy for my daughter," said Tlanik, "but it
is difficult to let her go."

Vor'Ran added, "She will adjust. He seems like a
decent fellow."

Takthan'Tor nodded and excused himself, saying
he needed to speak with Culrat'Sar. Just as he
approached the Leader of the Far High HIlls, Persica
intercepted him.

"And where are you off to in such a hurry?" she

asked, keeping step with him. Takthan'Tor caught himself and slowed down, realizing he was almost running away from Wry'Wry's parents.

"Was it rushing? I did not notice," he lied. "I am looking for your father."

"I will take you to him; come."

Culrat'Sar was in a conversation with Gontis'Rar of the Little River, Lair'Mok of the Deep Valley, and Tar'Kahn, Adik'Tar of the unnamed community.

"I am glad you are here," said Culrat'Sar. "We were just discussing whether the High Council meetings should continue or not."

Takthan'Tor frowned. It was the first he had heard of this. "Why would we discuss that?"

"Many of us feel we are not ready to come together with the other communities; we have much to work on in our own communities," said Tar'Kahn. "We could always start them up again later. If we wished."

"We need to meet together," protested Takthan'-Tor. "We need to keep continuity in the vision we have for our people and in the way we lead. We also have much work to do with the Brothers. There is wisdom in gathering and sharing ideas. I see no benefit in going off on our own, certainly not at this point. If ever."

"Adik'Tar, not all the communities are ready to move at the same pace you are. You speak of making contact with the Brothers, establishing relationships with them. We are not ready for that. We do not want

282 | LEIGH ROBERTS

to spend our resources in that direction. At least not now," said Lair'Mok.

"And how do you feel about this Culrat'Sar?" Takthan'Tor asked.

"I do not agree with any of them; I agree with you. But we are in the minority."

"And what of the Rah-hora?"

"We have not forgotten the Rah-hora," said Gontis'Rar. "We will honor the Rah-hora. We simply want to spend our efforts in another direction first."

Culrat'Sar turned to Takthan'Tor. "They want to find the Protectors. See if they can convince them to return to us."

"I see," he said. "And how do you think you will find them?"

"The Great Spirit will guide us," said Tar'Kahn.

Takthan'Tor was trying to get ahead of Tar'Kahn's argument but did not understand it. "Why would the Great Spirit guide you to find them? That would mean it was not the Great Spirit's will that they left us."

"Because we need them," Tar'Kahn replied.

"If we needed them, if the best thing for us would have been for them to stay, then why did they leave? Do you believe you are more connected to the will of the Great Spirit than they are—those who serve the Great Spirit in much greater harmony than we ever could? You think their leaving was a mistake, and going after them will rectify it? I do not see how you can think that." He was getting frustrated in spite of himself.

"We do not believe there is any better goal to pursue." Tar'Kahn said it with finality.

Takthan'Tor then realized there was no use arguing with them or trying to change their minds. He could see such fear in them, which he knew was greater than words could overcome. The Protectors were too much for him to compete against. The sense of security they provided, the ease of lifestyle, their towering presence. The Akassa paled by comparison. In the minds of these males, they could never provide the security for themselves that the Protectors had. So rather than bothering to try, they wanted to plead with the Protectors to return.

He looked at Culrat'Sar and then turned and walked away, leaving the other Leaders standing together. They were going to search for those who did not wish to be found. It would take them years, centuries, perhaps an age before they would admit defeat. Their fear was more powerful than their reason. They would do anything to go back to the life they had before. They could not see themselves as anything but inferior and thus had no confidence in their own ability to provide for themselves, their communities, or their loved ones. So instead of taking up the challenge, they would put all their time and effort into trying to go back. Chasing after what was instead of pursuing what could be.

Takthan'Tor walked until he had calmed down.

He came to a fork in the corridor and turned back the way he had come. Then he looked for Culrat'Sar once more and explained that though it was still early, he was going to his room and would be heading back to Kthama first thing in the morning.

"Let my daughter show you to your quarters." Culrat'Sar motioned for Persica to come over and tend to Takthan'Tor.

As they walked together, Persica remarked, "Forgive me, Adik'Tar, but you seem upset."

"It has been a long day," he replied.

"Is it conducting the pairings that has fatigued you?" she asked.

Takthan'Tor shook his head. "No, it is the short-sightedness that surrounds me and which threatens our future that has me concerned."

He walked a few more feet, "I am very tired and do not wish to oversleep. Will you please arrange for someone to wake me well before first light? I wish to return to the High Rocks as soon as possible."

Having had a short rest, Wry'Wry and Kant returned to the others. There were many congratulations and well wishes being shared all around. In between socializing she searched for Takthan'Tor. But she did not find him the rest of the evening. She was surprised at her relief, however, when she spotted

Persica. Wherever Takthan'Tor was, at least they were not together.

When Wry'Wry was standing alone, Persica came over and gave her a big hug. "Oh, I am glad for you. He seems like a fine fellow. I so hope you will be happy together."

Wry'Wry did her best to set aside the fear that her friend was interested in Takthan'Tor. "Thank you. I am going to do my best. Maybe you will come and visit me after I am settled in?"

"Of course. I would love to."

Nearly everyone had left the chamber, and Wry'Wry was legitimately tired now and yearned for sleep. Kant noticed she was having trouble keeping her eyes open and suggested they turn in.

He waited while she picked her preference on the sleeping mat, allowing her to settle before lying down beside her. He reached over and patted her hand and said, "Sleep, Wry'Wry. Have no concerns about expectations on my part tonight or any other night."

Wry'Wry drifted off to sleep, trying not to imagine the day to come, and the next, and the next after that.

But the next day did come, and Wry'Wry bid her mother and father goodbye and left with Kant for his home. She found herself wishing it had been a longer trip so she could make an excuse of fatigue to keep to herself in whatever living quarters she would be sharing with Kant. To keep her mind off her inner turmoil, she tried to focus on the cool air biting her face.

Kant's parents were waiting anxiously to meet Wry'Wry. They embraced her warmly and gave the couple a gift of dried fruits. Then they took her through their small cave system, showed her where key features were, and introduced her to others in their family.

Wry'Wry had no idea their community was so small, nor that the place they lived in was so compact. There was no expansive entrance, no weavings of tunnels and hallways leading from one level to the next. After living all her life at the complexity of the High Rocks, this could be a hard adjustment for her.

Another of the differences was the imbalance of males and females. There were far more males here than females. She wondered if that was because the females asked to be paired as soon as they were eligible so they could leave this small establishment.

After she had been shown around and Kant's parents had run out of people to introduce her to, Wry'Wry was left in Kant's quarters to settle in. She unpacked her carrying satchel, stacking her tools in the corner that Kant had indicated was hers to use, and carefully placed her Keeping Stone next to them. She then lay down on the sleeping mat. Not knowing what to do next and with her mind unoccupied, overwhelming loneliness swept over her. She missed her mother and her father. She missed her friend Tensil. She missed the High Rocks. She missed Takthan'Tor, and she missed the comfort of seeing him walking about, making decisions, protecting and providing for everyone through his leadership.

It had not even been a day, and already Wry'Wry was miserable.

Kant came to check on his new mate and heard her crying inside their living space. He left and went to find his parents to ask for help.

"She just needs time," his mother said. "This is a big change for her. It is far easier for you as she has to fit into the framework of your life, not the other way around. Everything looks different, sounds different, even our ways are different. Different enough to remind her she is not at home."

"Help her find a place for herself here. She needs a project, something to dedicate herself to," his father suggested.

"She is a toolmaker. I do not know anything else about her," Kant said.

"Then start with that," said his mother.

"I will talk to our toolmaker. He can tell me the best places to take her for her supplies. Yes, something familiar for her to throw herself into. Thank you."

Not long after, Kant—carrying a huge basket—went and fetched Wry'Wry.

"Where are we going?"

"You will see. Someplace I hope you will like."

He led her out into the forest to where their toolmaker had said they should go. Now that summer had long relinquished its reign to fall, the brightly colored leaves had let go of their hold on their branches and collected on the ground. The forest floor was covered with them. The smell of damp earth was a delight, and Wry'Wry let herself focus only on the moment at hand. All the Akassa found solace in the quiet solitude and ever-bearing provision of the forests.

It did not take her long to figure out why Kant had taken her there or why he was carrying the large basket. She immediately sat down and began turning rocks over, looking for those she wanted. Kant squatted down next to her and patiently waited for her to pick them out. As she did, he put them in the basket and waited some more. After having found enough to keep her working for a while, Wry'Wry stood up and brushed herself off. They had been there for some time, with never a complaint out of Kant.

"Thank you. That was kind of you."

"I want you to be happy here," Kant said. "I am glad you enjoyed this."

Wry'Wry smiled and looked up at him.

"You are beautiful," he said before he could catch himself.

Wry'Wry looked away. "Thank you," was all she could think to say.

"Come on," Kant said, lifting the heavy basket, "I am anxious for you to meet our toolmaker. He told me where to take you."

The three of them spent the rest of the day looking at the toolmaker's collection of tools and talking about the stones Wry'Wry had gathered. Though Kant was not following all of the conversation, he was content to see Wry'Wry relax and liven up, talking about what she loved doing.

That evening, when they retired, Kant edged himself the tiniest bit closer to Wry'Wry. He could feel her body heat and smell her sweet scent. He vowed he would wait for her to come to him, though, so he tried to squash his desires and pretended to be asleep.

Takthan'Tor threw himself back into the routine of guiding life at Kthama. He slept little, working himself into a state of exhaustion before he would turn in. He took long walks around Kthama, enjoying the drop in temperature. To the surprise of others, he had given permission for the preparation of the Leader's Quarters to be finalized. He had felt that his presence would displace whatever remained of Moc'Tor and E'ranale, but now seemed to be a time of beginnings and endings, so it seemed fitting.

With the help of some males, the females had done a great job in refreshing the Leader's Quarters. The walls had been whitewashed with caulk, giving everything a brighter appearance. All the elements had been replaced—new water baskets, seating stones, food storage gourds. He wondered what had become of the items that belonged to Moc'Tor and E'ranale but doubted they had been destroyed. He thought that they might instead have been stored somewhere out of sentiment.

Takthan'Tor had few personal items of his own to move in. The most important was the new 'Tor Leader's Staff. The first thing he did upon entering was to place the staff in the eastern corner. As he did, he thought of the thousands of times Moc'Tor had done the same thing with the original 'Tor staff. He could not help it; his thoughts drifted to Pan and her family. Where had they gone? What was their life like now? Like the others, he yearned for their return. But he knew it was not to be and that the Akassa's salvation lay not in trying to return to the past but in making the most of the present.

"It needs a female's touch," he caught himself saying out loud. But it was true. It was cold and empty, despite the others' attempts. Like everyone else, he had suffered a great loss when the Protectors left, and now Wry'Wry was gone. Lost to him forever, lying in the arms of another male. He willed himself to accept it, that this was the price of duty, just as he willed himself to fulfill the other obligations he bore. But his heart and mind struggled to make peace with it.

After staying only a few moments, Takthan'Tor left the newly prepared room, a place as empty as his heart.

It was always arguable which season was the most beautiful on Etera. The soft spring greens and blossoms proclaiming the rebirth of life, the warm summers with sacred nights lit by the moon and stars overhead, and the soft golden glow of the fireflies in the fields. And now, fall with its gently drifting leaves and rich smells of damp earth had almost come to a close. Soon it would be winter and sparkling white snow would blanket their world as if preparing it for rest until the cycle came full circle with the rebirth of spring.

Sitka had returned to her routine at the Brothers' village. She did not speak of Oh'Mah any longer but kept her head down and seemed to become a recluse, as if again in mourning. She and her beloved had been inseparable from a very young age, and when he died tragically, she had cut herself off from everyone else, just as she was doing now.

Tocho and Tiva were disappointed that there was no further talk of going to the oak tree. They did not understand what had happened, but their parents admonished them not to pester the Medicine Woman about it any longer.

Something had happened. The people of the village knew it. Some had seen Sitka come flying back, panic on her face. She had immediately gone to find the Chief, barely breaking from a dead run. And she had not come out of his shelter for a very long time. When she did, she was changed. She became distant, and no longer sang while she went about her ways.

Chief Chunta had been watching Sitka carefully since she told him about the last visit and what the unidentified female had drawn in the ground. Only he and the Elders knew about this, and though they could not understand how it could have come to be, the Chief did not allow her story to be discredited. But he also did not want it spread throughout the village. So nothing more was said of it, and life returned to normal, though there was an undercurrent of dissatisfaction that the topic of Oh'Mah had been dropped. When asked about it, the Chief answered, "Time will reveal the next step in this journey. We must be patient."

Sitka herself sometimes had trouble believing it was true. But she had no reason to believe that the female Tensil would have lied to her. What would have been the point? It was an incomprehensible story; no one would make up something so unbelievable. How was it even possible for Oh'Mah to have bred with her people? If it had happened, how would her people not have known about it? There was no talk about any of her people's men or women disappearing. And surely none of the women could bear a child sired by a Sasquatch. She could never bring it to term; it would burst her open. Sitka could not figure out how it had been done, and this question haunted her for some time. Finally, she surrendered it. She decided that Oh'Mah's ways were unknown to her and her people. It was said they could disappear right in front of your eyes. And that they could be watching you, and you would never know. So what other magic did they possess? Since the question was unanswerable, in her own wisdom, Sitka set it aside.

The winter snows were not long off. Much time had passed, and the Chief called for Sitka.

When she entered his shelter, she was relieved to see he was alone. She knew it must be about what had happened with the strange female as there was nothing else of any importance going on.

"Have you come to a decision?" Chief Chunta asked.

"About what?"

"About what you believe is the truth."

"What I believe is the truth does not matter because the truth is not knowable. But I will tell you I have made peace with whatever did happen. I came to realize that what little we do know of Oh'Mah leaves room for many wondrous possibilities."

"Are you ready to go back and make contact again?"

Sitka shook her head, and the Chief nodded his understanding and waved to signal she could leave. She did not know if she had displeased him and left feeling uneasy about the meeting.

As she walked away, Tocho and Tiva came running after her. They did not miss a thing.

"We saw you come out of the Chief's shelter. Are you going back to the oak tree?" Tocho asked.

"No, I am not. Please do not ask me about this again. If and when I am ready, I will let you know, I promise." Sitka then put her head down and continued on her way.

"What are we going to do?" asked Tiva.

"What can we do? We have to wait until she is ready."

"If she is ready. What if she is never ready? What

if they think we are mad at them now, and they will not ever talk to us again?" She was close to tears.

Tocho put his arm around his younger sister. "I do not think that is what is happening. Sitka was so unhappy when she came back from the last meeting that surely it was obvious to Oh'Mah. I am sure they understand that whatever happened upset her a great deal."

"Will we ever know what happened?"

"I do not know," replied Tocho. "Maybe not. And we will have to live with it."

"I do not think I can," Tiva whimpered.

It broke Tocho's heart to see his sister so sad. She had been so excited about being part of this great mystery, and now it seemed the light had gone out of her spirit.

"Let us go home. I will carve you a figure of Oh'Mah; would you like that?"

"Oh, yes." His sister perked up.

As the family lay together in their shelter, warmly bedded down for the night, Tocho could not stop thinking about Tiva. She was too young to be this unhappy. He knew something must be done about it, but what?

Over the next several weeks, Tocho continued to ruminate about how to help his little sister. Nothing he did cheered her up for long. The figure of

Oh'Mah did for a while, and then when that wore off, he made her a new hide doll, even working with Sitka to make some little clothes for it. Tiva had smiled when he gave it to her and slept with it every night, so he knew it pleased her. But nothing completely lifted her sadness.

He tried talking to his parents about the problem, but it seemed they did not really understand. In the end, he was convinced it was up to him to help her.

"Tiva, why are you still so sad?" he asked one day when they were out on a walk.

"I am sad because I keep thinking about Oh'Mah coming to the oak tree every day with no one there to greet him. What if he thinks we do not like him? What if he thinks he did something wrong? I do not understand why Sitka is not going back.

"I asked Momma about it, but she said we cannot speak of it any longer because whatever happened is between Sitka and the Chief. So I am without hope."

"Do not say that; there is always hope! We do not know what is going to happen. Perhaps it is not as bad as it seems."

"I am not a child!" Tiva objected, even though she clearly was. "We both saw Sitka running back here as fast as she could. Something happened. And it was not good."

Talking with Tiva had reinforced what he thought. He knew the only thing that would really make her happy was if someone made contact with the stranger again.

The next morning, Tocho arose before anyone else. He was very quiet and careful not to wake anyone. He had barely slept, not wanting to lose the opportunity to leave before the others awoke. He slipped out of their shelter and headed for the oak tree. It was a long way to go alone in the dark, but he was determined to make it there and back before the others got up.

It was colder now, but there was no snow yet. The hard ground made travel easier, and his foot coverings kept his feet warm and dry. He had to move slowly at first, not wanting the rustling of the dry leaves to wake anyone in the village. In his heart, he was happy he was doing something—anything—to help his sister.

Tocho made good time, mostly because he ran much of the way in an attempt to work off his nerves. He found the spot where Sitka had said they were leaving the stones to mark the days. He carefully squatted over the circle to see what remained.

It was clear something had disturbed the pattern. Sitka had described how they were lining up stones to mark the days, but now the stones were scattered about. No matter, he decided to start over. He removed the rocks, brushed the fallen leaves away, and smoothed the ground. Then he placed one rock in the cleared circle and stood up to look at it. He stepped away, and deciding it was now obvious that the area had been reset, looked around.

All he heard were the calls of the winter birds and a creature stirring in the brush, most likely a squirrel. He had not expected to meet anyone, he knew it was unlikely, but he still stood there a while, waiting. And hoping.

After a bit, he turned back toward home. He decided, as much as he wanted to tell her, he would not mention his project to Tiva until something came of it. It would be hard to keep it from her, as he knew she needed the encouragement. But in the end, he knew it would just be another big disappointment if nothing happened. So he kept it to himself.

Because Tocho had hurried, he was able to slip into their shelter unnoticed. He lay down, satisfied that he had done something.

The winter snow had finally come, but Tocho did not give up, still making his trek as often as he could, somehow managing to sneak out and back before the rest of his family even woke up. Except one morning, several weeks later, when he came back inside and found Tiva awake.

"What are you doing up?" she whispered, raising herself up on one elbow under her sleeping blanket and rubbing the sleep from her eyes.

"Shhh," he answered. "I was just out for a walk."

She looked down at his feet. "You must have gone far because you have clumps of snow all over your foot coverings."

Tocho had gotten so used to going out in the dark and was distracted by his nervousness that he had not even realized the significance of the snow that had fallen overnight. But it was not the snow on his foot coverings that was concerning him; it was that he would have left tracks.

He had become lazy. It had become such a routine for him that he had left his guard slip. But there was nothing he could do. Most people would think nothing of the tracks to the tree line unless they followed them and saw that they kept going. If that happened, he had no explanation. They could clearly be traced to his family's shelter, and then there would be questions.

Tocho crawled under his blanket and told his sister to go back to sleep. He lay there for some time, trying to think of an explanation for the questions that were sure to come.

Having spent the last few weeks trying to stay awake to leave very early, Tocho was now very tired. As a result, after he had lain there for a while, he fell asleep. When he awoke, he realized the rest of his family had gotten up. He wrapped his blanket around his shoulders and stepped outside to find them.

He squinted in the daylight. It was so bright. To his delight, he saw that it had snowed since he came home. He shielded his eyes with his hand and scanned the direction he had taken into the forest. Thank the Great Spirit, enough snow had fallen to cover his tracks. He breathed a deep sigh of relief and went to join his family at their fire.

"I let you sleep," said his mother. "You have not been sleeping well for some time. Your sleep has been fitful, actually. But what is the cause of your restlessness, Son?"

"Oh, I did not know you had noticed. I hope I did not keep you awake," he answered, braced for the next question that might be coming.

"Are you having digestive problems? I can ask Sitka to give you something."

Hoping for more information, Tocho did not answer. *Perhaps she thinks I am just going to relieve myself?* He did not want to lie to his mother. It was one thing to keep a secret but another to lie outright.

"You seem to get up and go into the woods early while it is still dark," his mother continued. "But I fall asleep before you come back. I just assumed you were not feeling well."

"I am sorry if I disturbed you," he apologized. He realized that he would not be able to keep this up much longer because if his mother went to Sitka, whatever Sitka gave her for him would work. At least, it would if that was the reason why he was leaving in the early hours. So, he could not let Sitka's medicine be discredited. It would have to 'cure' him, which meant he could no longer make the regular pilgrimage to the oak.

In all the trips he had made, there had not been any new stones added. Whatever had happened, it seemed Oh'Mah was no longer coming back to the site. But he was not about to give up. He vowed he would find them, one way or the other.

After Tensil told Takthan'Tor about what had happened with Sitka, she went back to the large oak for several days. Eventually, since Sitka did not show up, and no new rocks were added to indicate that Sitka had even been there, Tensil gave up. She had talked it over with Takthan'Tor, and they agreed to give it some time. Time had a way of putting things in perspective, and they hoped that after the shock wore off, the Brothers' Medicine Woman would try to make contact again.

Quite a bit of time had passed when once more she made her way to the site. As soon as she could see the clearing, her heart stopped. It was clear someone had smoothed the area out, and even under the blanket of snow, she could tell that the stones had been rearranged. She walked up to the circle and carefully brushed the snow off. There was a small pile of stones outside the perimeter and a row inside. Sitka must have started coming back, but Tensil had not, so Sitka's line of stones stretched out alone. There was nothing to tell her that Tensil would be back to try again.

Tensil's heart sank. There were so many stones. So many failed attempts on the Brothers' part to meet up with her again. She decided then that she would come back to check every day now, no matter what. She picked a bright rock from the pile and placed it alongside the first stone of Sitka's new lineup, showing that she had come. Of course, she had no way of knowing it was not Sitka who had faithfully added a stone day after day after day.

And even sadder, Tocho would not be back any time soon to know that Tensil had come back, as his trips to the oak tree were over.

They had missed each other by one day.

Tensil reported to Takthan'Tor what she had found. Like her, he was disappointed that the communication had been interrupted.

"I feel terrible that Sitka went back to the oak so many times, and I did not. If only she had not asked how we had come to be. If only I had pretended not to understand, stalled for the truth to come out after we had created a stronger bond. Then I would not have let her down like this."

"You did the right thing," Takthan'Tor replied. "It is best to be honest."

Even as the words were out of his mouth, he felt a pang of guilt. He was touting honesty, yet he had not been honest with Wry'Wry. If he had, he would have explained why he had backed off on their relationship. Would it have made a difference? She would still be the daughter of his High Protector.

Tensil broke his reverie, and it was as if she had read his mind. "Have you heard anything about Wry'Wry?" she asked. "I miss her."

"No, I have not, but then it has not been that long. She is only up the Mother Stream; you could take time to visit her. I am sure she would like that."

He did not admit that he would also like to hear how Wry'Wry was doing. He had looked Kant up and down at the Ashwea Awhidi when no one was watching. Takthan'Tor's impression of him was that he was a dependable fellow, looked to be in robust health, and had treated Wry'Wry gently during the ceremony—at least what he had observed. He so wanted to ask around to see what kind of male this Kant really was, but he knew he could not.

"Perhaps I will. I will let you know."

⟨❋⟩

Wry'Wry was thrilled to see Tensil. She gave her a tour of the small cave system of Kant's community, and then they sat outside to enjoy the winter beauty.

She told Tensil that everyone there was treating her well and seemed to be good-natured with few squabbles among themselves. Kant had gone out of his way to help her adjust, introducing her to their toolmaker as they had a shared interest.

"So then, why are you not happy?" Tensil asked.

"Did I say I was not happy?" Wry'Wry frowned.

"You did not have to. I can feel it throughout you. You are despondent. I would have said sad, but it is more than that."

"It is a big adjustment. The community is so small that I can practically predict what each person is going to do every day. They have their routines."

"The People at Kthama have routines too. It is our way of life. I do not understand why that is a problem here?"

Wry'Wry sighed. "I have no history here. And I miss my mother and father. I did as you suggested and talked to Mother about not being paired, but in the end, I changed my mind. Deep in my heart, though, I did not want to be paired, and I should have stood my ground. Run away if necessary. Oh I do not know—" her voice trailed off, and she looked at her feet.

"Is he good to you?" Tensil asked.

"Yes. And patient. I am trying to adjust, truly I am. He is a handsome fellow. I have no complaints. There is just no—spark."

"I see the problem. The stories of Moc'Tor and E'ranale and Pan and Rohm'Mok have filled your head with dreams of a once-in-a-lifetime romance. Do not feel bad; I believe every female wants that, but it does not happen for many."

"My mother told me she was not particularly fond of my father when they were paired, but that she learned to love him. I guess there are different kinds of love." Then Wry'Wry rose to her feet. "Enough of this, let me show you my new tools. Close by, there is a rich grouping of the rocks I need."

As they walked, Wry'Wry dared to ask the question which was burning in her mind. "Do you think Takthan'Tor is considering pairing with the daughter of Culrat'Sar?"

"Persica? Oh I do not know. He does not confide in me. Why, do you think it would be a good match?

"She seems to like him. She falls all over him whenever he is around."

Tensil shot a look at Wry'Wry. "You are in love with Takthan'Tor. That is why you are so unhappy. Oh, Wry'Wry. How could I not see that before now?" She turned to her friend and hugged her.

Wry'Wry could not keep up the pretense any longer. She had confided in her mother that she was once hoping to pair with Takthan'Tor, and she had told Persica there was someone in her heart, but she had never admitted to Tensil what the problem was. Tensil sat and commiserated with Wry'Wry for some time but could not garner much wisdom to comfort her with, considering that she was paired to Kant.

"You have to make the best of it, I am afraid.

Make a serious effort through the cold months and try to get to know him. Maybe it is as your mother says and you will fall in love with him. Who knows, by spring, you may feel totally different and be glad you are paired to him."

Wry'Wry wiped her tears on the back of her arm. "You are right. I will try. He deserves it."

CHAPTER 14

I ria and Visha had come to a truce. Though Visha still attempted to irritate Iria, for the most part, they went their separate ways. Visha had not yet announced she was seeded, leaving Iria feeling torn. She wanted Visha to be seeded because then her mate would no longer have to keep trying. But she also dreaded how much more arrogant Visha would become once she knew she was carrying Dak'-Tor's offling.

Kaisak had made few changes as there were few necessary. He still kept Useaves at arm's length, consulting with her as little as possible. He knew he needed her as she was their only Healer—though he would not call her that in front of the community as she had no official training. It bothered him that she alone knew about the plants and concoctions used to help heal sickness and wounds.

One day he called her over. She stood in front of

him, leaning on her stick while he remained seated at the fire. "You are to begin training someone else in what you know. You are getting older, and it is not good for us to have to rely on only you for help when we have an injury or sickness."

Useaves had not seen this coming and had to think quickly. As much as she would have preferred to defy him, she realized that his request was reasonable. After all, she was getting older—and if she were to fall ill, who would know how to care for her?

"I must be allowed to choose who. Not everyone has a leaning toward the practices. It must be someone meticulous, smart, and willing to learn."

Kaisak did not trust Useaves any more than Useaves trusted him, but he had to give her that concession. "Very well, you can choose who it will be. But be quick about it."

Useaves trudged through the snow to find Iria, her walking stick poking deep little holes down through the white blanket. Tucked under her arm, she carried the little toy Iria had brought for Isan'Tor.

"Oh, thank you for returning this! I do not know how I could have forgotten it!" Iria exclaimed, happily clutching the little figure to her.

"That is not the reason I came to see you." And Useaves explained.

"You want to train me? Why me?" Iria asked.

"I gave you tasks while you were living under Laborn's protection, so you have already helped me with gathering and preparing some of the plants I use. You followed my directions carefully, and you caught on quickly. It is an important role, and you are the best choice here."

"Why now? Are you ill?" Iria asked, trying to figure out what had prompted this.

"No, I am not ill. But for once, I agree with Kaisak; it is not good for there to only be one person with any kind of Healer knowledge."

"How is Kaisak going to feel about you choosing me?" she asked.

"He gave me the right to choose who I wanted, and I have made the best choice. He knows nothing about my craft; he is not in a position to argue about it."

"I will ask Dak'Tor," she answered. "If he agrees, how do I start?"

"Send someone to find me when you are ready, and we will begin right away. The winter is a good time to learn, as we are not busy planting or harvesting."

❦

Dak'Tor's natural reaction to anything coming from Useaves or Kaisak was to question the real motive. He did not mean to detract from Iria's abilities, as he was the first to admit she would be a great choice. But he knew that Useaves weighed every move against how it aligned with her ultimate goal, though he admitted he had no idea what that might be. In this instance, he believed choosing Iria was another way to balance power between him and his followers and Kaisak. And a balance in power kept everything in stasis. It was a way to buy time, but to what end? Useaves was an older female, and time was not on her side—and apparently, for whatever she wanted to accomplish, time was a key factor.

Iria started meeting with Useaves for half a morning each day. She found that when Useaves was focused on teaching, she was more likable, and Iria was not as suspicious of the older female as her mate was. Word soon got out that she was being trained, which irritated Visha as it meant an elevation in status. The truce between them took a hit.

Visha decided then that during the mornings, when Iria went to meet with Useaves, she would approach Dak'Tor and ask him to mount her under the guise of seeding her. Dak'Tor at first resisted, as it interfered with his tasks; however, the logic of it finally wore him down as Iria was preoccupied, and this way, it took none of his time away from her. He did not realize that Iria might view it differently.

"I hear that you and Visha are together many mornings while I am studying with Useaves," she confronted him.

"Yes. It was her idea. I thought it made sense since I do have to seed her, and it did not take time away from you and me or being with Isan'Tor."

"It is humiliating to me. People are saying that when I am distracted, you go to her."

"That is not how it is," Dak'Tor said. "I am merely fulfilling a duty."

"That is not how she makes it look. And she makes remarks to the other females about how kind you are to her and how attentive."

"You know that is not true. I do what I have to do and am done with it. I wish she would become seeded so that part could be over; it is definitely causing trouble between you and me."

"She makes it sound as if you spend the whole time with her that I am with Useaves."

"That is not true. From now on, when it is finished, I will make a point to walk through the common area so others see I am not lingering."

"Thank you."

Dak'Tor gently rubbed his mate's belly. "Soon, we will have another family member," he said, smiling.

"Not until spring," she corrected him. "I do not know which would be better, a male or a female. If it is a female, then we have no worry about her claim to Laborn's leadership. And therefore no threat to Kaisak."

Dak'Tor realized then that Iria, too, did not believe Kaisak's claims that he would honor the offling's heritage.

"If it is a male, then we can only hope it has your markings."

Dak'Tor squinted at her. "Are you saying you think the offling could be mine?"

"Do you remember the night Laborn released you and claimed me as his property instead? He allowed us to spend a few hours together, so it is possible you seeded me then," she said.

"Well, I meant it when I said that this offling would be as much mine as Isan'Tor is," Dak'Tor reminded her.

"I know. And I believe you. But it would uncomplicate things if it is a female, or it is a male with some silver markings somewhere."

He pulled her to him and rested his head on the top of hers. They both knew that if the offling was a male and had no markings to prove he was not Laborn's, they would have to be vigilant as Kaisak would have no intention of letting the offling live to usurp his leadership.

"Do you think Useaves thinks it is Laborn's?" Iria asked.

"As clever as she is, I would say she is prepared to work the situation to her advantage either way." Then he asked, "Why did you wait so long to tell me that I might have seeded you before Laborn—"

"I do not know. I was afraid to get your hopes up? But now that it is only a few months away, I thought we should face what might happen if Kaisak believes it is Laborn's." She pulled back to look up at him.

"I will not let him harm the offling, either way, I promise you."

"I have not let my parents know that the offling could be yours," Iria said, "but I will when it is closer to the time. I do not want it to be a shock to them, as they, along with everyone else, are thinking the offling is Laborn's."

Talk throughout the community had died down, though everyone was aware of Iria's growing belly. What they were waiting for was to hear that Visha was seeded. But no word came, and so Dak'Tor continued to mount her periodically.

Then one day, someone said to Iria that Visha looked as if she was seeded. Iria made a point of looking her over closely. It could be true. But if so, then Visha must have known for a while that she was seeded yet continued to lead Dak'Tor to mount her.

"Are you seeded?" Iria asked her directly one morning where they were collecting water from the river.

Visha looked over her shoulder at Iria. She finished filling her water gourd in the sparkling cold river and stood up. "I am not sure. I believe I may be."

"What are you not sure about?"

"I suspect I am, but I am not certain."

"Let us go see Useaves then," Iria said. "She will know."

"Ha," said Visha, "if I do not know, then how is that old female going to know?"

"She knows these things," Iria said. "Or do you not want to know?" All her good intentions of avoiding any more trouble were evaporating.

Visha let out a long breath. "Very well, if you insist. I do not know what business it is of yours, though."

Iria bit her tongue. Of course it was her business, since it was her mate who was trying to seed Visha. But she kept her eye on the goal, to have Visha declared seeded.

Useaves was downstream with another female who was helping her fill her water gourd.

Iria called out to her, and Useaves looked up as they approached.

"I believe Visha is seeded," Iria said, pointing to Visha's midsection.

"What does Visha believe?"

"I— I—" Visha stammered.

Iria knew what Visha was experiencing; that unyielding glare was unnerving. It seemed to cut to the center of who you were, but that was what Iria was counting on.

Useaves dropped her water gourd to the ground and motioned for Visha to come closer. Then she blew into her hand to warm it and reached out to lay it across Visha's belly. Visha stepped back to avoid Useaves' touch.

"Do you not want to know?" Useaves challenged Visha.

Visha looked around to see some of the other females now gathered around. "I— I— Yes, of course."

Useaves extended her hand again, rested it against Visha's belly, and closed her eyes. After a brief moment, she said, "You are seeded." Then added dryly, "Congratulations."

Iria smiled from ear to ear, then turned to Visha. "I am not going to ask you how long you have known and been keeping up this pretense. I suspect it has been for some time. But now it is over. You are seeded, and my mate will no longer need to service you."

Visha gave Useaves a dirty look before returning to the spot on the riverbank where she had left her water gourd.

Iria turned to Useaves. "How do you know she is seeded?"

"I do not. But Visha does. And if she were hiding anything, she would have been reluctant to let me check her. Females want confirmation, except those who have something to hide."

Word spread quickly, but not before Iria had found her mate and given him the good news. A great weight had lifted from Iria's shoulders because she would no longer have to put up with Visha's tricks and posturing. Of course, in time, Visha would have an offling sired by Dak'Tor. However, Iria thought, she had already dealt with that when Vaha's offling, Altka, was born. But even though everyone thought Vaha's daughter was Dak'Tor's, knowing the truth made it easier to handle. But in this case, Visha's offling would be Dak'Tor's. What would that mean, if anything? She was not sure, but was certain Visha would use it to her advantage however she could.

Iria pushed the thoughts out of her head. For now, she and Dak'Tor were free of Visha. And she would handle Visha's next shenanigans when she had to.

Useaves continued to teach Iria. Kaisak was not pleased with Useaves' choice as he did not want Dak'Tor's circle to gain any more prestige or influence, but having agreed it would be her decision, he said nothing. Then, over time, he started to see how he could use Iria's training to his advantage. In time, Iria would know what Useaves knew. And in time, he could force Iria to do away with Useaves using the very knowledge that Useaves had passed on to her. After all, Laborn had already demonstrated how much control he had over Iria through her son. Soon she would have two offling, and that meant even more leverage for him to use against her.

Dazal had continued to try to endear himself to Vaha. She seemed to appreciate his help and his company and made more time for him than he would have expected. He felt they had gotten close but did not know exactly where he stood with her, so one day, after they had taken a peaceful stroll together and were resting next to each other under some snow-covered branches, he decided to come right out and ask her.

"Vaha, are you happy being part of Dak'Tor's pod?"

"Dak'Tor and Iria are kind to me; it is like having a brother and a sister. I know that sounds strange since I had Dak'Tor's offling."

Dazal swallowed hard; he could not dodge the issue any longer. He had spent a great deal of time with Vaha and gotten to know her, and he found his love for her only grew and grew. They had laughed together and shared their private thoughts about life and what mattered most to them. They had taken long walks together around the area, enjoying the beauty of Etera. They had engaged in playful berry fights. So if, after all this time, she had not developed affection for him, then he doubted she ever would.

"But are you happy being part of their pod? Would you not want a—different arrangement?"

Vaha turned to him. Light snow was falling, dusting his coat with tiny flakes. She took a moment and looked deep into his eyes, "Do not feel sorry for me, Dazal. I am lucky to have such an arrangement; I do not want your pity."

Dazal rested one hand gently against the side of her cheek. She did not move away but instead tilted her face into his touch.

"Look at me," he said. She looked up at him. "I am not offering you my pity. I am offering you myself."

"You care for me?" she exclaimed. "Oh, I must be dense. All this time you have spent with me and the gifts you have brought, for Altka and for me, I thought you were just being kind. I thought you felt sorry for me being second place to Iria—though that is not really fair as I never expected Dak'Tor to have feelings for me."

"I am offering you first place because that is where you are in my heart. But, if you do not care for me the same way, then I understand. I just needed to know. I will still be there for you and Altka."

"No," she said. "You misunderstand. I do care for you, Dazal. Each moment we have spent together has left me wanting more. More time with you. More of getting to know you. And—other things."

Dazal was happier than he had ever been in his life. "Then you would pair with me?" he asked.

She leaned over and pressed her lips against his. Her admission and the gentleness of her kiss melted his heart.

He wanted to devour her with kisses and pull her onto the ground on top of him, but he held himself back. He had come to this point not quite daring to hope that she cared for him in return. It was more than he could have asked for.

"I think we should tell Dak'Tor and Iria together, yes?" suggested Vaha.

He chuckled, his heart overflowing with happiness. "And your parents, no doubt?"

"Oh, yes!"

They rose together, and he pulled her into his embrace. This time he kissed her a little more vigorously, but it was still only a pale version of the passion he felt for her.

Dak'Tor and Iria listened as Vaha explained that she and Dazal were to be paired and that she would be leaving the pod to live with him. Iria secretly squeezed Dak'Tor's hand in happiness for them. It would have been perfect except for one thing. Vaha did not know the truth that it was Dazal who had seeded her and not Dak'Tor.

A pang of guilt shot through Iria. The three of them had, in a very deep way, betrayed Vaha. And now, standing at the brink of happiness, this dark secret lay between Vaha and Dazal. In her heart, she knew they should tell her. That Dazal and Dak'Tor should confess to her what they had done, and why. But Iria feared it would destroy the love between them. And she knew Dazal feared that too.

She broke free from her thoughts and brought herself back to the moment. "I am happy for you. We both are. Would you like us to go with you when you ask Kaisak to pair you?"

Vaha thought for a moment. "I do not need a ritual delivered by such a false Leader as Kaisak is. Dak'Tor, you should pronounce us paired."

Dak'Tor looked at Dazal and then at Iria. "I am not the Leader."

"You are to me. And to many of us," Vaha said. "Whether acknowledged openly or not, you are our Leader."

"Kaisak will not recognize the union," Dak'Tor pointed out. "I appreciate your request, but it is just begging for trouble from Kaisak. He will see it as usurping his authority."

"I doubt he will care what we do," Dazal said. "And Vaha is right. You are the one we follow, not Kaisak."

Iria had a bad feeling about this. It did not take much to anticipate that Kaisak would vehemently object to any acknowledgment of Dak'Tor having any authority. Part of her wanted to exist peacefully and prevent things from stirring up. But she also knew that ultimately Kaisak wanted the annihilation of the Akassa and Sassen, and he could not be allowed to succeed.

"Kaisak is untested," she pointed out. "We do not know if he is as temperamental as Laborn. Do you really wish to start your lives together with a battle?"

Vaha turned to Dazal, "Iria is right. We need to respect Kaisak's authority—for now. We are not ready for a direct confrontation over Dak'Tor's role."

"What if he says no?" asked Dazal. "Then what do we do?"

"I will do what I can to make sure he does not," Dak'Tor answered. The last thing he wanted was to enlist Useaves' help. But if anyone could influence Kaisak, it was her.

"You want my help to convince Kaisak to let Dazal and Vaha pair?" Useaves repeated.

"Believe me, the last thing I want is to be beholden to you," he answered. "But they love each other. He could easily see it as an affront to his authority."

"The main reason it would matter to Kaisak is that it was not his idea."

Dak'Tor said nothing. He imagined Useaves was trying to figure out how this would advantage her, other than putting him in her debt.

"And what of Zisa? She was to be seeded by Dazal," Useaves said.

"It will never happen. Zisa will never let Dazal mount her."

"I will talk to Kaisak, but I guarantee nothing. You and Iria are the only young couple that is paired. I am not sure he wants to set a precedent.

Again, Dak'Tor did not say anything. At least she was willing to try.

Kaisak eyed Useaves with suspicion when she approached. He had heard what she had told Vaha down by the river. Useaves was clever, there was no doubt, and Kaisak was torn between needing her wisdom and wanting to be rid of her. He wondered if Laborn had felt that way too.

"What do you want?" he asked abruptly.

"I do not want anything. I came to tell you of an opportunity," she said.

"An opportunity to do what?"

"To gain favor in the eyes of our people."

"Do I need to gain favor? Is that what you are saying?" He was already irritated, and the conversation had just begun.

"It is easier to rule the grateful and happy than the resentful and discontented. That is something Laborn never learned."

"Tell me of this great opportunity then." Kaisak sat down, leaving her standing.

"Affection has grown between two of your people. They wish to be paired. And you have the power to grant them this."

"Who is it?"

"Dazal and Vaha."

"Why should I grant any favor to Dak'Tor's rebel followers?" he scoffed.

"Again, civil unrest is not your ally. You would gain favor in the eyes of his followers. If you do not, you only give them more reason to want you overthrown."

"You talk as if this is a popularity contest between Dak'Tor and me."

"Again, it is easier to lead those willing to follow than trying to control by force," she answered.

"And if I do this, what is to stop others from asking the same? Then I lose control of who mates with whom."

"Laborn ordered Dazal and Zisa to mate, and they have not. How can a Leader truly control that? Certainly not by force. It is folly. Unless you are willing to punish those who do not follow orders. And then what? More unrest, more dissent. Laborn tried to crush Dak'Tor and his followers instead of winning them over. And he returned to the Great Spirit shamed."

Kaisak let out a low grumble from deep in his throat.

"Then make it very clear this is an exception," said Useaves. "You know as well as I do that the majority of the males keep separate from the females. Relationships are unlikely to bloom as this one has. Most of the males want to mate, not be paired."

Kaisak stood up again and rubbed his chin with

his hand. "Tell them to approach me at the evening fire. If I am to be their benefactor, I need as large an audience as possible to make it work."

Vaha could tell that though her parents had been thrilled for her to be under Dak'Tor's provision, they were happy she would have a mate of her own. Though they did not say it, she could also see they were worried about Kaisak's reaction to their request. Other than when Laborn had paired Dak'Tor and Iria, no new couples had been promised exclusively to each other.

That evening, Dazal and Vaha approached Kaisak as instructed by Useaves. Dak'Tor had rounded up his followers so there would be as many in attendance as possible because Useaves had told him that the more people there, the more pressure on Kaisak to grant the request.

As usual, she had twisted it.

In hopes of their request being granted, Dazal had spent the previous few days straightening up his living space. He put up those of his belongings that Altka should not be able to reach. He enlisted the help of his sister to make a little nesting area for the offling, making sure it was extra warm to compensate for the cold—although he had also arranged that, for the first few nights after he and Vaha were paired, she would stay with Vaha's parents. Of course, after that, the three would be living together.

Kaisak did not want it to look as if he was waiting for something to happen. He poked at the fire, using a branch to stir the embers, causing them to flare and send sparks upward into the night sky. Not needed for warmth, the fire was just a routine they had gotten into having each night, a focus point for the people to gather around.

Out of the corner of his eye, he could see a group approaching but pretended not to notice until they were nearly upon him. He finally looked over to acknowledge them, briefly scanning to see how many of the community were in attendance. He smiled as if pleased with the numbers.

Vaha's father approached first.

"Adik'Tar," he said and waited for Kaisak to acknowledge him. "We come to you with a request that we humbly beseech you to grant." He motioned to the couple behind him, stepping aside to make room for them to step forward.

Kaisak looked Vaha and Dazal up and down. "What is it you want?"

"We recognize that what we are about to ask is an aberration to our ways," said Dazal. "But, out of our control and without intent, Vaha and I have developed feelings for each other. We ask if you would grant us to be paired."

Kaisak remained seated. He looked first at Vaha. "You bore an offling by Dak'Tor." It was a statement, not a question. Then he looked at Dak'Tor, "The female has been under your protection and provision within your pod. Do you object to this pairing on any grounds?"

Dak'Tor was ready. "No, I do not. I welcome the opportunity for any who have fallen in love to spend their lives together."

Kaisak, having never been partial to any one female, stopped himself just before he let out a laugh. He could almost hear Useaves' voice in his head advising him that such a reaction would seem disrespectful.

"Dazal, as a male, you are content with mounting only one female?"

"I am," he declared.

"And what of Zisa?" Kaisak asked.

"We have never mated. She will not have me," Dazal admitted. Several of the females chuckled.

"Where is Zisa? Bring her to me."

Within moments, Zisa was standing in front of Kaisak.

"Dazal says he never mounted you."

"It is true. I do not consent to be mounted by him. Or any male." She looked around with a scowl.

"Then I release you from Laborn's decree. You are free of the binding to Dazal," Kaisak said.

Zisa slipped quietly back into the crowd.

Finally, Kaisak stood. "Though I do not understand this feeling you speak of, I will grant your request because it appears you are sincere. But," he added, looking at the crowd, "this is an exception and not a request I expect to be presented with again." He turned back to the couple, "Stand before me."

Vaha looked up at Dazal, and he took her hand as they moved to stand in front of Kaisak.

After being declared paired, Vaha and Dazal both breathed a deep sigh of relief, and then both smiled ear to ear. Iria took Dak'Tor's hand and squeezed it.

In the background, Useaves waited to catch Dak'-Tor's eye, and when she finally did, she nodded just the slightest bit. *You owe me.*

Dak'Tor's group followed Vaha and Dazal back to their area of the settlement, all chatting gaily. When they arrived at Dazal's living area, Vaha's parents and the other well-wishers embraced each of them and said good night. Dazal and Vaha entered his living quarters, ready to start their life together.

Vaha looked around, pleased at how tidy it was. She had expected far worse. It was a fairly large area with more than enough room for the three of them. She looked down at the area prepared for Altka and expressed her gratitude.

"I want you to be happy here, always," Dazal said, taking her hands in his. "If you want to change anything, by all means, do."

"I am so happy; I do not know what to say."

"Me too. I am so blessed. This is more than I could have hoped for."

Vaha could see that Dazal was waiting for her to initiate their union. She stepped toward him and snaked her arms up around his neck. She looked deeply into his eyes and then tilted her head to press her lips against his. He responded with fervor, and she returned his passion.

She disengaged herself long enough to lead him over to his sleeping mat, which was now theirs. Kneeling down, she reached up, beckoning him to join her, and they lay relaxed next to each other.

"I never believed this would happen to me," she said, caressing his face.

He nuzzled her neck and answered, "Nor did I."

"I only wish—" Then she stopped.

"What?" Dazal continued his attentions, moving up to talk softly in her ear. "Oh, I do not wish you to have any regrets," he whispered. "If it is something in my power to change, I will. Just tell me—"

"It is not. I was going to say I wish I had never been mounted by any male but you. I wish it had only ever been you and me together."

"It is not important," he said.

"It is to me. I never expected to be paired to one male, but now that it is here, and it is you, I wish Dak'Tor had never mounted me. Nor seeded me. Oh, how I wish Altka was ours."

Tears formed in her eyes and threatened to overflow.

"Do not worry; try to put it out of your mind. It is just you and me now, and we have the rest of our lives to spend together."

Vaha sat up. "I am sorry. I did not want this to ruin our first night together."

"Maybe it is too soon," Dazal said. "Maybe we are rushing things? As much as I want you, I think we should wait until you feel ready."

"I just had to say it; I do not want secrets between us, and I did not want to start our life together harboring regrets."

Dazal sat up too.

Vaha could see that his face was pinched. "I have upset you; I am sorry!" she exclaimed.

"No. No, it is not that."

"Then what is it? You look so unhappy right now."

"Because you are sad. Please. Let us wait another night or so until there is less pressure. We have plenty of time, and I want it to be perfect for you."

Vaha conceded. "Alright. Perhaps it is best."

Dazal lay back down and stretched out his arms. Vaha joined him and rested her head on his shoulder. He wrapped her up in his embrace, his head against the top of hers. Soon, her breathing made it clear she had fallen asleep, though he did not join her in sleep for some time.

The community was abuzz with gossip over the pairing of Dazal and Vaha. Some found it a sign of hope that Kaisak would not be as restrictive as Laborn had been. Perhaps he would reverse Laborn's prohibition against any of the younger generation mating. Word of these conversations reached Kaisak through Gard.

"Usually, it is Useaves who tells me these things. Why you?" Kaisak asked.

"Not to influence you, to be sure. I thought you might want to know."

"Hmmph." Kaisak tilted his head and looked at Gard, sizing him up. "You and I have never had any problems between us. And other than that first alter-cation where Laborn gave you that scar, I do not believe you ever gave Laborn trouble either. Unless you count hitting him on the back of the head with a rock." He waited for Gard's answer.

"Laborn was not a Leader to be reasoned with. He wanted what he wanted. It was do as he said, or there would be trouble. You are aware of that," Gard defended himself.

"The people are waiting to see what kind of Leader I will be, no doubt."

"As are you, perhaps?" Gard said.

Kaisak chuckled. "Perhaps." He had never known Gard to be clever, had always thought of him as being dull-witted. "Perhaps there are many things I am yet to learn," he continued. "So tell me. What would you do in my place to win the trust of the people?"

Gard did not hesitate, "I would set out to make a record of those we have left. Determine who is related to who and how far back it goes. You cannot expect them never to mate. It is time to figure it out and move forward."

"I believe you are right. I do not know why Laborn made no movement in that direction. The males, in particular, are very frustrated. To continue to prevent them from satisfying their natural desires by mating is to invite unrest. Perhaps even revolution."

Though Kaisak did not tell Gard, he was thinking of Useaves' words that happy people were easier to rule than discontented and irritated ones. He was not sure if he totally believed this. Perhaps *happy enough* was the right formula. Not so happy that they would want more liberties than would be advantageous to give them, but happy enough that they could make peace with their lot. He would have to ponder this further.

Kaisak knew everyone in the community, and he knew who he would choose for the task of keeping records, but he wanted to hear Gard's recommendation. Not that it meant that much to him, but he was trying to understand Gard better. "Who would you suggest?"

Gard threw out two names. "Either of them. Both are smart enough to come up with a recording system and congenial enough that their approach would not be off-putting."

Kaisak nodded his agreement. "Have them both meet with us tomorrow. I will explain the need and see who comes up with the best plan."

"As you wish, Adik'Tar." And Gard bowed very slightly before leaving.

Useaves made it her priority not to miss a thing. So it was no surprise that she noticed Kaisak and Gard returning to the camp together. And later, that Gard was out among the others, obviously looking for someone in particular. Ever since Useaves revealed that it was he who had injured Laborn and not Dak'-Tor, she had felt a shift in their relationship. And now this. Kaisak was taking counsel from Gard instead of her. She had wanted Gard to be Leader, but not if he were to slip out from under her control.

She positioned herself in a place she was sure Gard would come by. And he did.

"What are you up to?" she asked casually.

"A task for Kaisak."

Useaves was perturbed when he did not elaborate. But she was not going to give him the satisfaction of questioning him about it. Nor of letting him know it bothered her that she was not in on whatever it was. She would find out soon enough.

Instead, she said, "It is good he is starting to trust you."

"He has every reason not to since you told him, and everyone, that I hit Laborn with the rock."

"I explained why I did that. Did you not understand?"

"Yes, I understood. I still do. I understand that you have manipulated everyone here for some time. Laborn, Dak'Tor, me. No doubt the females too. You say your end game is for me to be Leader, but now I have to say that perhaps I do not want to be Leader. Because the fact is, no one is really the Leader here while you are around. The real power is you, behind the scenes, controlling what people do."

"I am no different than anyone else, Gard. Everyone tries to achieve the outcome they want. Why do you judge me so harshly?"

"You may be right. But the difference is, not everyone is willing to betray those who trust them— even their own family—in order to get what they want."

This time Useaves refrained from slapping Gard for mentioning their relationship.

"So you see my plans to make you Leader as a betrayal?"

"You twist my words."

"I want to understand. Help me understand." She leaned forward in a conciliatory gesture.

"It is a waste of time talking to you. I see that now. Whatever your master plan is, you can leave me out of it. From now on, I will be loyal to Kaisak and hope that in time I can live down the disgrace of what I did to Laborn—and Dak'Tor." And Gard stalked away.

Useaves' mind was in a whirl trying to figure out how to fix this. Perhaps there was no way to fix it. Perhaps she must just abandon her plan for Gard to become Leader. If she had lost her control over him, he was no use to her anymore, anyway. If so, then it came down to who would be easier to manipulate, Kaisak or Dak'Tor? When she figured out which it was, that would tell her what she needed to do next.

Dazal was overcome with guilt. He had avoided mating Vaha the previous night, their first together, but knew he could not put her off for long, or she would start to feel rejected. Every female there knew the males were frustrated from not being able to mate. No healthy male would stall forever in taking a female he had a right to, not even a very considerate one. He should be trying to reassure her so they could consummate their pairing.

No matter how long he thought, he could not decide what to do. With all his heart, he wanted to confess to Vaha what he and Dak'Tor had done, so

Vaha would know he had been her first, and she had been his. That her wish was granted, that Altka was, in reality, their daughter. How he regretted having been part of this deception. He could not find a way to live with it, and he could not find a way to tell her without risking losing her.

Finally, he decided that no matter what happened, she deserved to know the truth. However, he would be breaking the Rah-hora with Dak'Tor. And that was also wrong.

So he approached Dak'Tor. "I need to speak with you. Alone."

They found a secluded spot in which to talk. The beauty of the area was in stark relief to the sadness in Dazal's heart.

"Are things not good with you and Vaha?" asked Dak'Tor. "I would have thought you would be beaming today."

"I have to tell her."

"Have to tell her? About what we did?"

"Yes. I cannot live with this for the rest of my life. She has a right to know."

"Dazal—" Dak'Tor let out a long breath.

"I know what trouble this will cause if she gets upset and tells others. But try to understand. Surely it bothers you that Iria does not know that Vaha's offling is not yours?"

Dak'Tor had to admit that it would if Iria did not already know. But he had already broken the Rah-hora and told his mate what he and Dazal had done.

So how could he expect Dazal to live with it when he had not been able to, either?

"We have made a mess of it," he said. "I have to tell you, I told Iria some time ago. She was so distraught that I had mounted Vaha; she believed I did not love her. So, I already broke our Rah-hora. I am sorry."

"I should be angry. But I am not. How can I judge you for not being able to live with it when I cannot? It was not a big deal before I developed feelings for Vaha. I believed, as we first said, that it was not an issue. Vaha would get her offling, and no one would be any the wiser. But we both underestimated how much lying can eat at your soul. I am sure you were relieved to tell Iria, and obviously, she took it well."

"Yes, she was very happy. But she also feels badly for Vaha. You are right. Vaha deserves to know the truth. We can only hope the truth is not worse than the lie. And that she does not go running to her parents and tell them how we deceived her."

"Or Kaisak—"

"Let us find Iria and decide how best to approach Vaha."

Iria listened to both Dak'Tor and Dazal. When they were finished, she said, "I am glad this is going to come out, but it is going to be very hard for Vaha. Perhaps in time, she will be happy about it, but it is going to upset her greatly at first. After all, Dak'Tor and I are the ones who took her into our pod and protection. And now, Dazal, you have paired with her. Who else is she close to in the world except her parents and us?"

"She will run to them immediately, and I cannot blame her," said Dak'Tor.

"Whatever happens, the most important thing is her," Dazal sighed. "Oh, how I wish I could go back and undo what we did. I have made many mistakes in my life, but this is the worst."

"I am not excusing what you did," Iria said. "But remember, this is not something either of you would have done had Laborn not put you under duress."

"Perhaps I deserve to lose her. Perhaps that is to be my punishment for this." Dazal hung his head.

"I pray we do not all lose her," added Iria.

"I wish there was someone whose counsel we could seek," Dak'Tor said. "But there is no one. We have to figure this out on our own." Once again, the cost of his bad behavior at Kthama was sinking in. How he wished he could ask Pan what to do. It was because of his poor behavior that he was far, far away from his sister and would most likely never see her again—unless he lived long enough to be there when she brought the Promised One.

That evening, Dak'Tor and Iria came to Dazal and Vaha's quarters.

Vaha greeted them warmly. It was only their second night of being paired, and she was hoping to be alone with Dazal, but could not deny she was happy to see her friends.

Iria sat next to Vaha while Dazal and Dak'Tor took a seat in front of them.

"I love you, Vaha," Dazal said. "I have for some time. And what I am about to tell you is something I never intended to. I hope that you will listen to the end before you judge me. I made a grievous mistake, and my prayer is that, in time, you will find a way to forgive me."

Vaha frowned and glanced at Iria in alarm.

"Just listen, please. And try to understand none of this was ever meant to hurt you."

"You are scaring me."

Dak'Tor started. "You remember when Laborn said I was to mount you so that you would produce my offling as part of his master plan to increase our population with the intent of eventually killing all the Akassa and Sassen?"

Vaha swallowed hard. "Yes, of course, I do."

"Obviously, this put me in a terrible position. I loved Iria, still do. And I never wanted to betray her like that."

"Yes, you explained this to me. You asked me to keep my eyes closed so you could pretend you were mounting her and not me. And I understand that it was because you love her."

"There is more to it than that. I could not go through with it. So, it was not me who mated with you in the little cave in the dark." Dak'Tor looked across at his friend. "It was Dazal."

"What?" Vaha sat up straight and looked at her mate. "Tell me this is not true!"

"It is true. Dak'Tor could not bring himself to do it, so I took his place. It was never meant to hurt you. At the time, in our stupidity, we thought it a victimless crime. You would get your offling to love and raise. Dak'Tor could remain faithful to Iria. No one would get hurt."

"But—but Dak'Tor, you went on to mate with Dara and now Visha? How is that not betraying Iria?"

"They did not know it would continue," Iria said, turning to face her friend. "In the end, I had to accept that this was Dak'Tor's role. That if he did not comply, then Laborn would have no use for him and would most likely kill him. I made a choice to live with his mounting other females. I could bear that more than I could bear his being murdered by Laborn."

Vaha stared at Dazal. Her eyes were burning with emotion. "So Altka is yours?"

"Yes. She is mine. She is *ours*."

"This is why you could not— Why you and I have not yet—"

"Yes," Dazal said. "I knew I had to tell you the

truth. No matter what. Oh, if I could take it back, I would. I would."

Vaha looked away, thoughts and emotions surging through her. Then she stood up. "I do not know what to say. What to think. I trusted you. All of you. Maybe not as friends at first, but as honorable people. Then later, when you took me into your pod, I was grateful."

She stared at Dak'Tor. "So it was guilt that made you provide for me?"

Dak'Tor jumped to his feet. "No. No, that is not true. I provided for you—Iria and I agreed to invite you into our pod—because we care for you. I admit it was a terrible thing Dazal and I did, but our feelings for you are true."

"If they did not care about you," Iria said, "They would not feel bad. They are good males; they just made a terrible decision."

Vaha covered her face with her hands. "I need to think. I need to be alone. Please go. And do not come back. Do not try to talk to me about this any further. Right now, I never want to see any of you again."

Dazal stood up and tried to approach her. She heard him step forward and looked up. "Do not try to touch me. I told you to leave, and I meant it. Now go!"

Once she was alone, Vaha fell to her knees. *How could they? How could they?* And Iria, too. She had thought Iria was her friend. Did they all think themselves so clever, pulling this off?

Vaha was broken. Everything she thought she knew was a lie. Her mind started to whirl, wondering who else knew about it. Did her parents know? Surely not; they would never have agreed to this. No, no, they did not. Her father had been so happy to learn that his daughter's offling would be by Dak'Tor. That it would elevate her status. Now what? What of Altka? Her daughter. No wonder her daughter did not have any of Dak'Tor's markings. She was not *his*.

Part of her wanted to be happy that Altka was Dazal's. She loved him. Had loved him. Did she love him still, after this? She was not sure. Did he love her? Had he ever loved her? Because how could someone do this to another person they loved? Or to anyone, for that matter. She wanted to run, to take her daughter and run away. But there was nowhere to go. She thought about returning to her parents, but that would just raise questions. What she needed was time. Time to think this through.

What she did not need was questions and more people getting involved.

Whatever she decided to do, she knew that decision would not be made today. She needed time for her feelings to settle down. She would do nothing until she could think more clearly and the gaping wound in her heart was not so fresh.

She wanted Dazal to find another place to stay, but she knew that would also raise questions. She would have to find a way for them to live together but ignore each other for now. Could she forgive Dazal, who was now apparently the rightful father of her offling? Could she ever forgive any of them?

One thing Vaha did know; the most important thing was her daughter's welfare. And no matter what, that would be at the forefront of any decision she did finally make. She prayed to the Great Spirit for wisdom.

CHAPTER 15

The winter had now set in. A particularly cold storm had dumped deep snow over everything. Knowing that few others would venture out needlessly in such weather, Tocho decided he would go and check on the oak tree one last time.

He bundled up as best he could and set out alone in the early morning hours. The cold air stung his lungs and bit his skin where it was exposed. He picked up a walking stick along the way; it just felt better to have something to poke ahead of him in the snow. He knew the way well enough, though the deep whiteness made everything look as if it was at the same elevation. Finally, in the distance, he could see the tall oak, its dark branches in stark contrast to the snow that now rested upon them.

He could just see the indentation of the circle where they had been lining up the rocks. He dropped his walking stick to the side and gently pawed away the snow. He took his time, not wanting to dislodge any of the stones underneath, for that would negate the whole reason for his trip—to see if any of the patterns had changed in all this time.

Finally, he was down to the bare ground. He could see where the stones were and gently wiped the snow away from their sides. He uncovered Sitka's side of the stones first, then he carefully felt around for the lineup of stones that would have been placed near hers, showing the days of any visits by Oh'Mah.

He smiled broadly when he realized there was a new stone at the top of his lineup. Whoever it was had come back. So the field of communication was still open. Tocho was so excited he did not know what to do. He wanted to tell someone. He wanted to tell Tiva so she would smile and make his world bright again. And he wanted to tell Sitka, though he was not sure anymore what she really thought about making contact with Oh'Mah.

He knew he should be heading back, but Tocho's curiosity got the better of him. What if their home was not that far away? Surely there was a group living together, not a lone individual, and they were obviously friendly as they could easily have hurt or killed Sitka if they had wanted. What if he could find them? How exciting would that be?

Against his better judgment and shored up by his adrenaline, Tocho decided to press forward out of the Brothers' territory and into *theirs*. It seemed that

Sitka was never going to try to meet them again, and he had come this far, so why not go a little farther? He still had plenty of hours before dark.

Tocho stepped past the huge oak tree. The terrain rose sharply, with scrub and small trees dotting the incline. He used the trees as handholds and made his way up, up, up. When he was nearly at the top, he had to stop and catch his breath. The biting cold was a shock to his lungs, and though he was used to hiding and hunting, it had been a while since he had gone on any expeditions with his father. In short, he was out of shape for such a steep, snow-covered climb.

When he reached the crest, he stopped to look at the incredible view that lay before him. Snow-topped mountains stretched far and wide, the bright sunlight glistening off their silver peaks. Without obstruction, the wind was stronger, and he held tight to a locust tree while he enjoyed the beauty around him. Eventually, his teeth started to chatter. What he did not realize was that he had lost so much body heat that he was slipping into hypothermia. His thinking was impaired.

The other side was just as steep going down as it had been going up. If it was a challenge coming up, with one false move as he descended, he could end up in a heap at the bottom of a long, dangerous slide down. But Tocho had come this far, and he had hours of daylight yet. Besides, he kept thinking about his little sister and how excited she would be if he could find any sight at all of Oh'Mah.

He brushed the falling snow from his face, took a deep breath, and started down the incline.

The moment Tocho took his first step, he knew he had made a huge mistake. He started to slide, grabbing frantically at the trees and saplings, trying to stop his descent, but to no avail. He was now tumbling down the steep slope. He hit his head on something hard, and he rolled downward, out of control. Finally, he landed, his body sinking deep. Soon the heavy snowfall would cover any sign of him.

The last thing he remembered was a pair of strong arms lifting him out of what would have been a cold grave.

(🐾)

On his way back from checking on the visitors, Culrat'Sar and Persica, Vor'Ran told Takthan'Tor that they had come to the High Rocks to speak with him.

"Welcome, Adik'Tar," Takthan'Tor greeted Culrat'Sar, his eyes flitting to Persica, noticing again how beautiful she was, how becoming was the black and brown hair that fell so gracefully to her shoulders. "Welcome to you both. To what do I owe this honor?"

"I want to talk to you about our people," said

Culrat'Sar. "The state of the community, if you have time."

"Of course. Will Persica be joining us?"

"If you do not mind. She is interested in such things."

Once they were in a private meeting room, Culrat'Sar began. "At our last discussion, you remember that Lair'Mok, Tar'Kahn, and Gontis'Rar decided we should look for the Protectors. Find them and bring them back."

Takthan'Tor shook his head. "It is folly, to be sure. Our efforts are better spent trying to help our people gain confidence in their own abilities. Looking for someone who does not wish to be found, especially the Protectors, is not a productive use of time or effort."

"Besides, it focuses their people in the wrong direction," added Culrat'Sar. "Back to dependence. Back to the past. It will not move us forward into a positive future of our own making."

"I agree. Do you have a proposal?" Takthan'Tor could feel Persica watching him. He knew she had an interest in him, and he also knew he needed to select a mate. No doubt she would be a fine choice, but he was still trying to rid his heart of Wry'Wry.

"Unfortunately, I do not. Neither you nor I have any influence over their communities. Nor should we. But we can more intensely focus our effort on our own communities. That we can do."

Takthan'Tor turned to Persica, "Do you have any opinions about this?"

"Only to state the obvious. Each generation passes their attitudes and beliefs onto the next. If the parents raising offling continue to demonstrate our inferiority in their actions and words, then that, in turn, will be passed forward. Generation after generation. If we do not turn this around, this belief in our frailty and the need for the Protectors in order to survive will only get worse."

"And we need not just to survive, but to thrive," Takthan'Tor added. "They had such an overpowering influence on us, I agree. The Guardian told us to stop speaking of them. I do not hear such talk in our common areas, but we know nothing of what is going on in their private quarters."

Culrat'Sar nodded. "But it is more than the talk. It is the impression that has been made on their souls. That we are less than they were, that we can never be as strong, as wise, as resourceful as they were."

"And we are resourceful," said Takthan'Tor. "Look at the improvements that have already been made. But, yes, they do not see that; their eyes are blinded by their grief."

"We all long for safety and protection," Persica volunteered. "It is natural."

"Unfortunately," her father added, "nothing else can compare with the feeling the Protectors' presence gave us. I fear I do not know the solution. They will never forget as long as they keep the memory alive."

"Then let us beseech the Great Spirit for wisdom. For a path forward," Persica said. "For healing for our people, who are suffering, and for our offling that they may not inherit the feelings of inferiority we all struggle with. If we lose the next generation to this self-depredation, I fear our community will never recover."

"Wise words," Takthan'Tor said. "Thank you. That is what we must all do."

Takthan'Tor felt a sense of relief in having others to discuss such matters with. And Persica was fair and reasonable. She did not seem to be emotional to the extent that it might cloud her wisdom. She was the daughter of an Adik'Tar, so she would have a first-hand understanding of the demands of leadership. Despite his longing for Wry'Wry, Takthan'Tor decided perhaps it was time he got to know Persica better.

Pan's restlessness continued. And the despondency that Rohm'Mok himself had noticed had not lifted. She took joy in little moments with him and Tala, but an undercurrent of unease was now always with her.

"Saraste'," Rohm'Mok said at last, "what can I do

to help you? I know you are struggling with something."

"I do not know the solution. Or perhaps I do not want to know," Pan answered quietly.

"The Great Spirit knows I do not presume to understand the burdens you carry, but perhaps it is time to seek the counsel of someone who would understand."

Pan looked up at her mate.

"Can you not call on your mother? In the Corridor?" he continued. "Can you ask to visit her—if that is what it is called? Or do you always have to wait for her invitation?"

"I have never considered trying to reach her. I do not know if it can be done," Pan said, her voice still low. "Perhaps I should try."

"I will take Tala and leave you be if you want to try now."

Pan nodded, and after they had left, she lay down on their sleeping mat and quieted her mind. She went deep into her consciousness and then called out from her soul to her mother. She waited, but nothing happened. She tried again, but there was no change. Then she remembered that her mother had told her help would be provided. *Irisa.* However, she tried one last time with the same result. So she got up and went to find Irisa.

"How can I help you?" the elderly female asked.

"I cannot shake this feeling," said Pan. "As if something terrible is about to happen."

"Is that coming from your soul? Or your imagination?"

Pan fell silent for a moment. "*Terrible* is a judgment on my part. It is more a feeling of something momentous. I suppose the term *terrible* comes from my fears."

"Fear is a powerful element. It can drive us either toward what is ours next to do or away from it," Irisa said.

"How can fear drive us toward anything?" Pan asked.

"Every action has consequences. But avoiding action also has consequences."

"So, fear of not doing what I should do might drive me to do it—"

"Yes. Fear is part of our natural state here on Etera," Irisa said. "Sometimes, it is fear for our personal safety. Sometimes it is fear for the safety of others."

Pan raised her brows. "I never thought of fear as being positive in any way."

"It depends on whether the fear is rooted in reality. In probable outcomes. Fear of a Sarius snake or a precarious perch on an icy slope at the top of Lulnomia are reasonable fears to have, based on the probable outcomes that both are dangerous situations that can result in tragedy."

"Thank you, Irisa. This has been helpful."

"I am glad. But I think the true help you need will come from my father."

Pan and Irisa stood before Wrollonan'Tor. From his considerable height, he looked down at them with soft eyes. "Your heart is troubled. You fear what will be asked of you," he said to Pan.

"I do, Guardian, since you told me much will be required of me."

"Do you fear what it is, or do you fear you will not be able to do it?"

"Both. Because I fear that I know what it is I have to do. And the enormity of it frightens me."

"Are you under the impression that Leaders do not have doubts?" Wrollonan'Tor's deep, rumbling voice was gentle. "That they do not struggle with their decisions, both before and after they commit to them? Your father had doubts. He doubted his decision to introduce the Others' blood into the veins of our people. He doubted how far he had let it continue, creating the Akassa. And he doubted his wisdom in choosing Dak'Tor over you to lead the High Rocks. But he did not allow those doubts to keep him from what he knew was his to do."

"What if I am wrong?"

"It is possible. We all make mistakes. And the greater our sphere of influence or control, the greater the impact of what we do. That is why we seek the guidance of the Great Spirit and trust that the Order of Functions has brought us to where we need to be."

Pan glanced away, squeezing back the fear that was starting to well in her eyes. "I know what I must do, but I fear it more than anything I have ever faced. And if I am to do it, I will need your help."

"I will help you, Pan. And you are right. You do need my help. What you are about to do is further and deeper reaching than anything that has been done before. We will spend time together so I can prepare you."

"For the final end to the Age of Darkness. For what is mine to do," Pan said.

"And for the consequences—"

"For others?"

"And for yourself."

Interview With the Characters

LR: Thank you for joining me. Let us start with Pan. How are you feeling about the series so far?

Pan: Since you asked, Leigh, I seem to be having a hard go of it. And it does not look as if it is going to let up any time soon.

LR: I know, Pan. I am sorry. But let me share some wisdom from my world. "To whom much is given, much is required." It is a heavy mantle to carry, I realize.

Pan: Wrollonan'Tor would love that quote. Speaking of which, finding out he was alive was a big shock. I do not think I am over it yet.

LR: You notice he is not sitting among you. I tried to get him to come, but he did not want to. I feel sorry for him; he has had a very long and hard life.

Pan: I hope that at some point, he finds the peace he is seeking.

LR: Irisa, how are you doing?

Irisa: I appreciate your compassion for my father. I have watched him suffer through the centuries. Ages, really. I am grateful my mother let me get to know him. He did not love her, and she knew that, but she did not stand in the way of us having a relationship.

LR: I give her a lot of credit for that. She did not know she had Guardian blood somewhere in her family background?

Irisa: No. It was only much later when I aged so slowly, that she suspected that was what it was. Then my father spent time with me and confirmed that was what it must be. I miss my mother. She was kind and loving—and patient.

LR: You will see her again one day.

Irisa: Yes. The Corridor. Our assurance that we will be reunited with our loved ones at some point makes the hardship of this life bearable.

LR: Who else would like to share something?

Kyana: I want to apologize. I am a bit embarrassed that I keep letting it bother me who Wosot mounted in the past. I am a grown female. I should be over such foolish jealousies.

LR: You are being too hard on yourself. We have all known times of jealousy, insecurity. Even though you know that Wosot loves you and wants only you.

Kyana: I do know that. Which is why I should get over it and just be happy we are paired.

Takthan'Tor: I want to say, I know it is my duty to pair and produce offling. I have to move on. (Takthan'Tor looked around the circle of those joining us.) I see neither Wry'Wry nor Persica is here. Perhaps that is just as well. I need to collect myself before the next book.

LR: You are the first Akassa Leader, Takthan'Tor.

Takthan'Tor: I hope history will remember me well.

(Just then, Dak'Tor and Iria joined us).

LR: Welcome. Have a seat and share your thoughts with us about how things are going so far.

Iria: Well, I am a little bit anxious waiting for my offling to be born.

Dak'Tor: *Our* offling. No matter if it is mine or Laborn's, he or she will be my offling.

Iria: I feel terrible about Vaha. I see she is absent, and so is Dazal. Still recovering from the most recent turn of events, perhaps.

LR: Yes. My heart also goes out to Vaha. People close to her who she trusted have deceived her. I hope that in time she will make peace with it. For all your sakes.

Iria: I still wish there was somewhere we could go. A fresh start. We would take our friends and my parents and leave. But even if Kaisak turns out to be a better person than Laborn was, we still cannot let him annihilate the Akassa and the Sassen.

Dak'Tor: We will not allow that. I do not know how, but if I live long enough and if it is the last thing I do, I will stop that from happening.

(A pause while Leigh waited to see if anyone else wanted to speak.)

LR: Well, thank you again for coming. Try to enjoy your time off until Book Five. I will catch up with you there.

PLEASE READ

Looks like we are nearing the end of Series Two. Book Five, Out of the Dust of Etera will most likely wind things up, although you could possibly change my mind lol. Book Five is available on Amazon. You can search for it under my author name or the book title.

Once again, at this point if you have not read Series One, I want to encourage you to still go back and read it. Series One, Wrak-Ayya: The Age of Shadows, covers the journey of the People thousands and thousands of years following what takes place in this series. There are some elements from Series One that are fleshed out in Series Two. Aren't you curious what you are missing lol?

Ways to stay engaged with me:

Follow me on Amazon on my author page at https://www.amazon.com/Leigh-Roberts/e/B07YLWG6YT

Or you can subscribe to my newsletter at: https://www.subscribepage.com/theeterachroniclessubscribe

I also have a private Facebook group at The Etera Chronicles

If you enjoyed this book, please leave a positive review or at least a positive rating. Of course, five stars are the best.

But, if you found fault with it, please email me

directly and tell me your viewpoint. I do want to know. But a negative rating truly hurts an author.

You can find the link to leave a product review on the book link on Amazon, where you purchased or downloaded the book.

Positive reviews on Goodreads are also greatly appreciated.

Until Book Five!

Blessings—
   Leigh

ACKNOWLEDGMENTS

Always–my husband, my friends, my readers. My fur family.
My wonderful editor Joy who is my right-hand and I could not imagine doing this without her.
The One-Who-Is-Three, who each day gives me a new slate to write on.

86742559R10215